Other Books by Marie-Nicole Ryan

Loving the Lawman Series
(Historical Western Romance)
Mastering the Marshal, 3
Pleasuring the Pinkerton, 2
Seducing the Sheriff, 1

Music City Heat Series
(Romantic Suspense)
Measure of a Man, 3
Because of You, 2
Love Me if You Can, 1
Beginnings, Short Story Prequel

David and Miranda French Stories
One Too Many (Mystery/Suspense)
Love on the Run (Romantic Suspense)

FBI Guys
(Romantic Suspense)
Broken Promises, 2
Holding Her Own, 1

Stand Alone Romantic Suspense
Too Good to be True
The Man for the Job
See You in My Dreams

Holiday Themed Short Stories
Valentine's Gift, 3
Pillow Talk, 2
Mistletoe and Mario, 1

HUNTED

Hill Country Lawmen 1

By

Marie-Nicole Ryan

RYANDALE PUBLISHING

Copyright

Edited by Wendy Ely
Cover design by Mary Varble
Cover photo © Bob Norris/Dreamstime.com

First Ryandale Publishing Print Edition: 2016
Second Ryandale Publishing Print Edition: 2019

ISBN-

Library of Congress Registration Number: TX 8-332-056

Dedication

To my mother who never got to read this story. I hope she would've loved it.

Chapter One

"They found two bodies, Sheriff," Dorothy, the dispatcher, said. "Your ranch...out by Simon's Creek."

"Who called it in?" Vince asked.

"Damn inconsiderate so-and-so hung up." She let out a loud huff over the phone. "Didn't leave his name."

"All right. Thanks." Sheriff Vince Tate punched the button, terminating the call. Now which of his ranch hands had made the call and upset the elderly dispatcher with his rudeness? No point in that.

Simon's Creek was a dry bed that wound through most of Los Marcos County, including the northern edge of the Tate ranch. Not the first time a flash flood had unearthed ancient remains. Better put in a call to the state archeologist, Abe Duckworth, who handled these cases.

Vince called Duckworth, giving him the details and location. "Meet you there." He disconnected the call, then headed to the outer office. Nodding at Dorothy, he stopped. "You know where I'm headed. Shouldn't be long."

"Should I notify Will, Sheriff?" She nodded, never once disturbing her tightly wound gray curls. "He's responding to a fender bender on Highway 18."

Vince shook his head. His chief deputy, Will Rasmussen, handled forensics. "Doubt we'll need him.

Probably native remains."

"Drive safe then."

"Always." Setting his Stetson on his head, he hid the smile threatening to break through. The dispatcher never failed to add her "Drive safe" warning when one of them left the office. A widow, she treated him and his deputies like the sons and daughters she never had. Not a bad way to start the day.

He stepped outside. The Texas sun beat down like Hell on steroids. Only May, but if today's temperature was an indicator, a blistering summer was already here. His Chevy Tahoe sat in the parking lot, waves of heat rising from the hood.

Welcome to Texas. Still, he wouldn't trade living here for any other state or country on earth. He opened the door, stepped back to evade the escape of super-heated air. He climbed inside, the seats still blistering hot through his jeans, and set his hat on the seat.

His com unit squawked. He grabbed the mic and nearly dropped the scorching plastic instrument. "Yeah?" he answered.

"It's Will. I'm over at your place."

"Thought you were working an MVA?"

"Finished. Didn't amount to much anyway. I was close so I thought I might as well..."

"I've already called Abe."

"Up to you, of course. These remains don't appear that old."

Not what he wanted to hear. "Okay. On my way." He reversed from his parking spot, flipped on his lights and siren, then headed down Main Street. He passed the drugstore, and his mind went automatically to pharmacist Abby Fields.

Yes, Abby Fields with silky dark, almost black hair.

And dancing green eyes.

A warm and willing body.

The only woman he'd ever loved.

Why couldn't she have just stayed the hell in Atlanta.

Her sudden decision to go to school at the University of Georgia in Athens, instead of UT in Austin as they'd planned—the final break in their relationship.

Was he supposed to forgive her for trashing their relationship after he'd left for college. No way!

Her father's murder six months ago brought her back to Kenton Valley. Oh hell, welcome to heartache round two. Still, he'd managed to remain professional and arrest her father's killer to boot.

After that, she really should've gone back to Atlanta. But no, she'd moved back and run her father's drugstore. Forever a daily reminder of her deception.

On top of everything else, he still couldn't find his runaway wife. If divorce papers couldn't be served, how the hell could he divorce her?

Dammit! He clenched his jaw. Jammed the Tahoe into fourth gear and headed east to Simon's Creek.

"I said it's over!" Abby jabbed the disconnect button then swore under her breath. Why wouldn't Rollo take the hint? No. She hadn't *hinted* it was over. She'd said so clear-as-day. Except real estate agent Rollo Moore was a stubborn jackass verging on stalker-dom and didn't seem to understand plain English. Maybe that tactic worked well with his clients, but it didn't suit her at all. What kind of name was Rollo anyway?

He was a distraction she couldn't afford. As the drugstore owner and pharmacist, she had a responsibility to the community. They deserved to have their prescriptions filled promptly and correctly. Lives were at stake, and he was an unwanted irritant and a complication.

After a single dinner date with Rollo, she knew all she needed to know about the man. Tall, dark, and handsome, yes. Arrogant and self-important to start—a big *no way Jose* in her book. She'd refused his offer to take in a movie. Not one to accept "No thanks" for an answer, he'd begun a barrage of multiple daily phone calls at the drugstore. Enough already.

At the moment, the store was free of customers. She walked to the front counter where her cashier, Ellen, was straightening the shelves. "Don't put any more calls from Rollo Moore back to my line."

Ellen frowned, then ineffectually brushed her too-long bangs from her eyes. "But what if he insists?"

"Tell him I'm busy and hang up. Can you remember that?"

"What if he's sick?"

"If he's sick, his *doctor* will call in a prescription. I don't want to talk to the man. Understand?"

"If you say so." Ellen blew her bangs from her eyes, then muttered, "I always thought he was a stud."

"That's just it. *He* thinks so too." Abby turned ready to head back to the pharmacy area. Hiring Ellen had been a favor to Abby's godmother who was best friends with Ellen's grandmother. Granted the eighteen-year-old was reliable and honest, but she wasn't the brightest bulb in the light fixture when it came to men. But then, who was at eighteen?

No doubt she'd learn the hard way. Abby had. The sound of a siren stopped her in her tracks. She turned in time to see the Vince Tate's SUV speeding down Main

Street. She ran to the front window and watched until he was out of sight. She let out a sigh.

Vince Tate—it was all his fault she'd even gone out with Rollo in the first place. She and Vince had dated—a lot—in high school, but he was barely civil since she'd come home to Kenton Valley. Yes, he'd come to her father's funeral, nodded, and assured her he'd find the SOB druggie who killed her father. And he'd kept his word.

Still, it was difficult to reconcile the bad boy to whom she'd lost her virginity in the bed of his Ford pickup under a star-filled, navy blue Texas sky with the stern-faced lawman who merely nodded when he glanced in her direction...and kept on moving.

He still had those sky blue eyes and the dark brown hair. But the twinkle in his eyes was missing. Unfortunately it had been replaced by an icy stare, and his run-your-fingers-through coffee-brown waves were cut shorter in an almost military style. Add that to the fact he acted as if he couldn't stand the sight of her. No matter how strong the sexual pull, she could never trust him again. She didn't need ESP to know there would be no rekindling of the fire that used to sizzle every time they came within five feet of each other.

Not anytime soon.

When she'd come back to the Valley, he'd avoided her, except when investigating her father's murder. And even then, it seemed he'd kept their contact to a minimum.

Technically, *he* was the one who'd broken her heart. Her choice of schools, her marriage to one of her fellow pharmacy classmates, and her ultimate decision to live in Atlanta for the last nine years certainly shouldn't have bothered Vince.

He'd had moved on. Oh yes, he had. He'd married a former high school cheerleader, Elizabeth Kellen. Although she'd run off with a bank official and a *lot* of money after only a couple years of marriage. If town gossips were to be believed, he hadn't been too broken up about her leaving, either. He was still in the process of divorcing her, complicated by the fact that she couldn't be located. So why was he determined to treat Abby like a stranger? Couldn't they, at least, be friends?

No point in obsessing over a man who didn't want anything to do with her. No matter how fast her heart leaped to her throat whenever she saw him. Heck, whenever she so much as *thought* about him.

The fax machine whined. She waited until the prescription finished printing and snatched it from the machine. "Wonderful." At last, was something to focus on, besides Vince Tate.

Vince took the back road, bypassing his ranch house to where Simon's Creek crossed his property. He spied his Chief Deputy's Dodge Durango. He hoped Will was mistaken about the bodies. Talk about a major complication.

He braked and exited the SUV, then set his Stetson back on his head. Striding over to the shaded area beneath a scrub oak where the remains were located. Will had already set up a crime scene perimeter. Due to the recent flash flood, the creek level was still high. He ducked under the tape. "What makes you think these aren't ancient remains?"

Will removed his cowboy hat, his reddish brown hair clinging to his forehead with beans of sweat. Pulling a bandana from his hip pocket, he shook his head. "Little thing like plastic wrap." He paused and wiped his forehead. "And modern clothes. What's left of 'em." He pulled back the tarp covering the bodies.

Vince's nose twitched at the familiar odor of decomp. He swore, then hunkered down. Two bodies. Wrapped like burritos. Modern day mummies. "Son of a bitch."

He pulled his phone from his hip pocket and called the state archeologist. "Not gonna need you, after all."

Abe responded, "You sure? I don't mind taking a look."

"I'm sure. Bastard plastic wrapped 'em."

"Well," Abe drawled, "that's good enough for me." The anthropologist rang off.

Vince pointed to a grove of cottonwoods. "Another twenty yards to the right, and all I'd have to worry about is the investigation. As it is, I gotta call in the Rangers. These bodies are square on my property."

Will pulled out his phone. "Want me to give Ben a call?"

Ben Rasmussen was a Texas Ranger, as well as Will's older brother. All the Rasmussen men were involved with law enforcement or the military. Vince shook his head. "No. Best go through channels. I'll step back. You handle the forensics like always. Need to follow procedure until the Rangers send someone."

With each word, a sensation of dread built up in his chest. Two bodies. His wife Liz and Ed Barnes, the bank president, had run off seven months ago with well over a hundred thousand dollars. The private detective he'd hired hadn't been able to locate her or Barnes. Seven months was a long time to lay low. Unless...

Unless they were laying in front of him.

On *his* land.

"You don't think—" Will broke off, clearing his throat.

Vince swallowed hard. "Lord, I hope not."

"But that's what you're thinking."

"Don't start speculating."

"Can't help it."

Vince turned and walked back to the perimeter tape, ducked under it, then turned. "Just do your job." That came out gruffer than he'd meant for it to. But dammit.

He ambled over to his vehicle, opened the door, and got inside. The Texas Rangers divided field operations for the state into regions. Most of the Hill Country was covered by Company F, headquartered in Waco. He called Company F and asked for Ben Rasmussen.

"Ranger Rasmussen."

"Ranger, I got a double homicide here in Los Marcos County. Last heavy rain washed up two bodies wrapped in plastic."

"Go on."

"They're on my property."

The Ranger grunted. "Any idea how they got there?"

"Not right off hand." He gave his address, adding, "Follow the road that circles behind the house and barn. It's about another two miles to Simon's Creek."

"I'm on it."

"Thanks. Will is handling the forensics. I haven't touched anything."

"Yeah. I'll take the lead on this."

"That's *why* I called."

"Sorry. Still, they're on your land."

"That they are."

The Ranger disconnected with a curt, "See you in

thirty."

Vince stared at the phone for a second. Disbelief. Denial. Or one of those other handy defense mechanisms wasn't doing its job. His gut told him one of those bodies was his wife Liz. And if that was true, the other had to be the no-good bastard who'd apparently tried to run off with his wife.

"Will!" He leaned from the SUV. "Find any money?"

"Not yet."

So where was the money?

"Did you hear? The rain washed up two bodies out on the sheriff's ranch."

Abby looked up from the prescription she was filling. "What?"

Dulcie Farmer stood in front of the counter, her cart laden with beauty products and vitamins. She was a trim fifties-something, aiming for another round at her forties.

Dulcie leaned her elbows on the counter, managing to display an inordinate amount of cleavage at the same time. "Well, I was in the sheriff's office selling band candy for my niece when I overheard Dorothy take the call. I'm telling you the sheriff took off like he'd been shot."

Abby kept a tight smile and refrained from an eye roll. Small towns. Nothing like 'em. Can't kill 'em.

"Do you even have a new prescription?"

"Oh no. Just these."

"I'll be another minute with this. Or you *could* take your items up front if you don't want to wait." *Please.*

"I don't mind waiting. You reckon Vince killed his wife and Eddie Barnes? I always wondered 'bout that.

You?"

"What?"

"Didn't you wonder if he'd done her in?"

"No. Never." Abby waited for the label to print and applied it to the bottle. She took her time slipping the script into a numbered bag. Maybe Dulcie would grow weary of waiting.

No such luck.

Abby stepped around to the register with a smile for her gossipy customer. "Now then, let's get you checked out."

She gave a sigh when the woman was finally out of the store. No, it had never occurred to her that Vince would ever do anything to harm his wife. While Abby hadn't returned to town until the week after Vince's wife and the bank president had run off, the town was still abuzz with the news. She'd heard it all. Small towns were good for that sort of thing.

Sometimes, too good.

She removed her white jacket and hung it on the wall hook. She smiled. High on a shelf, she spied her father's collection of antique apothecary jars. They were such a familiar part of the drugstore, she sometimes forgot they were even there. He'd collected them over the last thirty years, from short, squat clear glass jars, to stoppered brown jars to a single elegant milk glass one. His excitement when he found a really old one on eBay or his disappointment when he lost out on one at an auction—the jars kept his memory alive.

Walking toward the front of the store, she stopped at the front counter. "Ellen, I'm headed over to the Mercantile for a sandwich. Can I bring you something?"

"No thanks." Ellen reached under the counter and pulled out a brown bag. "I'm good."

***

The Mercantile, as the town called it, was officially known as the Wheaton Mercantile, established 1887, and had been run by the family ever since. Vince's cousins, Bethany and Lola Wheaton, had managed to modernize without destroying the vintage-style grocery. When the business next door closed, they'd bought it, expanded the Mercantile, adding a combined coffee shop, lunch counter, and cyber cafe with free Wi-Fi.

Abby walked to the back of the store and tapped on the glass door to the office.

Beth looked up, smiled, and beckoned Abby inside. "What has managed to pull you away from your cave of pills and potions?"

"Lunch." She rubbed her belly. "I'm starving."

Beth stood, her hands on her hips. "Madam, you've certainly come to the right place. I happen to know Eva made her special chicken salad today. Your choice of bread or roll."

"You can cut the sales pitch." Abby shot her friend a happy smile. "You had me at 'Eva made'."

Abby took a sip from her mocha latte then set it on the table. "Have you heard about the bodies found on your cousin's ranch?"

Beth's brown eyes widened. She straightened, then set her sandwich onto the paper plate. "Have I ever! Only every single person who's come into the store today has asked me if I'd heard the news."

Abby gave a shrug. "It's probably ancient remains. It's not unusual for a flash flood to wash those up." She really didn't want anyone she knew to be dead. Not even Liz Kellen Tate.

"Think what you will." Beth gave a toss of her blond curls. "*Most* folks think the bodies are Liz Tate's and Eddie Barnes's."

"I don't care what most folks think." Abby's cheeks grew hot. "Vince is *your* cousin. You know he'd never hurt Liz."

Beth gave a skeptical eye roll. "Wouldn't blame him if he had."

"Bethany Renee Wheaton. You should be ashamed." Appetite gone, Abby pushed away her sandwich.

Beth aimed a long manicured finger at Abby. "And *you've* still got the hots for your old hookup."

"It wasn't just a—oh, never mind. I went away to college. We both moved on."

"I *know* it was more than a hookup." Beth shot Abby a contrite look. "Sorry."

"Me too. I just hate how people are going to talk about nothing else. Still, I'd better get back." She scooted her chair back and stood. "Folks like to have their prescriptions filled on their lunch hour." Anxious to escape, she quickly paid for her lunch and left Beth shaking her head.

Vince would never break the law. Murder someone? No way. Much less murder two someones? *Hell no.*

"Excuse me, Abigail. Did you say something?"

Of all people to bump into. Smelling of expensive men's cologne, trim, tan, and dapper in his gray and white seersucker suit and highly-polished black Western boots, Jamison Darwin, the minister of the Kenton Valley Methodist Church. "Oh, Brother Darwin." Had she spoken aloud? Had the minister actually heard her curse? "No, just muttering to myself."

"Sorry. My mistake." He gave her a benign smile that told her, indeed, she had cursed right in front of her minister. "Is everything all right with you, Abigail?"

"Yes, I'm just in a rush to get back to the drugstore."

"Yes, your responsibilities keep you pretty busy."

"Yes. Yes, they do." She moved to go around him. He moved in the same direction, with a chuckle. "Shall we dance?"

"I didn't think Methodists danced."

"No, that's those Baptist folks."

"Got it." Good heavens what was she doing having such an inane conversation with the preacher.

"Hope to see you at services *this* Sunday, Abigail."

"If I'm not working. People need prescriptions on Sundays too," she hastened to add, ignoring the fact that she only covered the pharmacy every other odd weekend. Her relief pharmacist, Darla Murray, worked the other weekends and alternate evening shifts.

"Of course," he said with a nod. He stood aside, allowing her to pass.

She flashed him a quick smile and hurried across the street. Word on the street was half the single women over forty in town were after him, ever since he'd been hired a year ago. She couldn't see the attraction. He was too polished and a little too smug to suit her. Of course, she was well under forty, so that fact might color her perception.

And she wasn't desperate, either.

Chapter Two

Vince drummed his fingers on the steering wheel. Ranger Rasmussen was certainly taking his sweet time. Sitting idly by while his chief deputy did all the work...

A glance at his watch told Vince the Ranger was still a good ten minutes away.

He itched to climb from his SUV and assist Will. But that wasn't procedure, and Vince wouldn't go against procedure.

The nearby creek rushed along, still swollen with the recent rain.

His stomach growled. Breakfast was a distant memory. Lunch wouldn't be anytime soon. Maybe he'd stop at the ranch house before he headed back to town. Marti, the housekeeper/cook, would be sure to have a spare sandwich or two stowed away.

Vince heard the roar of a motor behind him. He glanced into the rearview mirror. The Ranger's SUV.

Finally.

The Ranger parked and exited his vehicle. Setting his white cowboy hat on his head, he nodded at Vince. Like all the Rasmussen men, Ben was a couple inches over six feet, broad shouldered, and fair-skinned. He had the same reddish-brown hair of his younger brother. Ben was thirty-five, five years older than Vince, and had joined the Texas Rangers only last year.

Vince emerged from the Tahoe. “Ben.”

The two lawmen shook hands. “Vince.” The Ranger nodded. “Forensics team’s coming. They’ll be here in another ten. I’ll see what my baby brother’s doing over there. Hope he hasn’t mucked up my investigation.” Ben’s tone was teasing and good humored.

“I heard that,” Will grumbled. “Haven’t mucked up anything.”

Ben gave a half smile. “Have to keep the young ’uns on their toes.”

Vince nodded. “Agreed.”

He watched the Ranger duck under the yellow crime scene tape. “Let’s see what you have here.”

As promised, the forensics team arrived and took over. Will shook his head and surrendered what he’d collected. Still shaking his head, he walked over to Vince. “I hate this. *My* crime scene.”

“*My* damn ranch.”

When Darla Murray arrived for the evening shift, Abby left the drugstore and headed home. After her father’s murder, she’d returned to the Valley and, once again, lived in her childhood home, an American foursquare of tan brick, built in 1913 by her great-grandfather, Edgar Fields. He’d moved from northeast New Mexico to Kenton Valley, Texas, and built it for his new bride. The house was too big for one person, but she didn’t have the heart to sell it. She loved the old house with its wide front porch and large rooms. Her parents had just remodeled the first floor to an open floor plan when her mother had a heart attack and died. Less than a month later, her father had been murdered.

Their sudden and early deaths had rocked her world. So many regrets. Too few visits home from Atlanta. Too few phone calls. And definitely too little time spent with her parents. They would never know their grandchildren—if she ever had any. Her father had walked her down the aisle once—thank heavens, he hadn't known her marriage was already on the rocks.

His murder had forced her to climb down from the fence and make a decision. She'd left Atlanta and the handsome William Armstrong Cavendish in the dust, along with his blue-blooded pedigree and his arrogant air. The very things that had attracted her to him in the first place.

Her family, the Fields, had been of solid upper middle class stock. Her great-grandfather was the younger son of a New Mexico cattle rancher and an aristocratic Spanish woman. William never quite got over it when he discovered her *mixed* heritage.

Get real, dude. We're all mutts of one kind or another.

She stopped before opening the front door and glanced around. She especially loved the wide porch. So many memories. Necking with Vince in the swing until her father turned on the porchlight, his signal for Vince to beat it.

The shady yard with its tall American red maples and one old live oak. In the back tall pecan trees provided a bounty of thin-shelled pecans each fall. A Tonto crape myrtle bedecked the tree-lined street with a splash of color from early June until fall, festooned with bright pink blossoms.

Maybe someday the house would be a real home again with a husband and two or three kids. She opened the door and imagined that distant day when she would hear the boisterous laughter of children and her husband's heavy tread as he came to greet her.

Hah! Fat chance of any of that coming true. Might as well rid herself of silly romantic notions. The only man she ever envisioned as her husband happened to be Vince Tate, and he, sure as heck, didn't feel the same. Working to keep the drugstore going, fulfilling her father's legacy didn't leave much time for socializing.

Her stomach growled, reminding her she hadn't finished her lunch. Ready to head into the kitchen, she walked into the open-plan living room/dining room and stopped.

The living room was a shambles. Pillows ripped open and dumped onto the floor. Her mother's newly upholstered wing chairs had received the same treatment. The roll-top desk in the corner had been broken into, the drawers pulled out and the contents strewn around the room.

Her hands shaking, she reached into her purse for her phone. Too late. A strong arm wrapped around her neck and pulled her off her feet. The intruder slung her purse across the room.

"Where is it, bitch?" The voice was harsh, unrecognizable. Terrifying.

Her feet scrabbled for purchase. Her back against his chest, she reached back, trying to claw her attacker's face. "What?" she gasped, attempting to catch her breath. "I have some cash—not much. You can have it."

"You know what I want." His breath blew hot against her neck. "Where is it? Where did he hide it?"

He?

Did he mean her father? Surely, her father wouldn't have had anything to do with the likes of this man. And a man he was, for sure. He smelled of a familiar men's cologne and an underlying odor of nervous perspiration.

"I don't know!" She struck back with her elbow and stomped his instep.

With a yelp, he slammed her head into the wall and took off, his sharp footsteps echoing on the oak floor, then fading as he ran out the backdoor.

She leaned against the wall to steady herself, taking slow deep breaths. She spied her purse and took a step toward it. Her head spun. She grabbed an upended wing chair for support until her head cleared.

Carefully, she made her way to the purse. She sat on the ottoman and rummaged for her iPhone. She swiped it open and called 911.

"Codes 10 and 4 at 501 Elm Street."

Recognizing the codes for burglary and assault, as well as Abby Fields's address, Vince grabbed the mic. "Unit one responding." Might as well since he was restricted from doing anything at the present crime scene.

"Thought you were tied up," the dispatcher said.

"Had to call in the Rangers. They're here. I'm free." He started the motor and shoved the gear lever into reverse. He backed up and headed out, the Tahoe bumping over the rough backroad.

Now what the hell was going on at Abby's place? Burglary and assault? Most likely, someone spied a nice big house and decided to have a go. And then she'd walked in on him.

"How bad was the assault?" he asked the dispatcher.

"She sounded shaky but okay. EMTs dispatched."

"I'll be there in ten." Circling around his ranch house,

he pressed the pedal to the floor.

When Vince arrived at Abby's, the Los Marcos County ambulance service was already on scene. He parked, spying Abby sitting in the rear while a female EMT checked her blood pressure.

The sight of a bandage on her head, along with her pale cheeks socked him in the gut. Abby Fields was a small, shapely beauty. And clearly no match for a thug. *Son-of-a-bitch.*

Yes, he still cared about her. And no, he wasn't happy about it. Not one damn bit.

He got out and walked over to the ambulance. "Abby," he said with a nod. "What happened?"

"One minute, Sheriff," the redheaded EMT interjected. "I'm not through with her."

"Is she all right?"

The redhead removed the blood pressure cuff. "She is, for now, but she needs a skull film before we can say for sure."

"Oh, no!" Abby held her hands up. "I'm not going anywhere. I'm fine. And I have a mess to clean up."

"I understand." Vince nodded. "But I still have a few questions. *Now* would be best."

The EMT's cheeks flushed. She let out a huff. "She needs to sign—"

"I'll sign your waiver," Abby said, "but no way am I going to the hospital."

"Whatever." The redhead wrinkled her nose. "It's *your* brain."

Abby squared her shoulders and leveled a sharp look at the EMT. "Suzanne Griggs, I know it's *my* brain. I helped you study for your EMT exams, and don't you forget it."

Vince held back a groan. "Enough, ladies! I need to find out what happened here. Abby?"

Abby held up a finger. "One minute, Sheriff." She turned to Griggs. "I'll be fine, but if I experience nausea, blurred vision, or increased pain, I'll take myself to the ER." With a sweet smile, she turned back to Vince. "Okay. I'm ready to answer your questions."

The assault hadn't done much to dampen Abby's attitude. She'd always been on the lively side. He jerked his head in the direction of the house. "Let's sit on the porch. We can talk there."

Her gaze caught his. "The porch? Wanna sit on the swing, too? I seem to remember..." Her voice trailed off, her meaning clear.

Damn. Now why had he chosen the porch to question her? The same wide porch with the same seductive swing where they'd necked as teenagers. Damn. Why couldn't he keep from thinking about the old days?

"Chair 'll be fine," he said, his tone gruff. *Keep your mind on the business at hand.*

She walked ahead of him on the flagstone walkway. Her almost black hair, cut shorter than when they were in high school, skimmed the collar of her red top. Red—her best color. Tan slacks encased her long legs and fit her hips just tight enough.

Those long legs and how they'd wrapped around his waist their first time together—the first time for both of them as it turned out. There was no way he could keep his mind on anything but her. He swore under his breath.

She looked over her shoulder. "What was that?"

"Nothing."

"If you say so." She shrugged, giving him a playful glance.

"Have a seat." Remaining standing, he pulled out his case notepad.

She sat on a flowery cushioned chair. She shot him a wry smile. "You know this is the most you've had to say to me since the night you told me you'd arrested my father's killer."

"Tell me what happened," he said, ignoring her comment. The past was the past. Better left that way.

"I came home. Unlocked the door—he must've come in the back way. I walked into the great room and saw the mess where someone had been ripping the place apart."

"Then?"

"All of a sudden an arm was wrapped around my neck. 'You know what I want. Where is it? Where did he hide it?' That's what he said. I offered him money. He didn't want that."

"Can you describe him?"

"He was *behind* me. I elbowed him in the ribs. Stomped his instep. He slung me against the wall. Banged my head." She fingered the bandage. "That's how I got this. Then he ran out the back way. His footsteps were heavy and sharp as if he wore boots."

Boots in Texas. Go figure.

"How tall was he? Could you tell his race?"

"He was rather solid. Not quite as tall as you, though. He wore leather gloves, but I saw a gap at the wrist between the glove and his jean jacket. He was white. Do you think this might have anything to do with the bodies found at your ranch?"

Vince shook his head. "Doubt it." He skimmed his notes. "And you only saw the one man?"

"That's all. Just the one. He was enough to scare the cr—well, you know what I mean."

Vince bit his lips to keep from smiling. "Yeah." He

closed the notepad and slipped inside his hip pocket. "I'm going to check the rest of the house. You wait here."

He walked inside the house. Just as Abby had described, the "great room" was a mess. Someone had definitely been looking for something. And they hadn't found it. Meaning, they would be back.

He continued into the kitchen area. If it weren't for the general chaos, it would've looked like one of those remodeled kitchens on the DIY channel. He strode to the back entrance and found where the intruder had effected entry. Shards of glass from one of the French doors littered the floor.

Intruder'd worn gloves. No point in dusting for prints.

He came back to the entry hall. Better check upstairs. Just because she hadn't seen or heard a second person didn't mean there wasn't one. He ran upstairs, taking two steps at a time.

Vince opened the door to what had to be Abby's bedroom. Damn. Bastard had been thorough. Closet door stood open. Drawers were pulled out and contents scattered around the room. Lots of colorful lacy underwear. What he wouldn't give to—

Hell. Keep your mind on the business at hand.

Even the mattress had been pulled off the bed and ripped open.

Bastard was definitely looking for something. But what?

Tired of waiting, Abby jumped up, entered the house, and met Vince as he was coming downstairs. "Well?"

"Well, what?" he asked.

"Who did this and what did he want?"

"I could ask you the same."

"*I* don't know. Maybe there's some gang going around breaking into houses. I'm a pharmacist. Maybe he was looking for drugs. You'd know more about that than I would."

"He was looking for something all right. Any idea what?"

"No!" She chewed her bottom lip for a second. "He asked where 'he' hid it. Could it be something related to my father's murder?"

Vince's brows drew together in a frown. "Have you come across anything you couldn't explain when you were going through your father's things?"

She sighed. "I haven't really gone through them. I donated his clothes to the Goodwill, but after I skimmed through his paperwork, I boxed it up in the basement." She shivered at the thought of the dark confines of the basement.

"It's not safe for you to stay here. This guy didn't find what he was looking for. He'll be back."

"I could stay with someone. Beth, maybe."

"I don't like the idea of you two—" Vince shook his head. "You can stay out at my ranch. He won't look for you there. I'll put the boxes in the Tahoe. We'll go through the paperwork together. See what we can find."

Her chin dropped at his suggestion. But she recovered, offering him a half smile. "*Stay at your ranch*? I'm not looking for a bootie call. And I don't need a bodyguard."

"Maybe you—"

"What? Maybe I *am* looking for a bootie call?" *The nerve.*

He scowled. "You have a bad habit of interrupting. *Need a body guard* is what I was going to say."

"Before I so rudely interrupted you. I see." She set her hands on her hips and glared back.

The corner of his mouth lifted in a crooked smile. "I'm glad you've recovered from your recent ordeal. That's good, but I'm still concerned. Your intruder didn't find what he was looking for. He'll be back."

"So I'm just supposed to abandon my home and let him try again? I don't think so."

"No." He wearily shook his head as if he was getting exasperated. "I suggest," he said none-too-patiently, "that you engage that expensive security system your daddy installed before..."

Realization dawned, sending a sinking feeling to the pit of her stomach. "Do you think Daddy knew someone was after something? What? But you caught his killer. He's already in jail and waiting for trial, so I don't understand what one could have to do with the other."

"When we arrested Tim Dill, we assumed the motive was drug-seeking since he's is a well-known druggie, and he killed your father just as he was ready to close. But there may been more to it."

"Why now? Why wait this long?"

"That's what I need to find out, Abby. And I can't investigate fully if I'm concerned about your safety."

Concerned for her safety, was he? Somehow that thought pleased her more than it should've. "I can't just take off somewhere. I have the drugstore."

"My offer of the guestroom still stands. I have an excellent security system, plus my brothers run the ranch. They'll be around."

"You expect me to stay with you and your brothers?" She could just visualize the mess left by three single men. Imagine the small town gossip such a move would generate.

"There's plenty of room. We have a live-in housekeeper and cook—Marti Mills. She'll make a proper chaperone."

Before she could respond, Vince's cell phone chimed.

"Gotta take this." He turned away and walked outside.

She hesitated until she saw him end the call then followed him onto the porch.

His expression was grave as he turned to her. "Pack a bag. I have to run by the office. Then I'll take you to the ranch."

"What's wrong?"

"Something's come up. I've been put on full administrative leave. Gotta hand in my badge and service weapon."

"Why?"

"Those bodies. Looks like one of 'em might be my wife's."

Vince pulled up and parked in his reserved space. The Los Marcos County Sheriff's office building was only two years old and equipped with the latest in computers and other technology. Two years ago, an arsonist with an ax to grind had set a fire that wiped out an entire block of derelict storefronts. The county had voted to build a new sheriff's office and county jail in the resulting space. Only two blocks from the county courthouse, it was a pleasant and convenient place to work.

He opened the door and exited the SUV. "Wait here. I won't be long."

"But if you're off the job and can't investigate the break-in, don't I need to come in and give the details all over again?"

"Don't worry about that. I'll give them my case notes. As for investigating, I won't be doing any 'til they find whoever killed my wife. Not officially, anyway. But we can still dig into your dad's papers and other effects."

"But they're taking away your gun."

He chuckled. "This is Texas. You better believe I've got more than one weapon."

"Right," she said, her voice a little tremulous.

Concern was written across her pretty face. In spite of her spirited attitude, her cheeks were still pale and her eyes were wide. Maybe it was just now hitting her how much worse things could've turned out.

He gave her a casual salute. "Be right back."

On entering the lobby, many of his deputies nodded then found a reason to look away.

"Only Dorothy, the dispatcher, had the courage to speak." Sheriff. It'll be all right. You'll see."

He offered her a smile and opened the door to his office. Will Rasmussen was seated at Vince's desk. He rose. "Sir."

"Will," he acknowledged, his chief deputy. "Mind explaining how you discovered her identity so quick?"

"Driver's license. Ed Barnes, too. What's left of their clothes matches the description of what they were wearing when last seen. DNA will take a while, but Ben said they'll put a rush on it."

"So I'm the prime suspect?" Husbands and significant others were always the first to be suspected—with good reason.

Will's gaze widened. He gave a quick shake of his head. "Of course not. It just has to be investigated. Wouldn't look good otherwise."

"Of course. No getting around that."

Vince removed his badge, remembering the day, four

years ago, his predecessor and father, Nathan Tate, had pinned it on him. He set it on the desk then removed his department-issue service weapon, a very nice Glock 27. "That's it. Anything else?"

Will had the grace to blush. "Keys to your official vehicle."

"That's going to make driving Abigail Fields out to my ranch a little difficult. By the way, I need to file a report on the break-in and assault at her house."

"You can give me the details. I'll enter them." He looked up sharply, as if the name had just registered. "Is Abby okay?"

"She's fine."

"I'll drive y'all out to the ranch and bring the Tahoe back. I reckon you have another vehicle to drive."

Vince nodded. "Yeah." He handed over his case notebook and the keys to the Tahoe. "It's all there. Somebody was looking for something. That's why I'm taking her out to my place. Don't want her there if he decides to come back."

"Understandable."

Will cleared his throat. "Ranger Rasmussen will want to interview you."

"How about I get Abby settled at the ranch. I'll come back—" He glanced down at his watch. "Make it around five."

"Fine. I'll let him know."

Vince squared his shoulders. He'd done nothing wrong. Nothing to be ashamed of. Luckily, his father had retired south to Galveston. Translation: his father wouldn't be around to stick his nose into the investigation. If luck was on Vince's side and the case cleared quickly, his father would never have to know.

All this time. Liz and Ed Barnes had been buried

somewhere on his ranch. Go figure. Who hated him enough to frame him for the murder of his wife and her lover?

He gave Will a sharp look. "Who made the call about the bodies being washed up? Which one of my hands?"

"We'll be checking into that. According to Dorothy, the caller didn't leave a name."

So...someone had been keeping track of the bodies. Had the recent rains uncovered the bodies, or had someone moved them in an attempt to place the blame on him?

His mind full of possibilities, he walked out to the Tahoe. Will followed.

"Sheriff Tate? Is it true?" Ed Barnes's wife, Rosalie, was standing between him and the Tahoe. She grabbed his wrist. "Did they find my husband and your wife?"

"Official statements will come from the Texas Rangers, ma'am. I can't say anymore."

"Did you kill my Ed, Sheriff? Did you?"

"That's a definite 'no,' Mrs. Barnes." He peeled her hand from his wrist. "Now, if you'll excuse me..."

Abby's eyes widened when Will entered the driver's side, and Vince the rear, but thankfully, she said nothing. Would she continue to believe him, even if, right now, it looked like he was the prime suspect?

Chapter Three

All throughout the ride to Vince's ranch, Abby kept her thoughts to herself. She'd noted definite tension between Vince and his deputy. Will had asked her a few basic questions about the intruder. And she'd responded. Vince—not at all. At least he wasn't under arrest. She could never imagine him do anything illegal, much less kill his wife and the bank official. No matter how angry he was.

While she and Will had shared a lot of the same classes in high school, Vince was a year ahead. He'd been the senior class president her junior year. He'd played football in the fall and baseball in the spring and summer. They'd started dating at the end of her sophomore year, even though her father wasn't thrilled. Fortunately, Vince was the kind of young man fathers liked. Polite. Respectful. Never in trouble.

They pulled up in front of the Tate ranch house. Southfork it wasn't, but the house was a large rambling two-story structure of field stone and wood. The dark green metal roof looked new.

Vince cleared his throat. "We have some things of Abby's stowed in the back."

"Sure thing." Will opened the door and jumped out. "I'll give you a hand. I don't think Abby ought to be exerting herself after what she's been through."

She shot him a quick smile. "Thanks."

Vince picked up her bag. He stepped onto the porch then opened the front door. "After you."

The housekeeper came rushing forward. She was a slightly plump, dynamo of a woman with a head of curly, and surely dyed, bright red hair. "Sheriff, I wasn't expecting you home this early. What the heck is going on? Nobody will tell me anything."

"It's complicated. Marti, you already know Abby. She's is going to spend some time with us."

"Of course I know her. Shop at her drugstore at least once a week." Beaming, Marti wiped her hands on her apron. "She can take the yellow room. It's freshly aired, and I just washed and ironed the curtains day before yesterday."

Abby smiled. "I'm sure it will be fine, Ms. Mills."

"None of that 'Ms. Mills' stuff. Call me Marti like this big galoot and his brothers do."

"Thank you, Marti. I'll try not to be any trouble."

"Little gal like you won't be any trouble. Now this one—" she smiled up at Vince, "and his brothers—that's what I call trouble." She set her hands on her hips. "Are you going to carry her bag upstairs, or do I have to?"

"No, ma'am. I'm on the job." He laughed, then added, "Marti's supposed to be our employee, but somehow she thinks she's the boss."

Marti smiled. "Men, young 'uns especially, need a firm hand. When it comes to keeping the house and cooking their meals, I'm the boss all right. And they know it."

"Wouldn't have it any other way," Vince said under his breath then picked up the carryall.

Abby chuckled and followed him upstairs.

"Second door on the right," he said. "Has its own bathroom. You won't have to share."

"Thank you. But you've really gone above the call of duty. I'll try not to get in your way."

He opened the door to the yellow room—her home away from home. "I'm across the hall...if you need me." His tone was low and somewhat gruff, but the pleasant rumble send a thrill through her body.

"I'll unpack and then we can go over my dad's papers."

Abby crossed the threshold into the room. Vince followed with her bag. He set it onto the bed. "Thanks."

Vince with his oh-so-rugged he-man body seemed out of place in what was definitely a pale yellow, girly room. It had been furnished with white ruffled Cape Cod tie-back draperies, and a spring-like yellow and green flowered quilt on the white-painted iron bedstead. An oak rocker sat in the corner across from a tall oak armoire. Most likely called a chifforobe in its heyday.

"I'm afraid this part of the house doesn't have many closets," Vince said. "My four-times-great grandfather built the house back in the late 1880s. There've been a couple additions since then, but this is part of the original house.

"You have a lovely home, and this is a lovely room. I'll be very comfy here."

Don't get too comfy. Vince won't like it, even if it's his idea to move you out here. The move was just for her protection. Might as well put paid to any fanciful or wishful notions she might have.

He must've felt her discomfort, because his gaze drew inward. "Well, uh, I'll leave you to it."

"I'll be downstairs in a few minutes...to help with his papers."

"Good enough. I'll be in in my office. Marti can point you in the right direction."

"Thanks, again."

His gaze met hers. He took a step toward her. "You

don't have to keep thanking me."

"I know." Her mouth grew dry. "You're just doing your job."

He took another step, closing the distance between them. "It's more than that. And you know it."

Her heart sped up. "I do?" Months without a glance or word in her direction. How was she supposed to know?

As if he'd read her mind, he said, "I wasn't free."

"Well, you are now," she couldn't help adding. Too soon?

"No. Not 'til I'm cleared." He stepped back. Turned. Left the room and shut the door.

She blew out a sigh. What was he playing at? One minute he was hot. Then the next, cold.

Cold as ice.

Abby found Marti in the kitchen whipping up something sweet that smelled like heaven in a pink Pyrex bowl. "Vince said you'd point me toward his office."

Marti turned off the red Kitchen Aid mixer and faced Abby. "Go down the back hall. Last door on the left. It's in the newest part of the addition. What he needs with all that computer stuff is beyond me. Being that the sheriff's new office building is equipped with every piece of technology under the sun."

"You haven't heard."

"Heard what?" She gave an eye roll. "Nobody tells me a blamed thing."

"They found Vince's wife and Ed Barnes."

"I knew it." Marti nodded vigorously. "Somewhere off in Europe most likely. I never knew Liz very well. I didn't come to work here until after she ran off. She always seemed just a little too sharp around the edges."

"No. Here on the ranch. They're dead."

Marti registered the shock. "Sorry for speaking ill of the dead, even if I didn't know at the time." She glanced out the kitchen window and nodded. "I knew something was up. I saw all the traffic, but I was too busy to worry about goings-on and such."

"Vince has been placed on administrative leave. They even made him hand in his badge and gun."

"Merciful heavens. *That's* why he came home early." Her mouth twisted to the side. "Now if you don't mind me asking, just what are you and all those boxes doing here?"

"There was a break-in at my house. An intruder looking for something, and he attacked me. Vince thinks he'll come back since we know he didn't find whatever he was looking for."

"He did the right thing then. Mr. Vince always does the right thing. But taking him off the job—now that's the stupidest thing I ever heard of."

"I agree, but he says it's procedure."

"Hmph!"

Maybe she should've waited and let Vince tell Marti the news himself. Oh well. Too late now. "I'd better go find him. We have a lot to sort through."

"You go on. Tell him supper's at six. Fried chicken—his favorite. That'll perk him up some."

Abby smiled. "I'm sure it will."

During the last remodel Vince's wife had instigated on the ranch house, he'd claimed a room for his office. "Man cave," she'd called it in that derisive way of hers. No matter, he'd claimed it for his own. He'd made certain he had upgraded cable and Wi-Fi. The furnishings were comfortable, an antique oak desk, a leather couch, and a

Navaho rug, suitably masculine in shades of red, black, gray, white. The room was his. His haven whenever he needed respite from Liz's sharp tongue.

From his desk he could enjoy a view of the lush Texas Hill Country landscape. Beyond the patio and pool, a wide expanse of tall cottonwoods grew along on one side, and scrub oak dotted the hills on the other.

When Abby entered his office, he looked up and smiled. "Thought maybe you got lost."

"No. Marti and I talked a bit. I'm afraid I spilled the beans about your administrative leave."

"Is she very upset?"

"Only over how stupid the powers that be are."

He favored her with another smile, unable to keep from enjoying her presence. "Having loyal friends and employees around, it's good."

"But somewhere or sometime, you've made at least one enemy."

"True enough." He scratched his head. "More than a few in the last four years."

"Who do you know that would kill two people just to blame you for the murder?"

He ran his hand though his hair. "No sane person would do that. More likely, this person had a reason to kill Liz or Barnes. Could've been spur of the moment situation that got out of hand, and, as a bonus, the perpetrator decided to fit me up for the murders.

"It doesn't make sense that they were killed on the ranch. I think the bodies must've been moved."

"That's what I'm thinking. Being on the sidelines doesn't sit well with me, but I have to trust the Rangers will get to the bottom of it. In the meantime, pick a box."

She walked over and selected one. "I'll sit on the floor so I can spread out."

"Be my guest."

She sat cross-legged and smiled up at him. His heart sped up. He couldn't help but smile at the familiar sight. "That's how you used to do your homework. Remember?" Sometimes, he'd done the same. Just to be closer to her while they "studied."

"Yeah. Daddy hated it when I did that too. Maybe he didn't trust you with his little girl." Smiling, she lifted the lid and started removing the contents. "This box is dated the year he was killed. I'll go through it first. Then if nothing stands out, we can work backwards.""

She skimmed the first few sheets then set them aside. "Most of this is hospital and medical bills from when Mom died. And then older receipts from all the work done on the house. Bills for the architect, the designer, and new furnishings."

"Look for anything that looks out of place. Overcharges. Anything like that. I'll go through these bank statements." He indicated that box with a jerk of his head.

"Right." She started separating the receipts into individual piles. "Maybe something will come to me if I look at it long enough." She sighed. "It's a pity. They spent all this money and had so little time left to enjoy the changes."

"Losing your mom and dad so close together must've been tough." Losing his mom when he was fifteen had been devastating.

"Still is. There's not a day that goes by I don't think of them."

"They'd be glad you came home. I am."

"I didn't come home soon enough," she choked out. "I have so many regrets."

Tears welled in her green eyes. Damn. What should he do? If he followed his instincts and comforted her, would she object? Hell. Feeling so awkward around her sucked. He eased from his chair to sit beside her on the floor, setting his arm around her waist and pulling her close. She lay her head on his shoulder and began to sob. Holding her, comforting her felt so right. Liz had never fit into his shoulder the way Abby did. For the twentieth time he mentally berated himself for ever thinking she would fit into his life.

Finally when her tears abated, she straightened. "Sorry," she said wiping her eyes.

"It's all right. I've never been afraid of a few tears."

"But I've gotten your shirt all wet." She gave an undignified sniff.

Resigned, he reached for a box of tissues. "Normally I wouldn't have these, but Marti insists on scattering them throughout the house."

Wiping her nose, she said, "It's a woman-kind of thing."

He chuckled. "Must be."

"I cried a bucket of tears for my mom, but when Daddy was murdered, I was too stunned and angry to cry. There was so much to do. The funeral. Packing up my stuff in Atlanta. The move. I was so focused on what needed doing that I never had time to grieve properly. She blew her nose. "How's *your* father? I haven't seen him since I've been home."

"He retired to Galveston. He's the hit of the senior citizen center with more female companionship than he can handle." Vince laughed, shaking his head. "But all he really cares about is fishing."

"He's happy then?"

"Yeah. Just hope the Rangers clear this case before he finds out. The one thing I don't want is for him to come back and stick his nose in."

"Would he do that?"

"Oh yeah. In a heartbeat."

"Makes sense," Abby said. "Once a parent. Always a parent."

"More like once a cop, always a cop." Then switching the subject, he said, "You and your husband didn't have kids."

"Oh no." She straightened and gave an arrogant shake of her head and shoulders. "He was too self-centered to share his life with a pet, much less a child."

And in any other universe, Abby was the kind of woman who should've had children, his children, and lots of 'em. "I'm sorry about the circumstances that brought you back to the Valley, but I'm glad you're here."

Especially now.

He reached to caress her cheek, but stopped when Marti knocked on the door. "Weren't you supposed to go back to the Sheriff's Department at five? Your deputy said to remind you before he left."

He jumped up, swearing. "Right. I told them I'd be back at five. I'd almost forgotten."

Abby started to rise. "Do you need me to come?"

"No. This is about the bodies. Keep on going through your father's papers."

To Marti he said, "Don't wait dinner on me. Don't know when I'll be back."

Or if...

The whole town was abuzz with the discovery of Liz Tate and Ed Barnes's bodies being found on the sheriff's ranch. Why hadn't he been arrested? Everything was going to plan. The Texas Rangers had been called in. Tate was apparently on administrative leave. How much more evidence did the Rangers need to make an arrest?

Moving the bodies had been tricky. He'd buried them in a shallow grave, having approached from the rear of the Tate ranch. He hadn't risked going in from the front. Too many eyes. He moved them because the weatherman said the rains were coming with possible flash flooding. Perfect for his timeline.

Shallow grave. Flash flooding. Bodies discovered. Drop a dime. Discovery. Perfect.

All he needed now was for the Texas Rangers to get off their collective asses and arrest the sheriff for murder.

Once Vince had left, Abby let out a sigh of relief. His presence was a great big old distraction. While she'd appreciated his comforting her, she couldn't help but be relieved when they'd been interrupted.

Once she'd separated the papers into like piles, she retrieved the box of bank statements Vince had been going through. Really she should've already shredded the lot. And after she'd gone through them thoroughly, that's exactly what she'd do.

A light knock on the door. "Abby?"

Now what? "Come in."

One of Vince's younger brothers, Chance, stuck his head in the door. He and his twin, Chase, were a year younger than she and two years younger than Vince. The twins were fraternal, but almost identical, except for their hair color. Chance's was a deep brown like Vince's. Whereas Chase's was the color of rich honey. "Just wanted to say *Hi* and welcome to the ranch. Marti says supper will be ready in about fifteen minutes."

"Thanks." She glanced at her phone for the time.

"I really meant that welcome, Abby. It's nice to see

you. You were gone a long time."

"Yeah, but I'm home now," she said, flashing him a smile while wishing he would leave her to her work.

"Well, anyway, see ya at supper."

Abby nodded and turned back to her father's papers. She heard the door close.

Good.

Fifteen minutes to go through years' worth of paperwork. Of course there was no reason she couldn't continue after dinner. Vince would expect her to make some kind of progress.

The numbers were about to make her eyes glaze over when she came across a payment to the county clerk, denoted as a filing fee for some real estate.

What other real estate was there? Just the house, lot, and the drugstore. This seemed to be a recent purchase. If so, where was the deed? Was a deed what her intruder was looking for?

First thing tomorrow, she'd go to the courthouse and check with the county court clerk.

Vince ambled into the Sheriff's Department. Ranger Rasmussen met him with a nod and an outstretched hand. Immaculate in his dress, as required by the Rangers dress code, he wore a navy suit and tie. He held his cattleman's-style white hat at his side. His reddish-brown hair was cut short. All in all, he presented an unflinching aura of the professional lawman. Only the warmth in his expression conveyed any sign of the close friendship they'd shared for the last five years.

"Where do you want me?"

Ben nodded. "Interview one. Just to make it official."

"I'd appreciate knowing what you've found, Ben."

"In good time."

Hell of a thing. Feeling like a perp. in his own office. He squared his shoulders and entered the interview room. He paused, almost making the mistake of sitting on the interrogator side of the table.

He shrugged and took the chair on the opposite side.

"Interview with Vincent Tate, Sheriff of Los Marcos County. Texas Ranger Benjamin Rasmussen and acting-Sheriff Will Rasmussen in the room."

He stared at the two men, men he'd always considered friends. "Well—going to read me my rights?"

"This isn't an interrogation, and you aren't under arrest," Ben said, pulling a notebook from his jacket pocket. "It's an interview. I need to go back to when your wife, Elizabeth Diane Tate, disappeared." He opened the file folder that was on the desk. "I have here the missing person report you filed on December 20, 2015. The record states the last time you saw her was when you left for work the morning of December 18, 2015. Is that correct?"

"That's correct. She was still in bed. At least, I assumed she was. We'd had a disagreement the night before, and she opted to sleep in the guest room."

"What was the disagreement about?"

"We talked of separating. It wasn't a knock-down drag-out. Just heated words." He gave a casual shrug, but hashing over details about his marriage was anything but. "She often picked a fight when all she really wanted was to sleep by herself."

Ben shot Vince a skeptical glance. "And how often did your disagreements become knock-down drag-out affairs?"

Vince tensed, his back rigid. "*Never*. It was just an expression. Around the time she ran off—because that's what I thought she'd done, we were arguing every night."

"What did you argue about, other than about

separating?"

"I was certain she was seeing someone. Mostly about that." Vince clenched and then unclenched his fists.

"Did you know who?" Ben made notes in his notebook.

"No, but when the bank VP disappeared with 150-thou of the bank's money, I assumed he was the man she'd been seeing. Figured they'd run off together. Like everyone else in town."

Ben made more notes. "I need to know how you spent the day of December 18th."

"I'll need to see what I can pull up in my records. Nothing sticks in my mind. It was seven months ago, Ben." What a nightmare.

"We've checked your phone and bank records."

"Then you probably know more about how I spent that day than I do."

"Surely, you can remember something about the day your wife disappeared."

"First of all, I didn't know she'd disappeared until she didn't come home later that night. And it wasn't the first night she hadn't come home." Vince blew out a puff of air. "How were they killed? Do you have ballistics? DNA? You gotta give me something." He half rose, thought better of it, then sat.

The Ranger, no sign of the friend he knew so well, kept a stone-faced expression. "I know it must be frustrating to be on the wrong side of an investigation. It's too soon for any reports. The remains have been sent to the state crime lab in Austin. Autopsies tomorrow morning."

"Go ahead. Give me a polygraph. Search my house and ranch. No need for a warrant. Just don't disturb Abby Fields. She's staying there since the break-in at her house. And she's going through her father's papers, and they are *not* a part of this investigation."

"Understood. Appreciate your cooperation, Vince. You're free to go…for now."

Vince rose. "I will remain available for questioning anytime you need me."

"I can get the lie-detector testing set up for tomorrow afternoon. That's the earliest."

"Appreciate that. I want these murders cleared up as fast as you do." He stood. At least he wasn't under arrest, and he could still walk out under his own power.

The dining room wasn't a formal one. Just off the kitchen, it was comfortable and warm. Vince's brothers chowed down with the appetites appropriate to men who lived and worked on a ranch. The top of the large oak table was covered with food. Only Vince was missing.

Tempted to loosen her belt, Abby could testify to one thing: Marti Mills was a superb cook. No wonder the Vince and his brothers allowed her full rein in the kitchen and house. Crisp fried-to-perfection chicken. Fluffy mashed potatoes. Home grown green beans. Sweet corn on the cob. Yeast rolls, sweet and light enough to be dessert, slathered with all the sweet butter she could eat. Ready to reach for a piece of lemon meringue pie, she stopped at the sound of a vehicle in the front of the house.

"That better be Vince," Marti said with feigned heat. "Or I'll have his hide for missing supper."

No doubt she would too, Abby mused. Honestly if she stayed any longer, she stood in danger of growing as big as a house. No second helpings, she cautioned herself. But the woman could definitely cook. Good. Tasty. Comfort food. Nothing fancy, just perfect.

Marti rushed to the front door. "I'll pull your plate

from the oven. Just put it in," she muttered. "Another ten minutes and it would've been ruined. Just ruined I tell you."

Abby heard Vince's deep bass chuckle as he ambled into the dining room. "I brought some guests," he said. "Will and Ranger Rasmussen are coming right behind me. They're going to search the house and grounds."

Marti screwed her face into a frown. "They got a warrant?"

"Don't get your apron in a twist. I gave permission. This is the quickest way to clear my name."

"Well, I don't suppose they'd like some supper first? We've got plenty."

Vince shook his head. "Might be construed as a bribe. I guess they'll have to wait for another time. However, I'll take that plate if you don't mind."

Abby hid a grin. Another man with a hearty appetite. Good sign he wasn't letting the suspension get to him.

"You'll need to show them which papers are yours, Abby. They won't disturb those. Will you?"

"No, ma'am," the Ranger said. She always found the Texas Rangers so solemn and imposing. The white hats. The silver-star badges. Ben Rasmussen was a perfect example of the breed. Tall. Handsome. Charming when the task called for it. But deadly and uncompromising, more often than not.

"Ranger Ben Rasmussen," he said, introducing himself to Abby.

She nodded. "Abby Fields. I remember you. You were a senior when I was in middle school."

He nodded. "We'll have a full forensics team in here tomorrow morning. This is more of an informal survey. We'll be taking in your guns, Vince. If they check out with ballistics, they'll be returned."

Vince turned as if something had caught his attention. "You're checking ballistics. So they were shot?"

The Ranger raised an eyebrow. "No comment at this time."

"Still, it's something to go on." Vince nodded his satisfaction. "Don't like being left out of the loop, though."

"Understood." Ben nodded.

Abby was dying to know what was going on, but she had even less right to know than Vince. So he had to be churning with frustration. The quicker the Rangers could clear him, the quicker their lives could return to normal.

Will—aka the acting-sheriff—and his brother departed with every firing weapon in the house, promising to return the next day for any weapons belonging to his ranch hands and any found in the stables and barn. Vince walked out to the back patio, breathing a sigh of relief. There was no way in hell any of those were used to shoot Liz and Barnes. With luck, another twenty-four hours at most, he'd be back on the job.

Abby joined him, sinking wearily onto a chaise. "Marti wants to know if you're ready for some lemonade."

Vince shook his head. "Hell of a day. Make it a beer."

She flashed him an understanding smile. "I agree. I think I'll have a glass of merlot."

He turned to go inside and met Marti carrying a tray holding a tall cold beer and a glass of wine. "You read our minds."

Marti chuckled. "Doesn't take much work to read yours."

"Have I mention lately how lucky we are to have you riding ramrod for us?"

"Come to think of it you haven't, but I already know

how lucky you are." She smiled up at him. "And I'm lucky too." Her voice was low but he caught her meaning. Her husband had died in a car wreck the same year Vince took office. It was his first MVA involving a fatality. He'd made the death notification. to Galveston, and Vince hired Marti as their live-in cook and housekeeper two days after Liz had run away.

Smartest move he'd ever made.

Marti set the tray on a table and discreetly left. Vince handed Abby the glass of red wine then took a long pull on his icy cold beer. "Come across anything in your dad's papers?"

"Yes!" She leaned forward. "I almost forgot. I found a county court clerk fee debited to his account the month before he died. I'm going to the courthouse tomorrow to see what that's about. *After* I speak to his lawyer. He may know something about it, but no mention was made while we were going through probate."

Abby leaned back and sipped her wine. The moonlight shone on her sleek dark hair. "I really appreciate this, Vince. You have a lovely home and ranch."

"It belongs to all of us. My brothers run it and take care of day-to-day ranch business while I play at being a lawman."

"So *any* of you could be suspects. Not just you. I know she was *your* wife, but either Chance or Chase could've—or one of the hands even—I'm just sayin'." She held her hands up in a who-knows gesture.

"True—technically."

"But the Ranger—Ben—he's really focused on *you*."

"I'm the husband. We'd argued. If it was anyone else, I'd be looking at me too."

"Sorry didn't mean to stir things up. But someone would have to have access to the ranch."

"Could've come in through the back part of the spread."

"Two bodies. Bodies are heavy, aren't they?"

"He'd need a vehicle to get them down to the creek, but there are access roads, if you know where to look. No need to come in from the main entrance."

Leaning back, he closed his eyes. The soft sound of her voice calmed him, even if she was talking about his wife's killer. Abby was just as easy to be with as she'd been in high school.

It was a night such like tonight. He'd taken her virginity in the back of his Ford pickup truck. A starry indigo sky. A warm inviting breeze. He'd been as inexperienced as she was. At the memory, his heart sped up. His body heated. "You remember?"

"Oh yeah." Her words, as soft as a sigh. "I remember."

He reached across, took her hand, and gave it a squeeze. "You were so sweet and so hot. I thought I'd died and gone to heaven."

"I *definitely* remember. We went there together." She let out a low chuckle that made his jeans grow snug. He shifted uncomfortably in his chair. This was no time to be reminiscing. It was too late. And too much was at stake.

Wineglass still in hand, Abby rose. "It's been a long day. I think I'll turn in for the night."

"Night. Sleep well." Perhaps, she'd read his mind. Back in the day, they'd almost eloped. They were *almost* comfortable in each other's presence again. No point in getting too comfortable. Not now.

Chapter Four

Vince got up at five. Too early for breakfast, but not too early for a much needed ride. He saddled Copper, his chestnut gelding, and headed for the back of the ranch. Maybe he could find where the perp had driven in with the bodies. With enough rain last week for a minor flashflood, they could've been washed down the creek for quite a ways.

And to be honest, he didn't want to face Abby at breakfast—not after the sex dream he'd had last night. Maybe bringing her out to the ranch wasn't such a good idea, after all.

After a full gallop, badly needed for clearing his head, he slowed the gelding when he reached the site where the bodies were found. Slowly, he rode along the creek bank beyond, surveying the ground for any vehicular tracks. He rode another mile and then another until...

He spied what appeared to be the tracks of an ATV. Yeah, that would work.

Copper stopped and nickered. He was a great horse, and Vince didn't work him often enough. With a blaze and two front white socks, he was a damn fine looking horse. The gelding nodded, his hooves moving restlessly. "What is it, fella?" Vince sat straight in the saddle, looking for whatever had spooked the gelding.

The whine of a rifle shot whizzed past his shoulder. "Damn!" He spurred the gelding and headed for cover. Someone shooting at him. On his own damn land. He leaned low as he aimed the gelding for cover.

Abby awoke to the smell of fresh coffee and frying bacon. Only two pieces. Because going up a clothes size wasn't on the agenda. She showered, dressed quickly, and went down for breakfast.

Vince was nowhere in sight. Bummer. Just as well. He'd figured largely in her dreams last night. Yeah, large all right.

Marti was pulling something from the oven. "Coffee," Abby begged, lying dramatically across the kitchen island with her hands outstretched.

"Coming right up." Marti set a pan of cinnamon rolls on a trivet, poured a large cup of coffee, and handed it to Abby. "Sugar or sweetener? Cream or powder stuff?"

"Sweetener and powder's fine. I can get 'em. Just tell me where. I don't expect you to wait on me."

"Bless your heart. It's my pleasure, but suit yourself." She opened an upper cabinet and pointed.

Abby grabbed the yellow packets and the creamer from the shelf. "I'd die if I couldn't have my coffee every morning." She stirred in the sweetener and the creamer, inhaling the fragrant brew. After a careful sip, she let out a moan. "Heaven. Absolute heaven, Marti."

After an iced cinnamon bun and two pieces of bacon, Abby rose from the table. "Thank you so much. It was delicious."

Marti smiled. "Since you're so appreciative of my cooking, I won't make any stupid comments like you don't eat enough to keep a bird alive."

"Good."

"But you don't."

Anxious to change the subject, Abby said, "Is Vince up yet?"

"I heard him get up at dawn. I think he might've gone for a ride."

"Oh." In spite of her dread of facing him, not seeing him was a disappointment. But what did she expect? A passing reference to their past relationship wasn't a precursor for more to come. No matter how much she wished it were. "Then I guess I'd better get to the drugstore. Working girl and all that."

After the morning rush, Abby took a break and drove to the courthouse. She pulled into a space and parked. Now, maybe she'd find the answer to at least one question. Calling her father's lawyer, Samuel Dunaway, hadn't been fruitful. He'd known nothing about any land transfer or purchase. Naturally, it should've been part of her father's estate, but probate had closed and hadn't shown anything. She promised she'd bring him a copy of the deed as soon as she obtained it from the county court clerk.

The Greek revival courthouse was built in the early twentieth century, and the gabled two-story Doric columns on all four sides signified history and stability. She couldn't imagine the public square without the magnificent edifice.

At the clerk's window, she pulled the bank statement from her shoulder bag. "Is there any way to cross reference the date of this registration fee with the deed? I'm my father's executrix, but neither his lawyer nor I, know anything about the property."

"What date was the fee debited from his account?"

"November 16th last year, so he probably was here the

14th or 15th of the month?"

After several keystrokes, the clerk looked up the computer screen with a quizzical expression. "It appears there is a deed but it is currently in the process of being transferred to a Macedonia Corporation."

"I've never heard of a Macedonia Corporation. When was the transfer initiated? My father passed away just over six months ago. Is it local?"

The clerk frowned. "This is most unusual. The transfer request was made six weeks ago online. I'm not familiar with the Macedonia Corporation. To my knowledge, it's not local."

"How can this be going on without my father's attorney knowing anything about it?"

"I assume Mr. Fields was handling it himself."

"But that's impossible. As I said, my father's been deceased for over six months."

The clerk scrolled farther. "There does seem to be a hold on the process."

"Maybe they're looking for the deed. I need to see the deed. And I'll need two copies. One for me and one for my attorney."

"Are you sure you don't have the original somewhere in his files?"

"I'm in the process of sorting through his paperwork now, but I haven't found anything like that. And it certainly wasn't with the deeds to the house or the drugstore."

"That will be fifteen dollars each for the copies."

Abby paid the fee, took the copies, and headed for her car. Surely, the attorney would find the information enlightening, even if she didn't.

Since she'd already taken more time away from the drugstore than expected, Abby left the documents with Dunaway's paralegal and rushed back to the drugstore.

Thankfully, only two people had left prescriptions in her absence. She'd have Ellen deliver them as soon as they were filled. As a rule, she didn't leave the pharmacy without a backup pharmacist. Today was an exception.

Vince rode Copper into a stand of cottonwoods. There'd only been one more shot, but he wasn't taking any chances. He pulled out his cell phone and called dispatch to report the incident, giving his approximate location. The dispatcher put him through to Will Rasmussen.

"I'll have someone out there right away. Just stay put."

"Right." Like he had a choice, being unarmed. "It was a damn close thing. I'd just found what looked like ATV tracks a couple of miles beyond where the bodies were found."

"Not supposed to be investigating this on your own."

"Guess I can take a damn ride on my own ranch."

"Like I said. Stay put. Stay safe."

"I'd be a lot *safer* if you and your brother hadn't confiscated all my firearms."

"Sorry. Had to be done."

Feeling as useless as tits on a boar without a weapon, Vince followed his deputy's instructions. He stayed put. Only when he observed Will's Durango did he break cover, leading his gelding.

Will climbed out and ambled over to Vince's position.

Vince motioned toward the hills. "Shots came from over there. Copper got skittish just before the first shot was fired. As far as I could see, the shooter hid in that grove of scrub oak. Thick as it is, that's what I would've used for cover."

"And the ATV tracks you mentioned."

"They came in from the hillside. Easy enough for an

ATV. Far enough from the house that they wouldn't be heard."

"Over here," Vince motioned. "Here's where the tracks stopped."

"Sure looks like a four-wheeler to me," Will agreed.

Vince cut his gaze to the hillside. "I never heard the shooter leave. Must've been on foot or horseback. That's what spooked Copper."

Will offered Vince his backup. "Just in case."

Vince nodded and took the Sig-Sauer P938. "Nice choice." It was the same type of firearm he used as a backup.

They climbed the hill and stopped at the only grove of scrub oak thick enough to conceal a shooter and his ride.

"Tracks, human and equine," Will said, indicating where the ground had been disturbed.

"He policed his brass," Vince said. "Someone careful. Someone determined not to get caught."

"I'll let Ben know. He'll get the forensics team out here again." He pulled out his cell phone. "They're already at the house. They'll head out here as soon as they're finished checking the house."

"I know. For blood spatter. Any sign whatsoever that I killed my wife. Like I would do that in my own house."

"Just a formality."

"Yeah," he grumbled. Being a person of interest in a murder investigation pretty much sucked. "In the meantime, I'll let my brothers and ranch hands know about the shooter and to step up security."

"Good idea."

Will removed a forensic flag from his case and marked the spot where the ATV tracks began. "I'll stay here until the rest of the Rangers' forensics team arrives."

"Then I'm heading back to the house."

Another person he needed to warn was Abby. Given the area covered by the ranch, it wasn't as safe as he'd thought. Still, as long as she kept to the house, she'd be safe.

But the question remained: was there a connection between the murders and the intruder at her house? He'd never put much faith in coincidences. Had to be a connection. Now he had to find it.

After he handed Copper over to one of his ranch hands, Vince entered the house. He inhaled the aroma of coffee. Just what he needed. He found Marti in the kitchen loading the dishwasher. "Where's Abby?" He grabbed a mug and poured himself a cup of coffee.

Without stopping her task, she replied, "Gone to the drugstore."

"She's supposed to stay *here*. And I want you to keep to the house today until we catch this shooter."

Marti straightened, facing him. "There's a shooter?"

"Yeah. One took a couple of potshots at me this morning. That's why. I'm hitting the shower then I'll head to town. Abby had a break-in yesterday. No business being in town."

"So that's why you brought her out here. Silly me. I had all sorts of romantic notions about the two of you."

He scoffed. "Couldn't be more wrong."

"Well, she has a business to run. You can't expect her to shut down just because of a little break-in." Marti poured in the dishwasher detergent, shut the door, then hit the power button.

"There was more to it than that. "

"Now then, I figured as much." Eyeballing him over her glasses, she set her hands on her hips and gave him the familiar fish-eye. "What *else* have you forgotten to tell me?"

"It wasn't just a burglary. He attacked her. He was searching for something. And he could return."

Marti reached for the coffee pot and poured herself a cup of coffee. "He's not likely to attack her in public and in broad daylight, is he?"

"She's at risk no matter where she is." Vince took a swallow of his coffee. *Ah, hazelnut today*. Coffee made life worthwhile.

Marti's expression grew concerned.

"But don't worry." He set his cup on the counter. "You're safe here. We're stepping up security."

She snorted. "Do I look like some shrinking violet to you? I can handle a shotgun."

"But the Rangers confiscated all the ranch's firearms for ballistics."

"They didn't get *mine*." She shot him a smug smile.

"*You* have a weapon?"

"You better believe I do. I keep a .38 Special under my pillow and a twelve gauge in my closet. This *is* Texas."

His fifty-eight-year-old housekeeper packed heat. Would wonders never cease?

Abby was alone in the pharmacy when the bell over the door jingled. Since Ellen was making a couple of deliveries, Abby was keeping a watchful eye on the entire shop.

Crap. Rollo Moore. That was all she needed.

He sauntered back to her counter. "Mornin', Abigail."

She mustered a polite smile. "What can I do for you?"

"Heard about your trouble yesterday. Wanted to see if you were all right. Didn't hurt you, did he?"

"Of course not. I'm pretty tough."

He chuckled. "I bet you gave him a run for his money."

Thankful for the tall counter between them, she said, "As you can see, I'm fine."

"So abrupt. You didn't used to be like this."

"Like what?"

"Brusque. Business like."

"You are in my place of business. If you don't need a prescription filled or a men's hair product for your receding hairline, then I'm afraid I have other things to do."

He glanced around the store. "I don't see any other customers. Aren't you afraid being here all by yourself? I mean..." He shrugged.

"What do you mean?" She sucked in a quick breath. "That sounded like a threat."

The bell over the door jingled again. She relaxed, emitting a little sigh.

"What's going on?" Vince's bass tone, came across as gruff and very I-mean-business.

He headed toward her, glancing from her to Rollo and back. "Moore, are you bothering Ms. Fields here?"

"He was about to tell me whether he had a reason for being here, or he was warning me I might not want to be alone in my place of business."

"Warning or threatening?"

"You know, I'm a little fuzzy about that. Almost sounded like a threat."

Rollo backed up, holding his hands up in front of him, gesturing surrender. "Now, hold on there. I just expressed a concern. That's all. Especially, after what happened yesterday."

Vince's steely blue gaze, fastened on Rollo. "And just what do you know about what happened yesterday? Hm?"

"Nothing. Not a thing, Sheriff." Rollo shrugged, giving

Vince a smug grin. "But you're not the sheriff right now, are you?"

"Temporary situation. That's all."

"We'll see about that. I may just have to report you for misuse of power."

"Be my guest." Vince tipped his hat forward. "*You* could be charged with harassment. Isn't that right, Ms. Fields?"

"Since he apparently doesn't need a prescription filled, and doesn't want any men's haircare products—although I could and would recommend something for your early male pattern baldness—I would like it very much if he left my drugstore."

Rollo's cheeks flushed and his hand went to his scalp. "Fine. You won't see me here again. In fact, I'll drive to Mason when I need the services of a pharmacist. And I'll *recommend* my friends do the same." He huffed, spun on his heel and made tracks.

Finally, he'd gotten her message. Insulting customers wasn't part of her usual wheelhouse, but she had to smile.

Vince eyeballed her, his azure eyes shining with merriment. "You were pretty tough on him." He gave his hair a tug. "Could you recommend something for me?"

Abby smiled, tamping down the impulse to give him a big hug. "I think we can wait a while. Quite a little while, in fact."

"Good to know."

"So why are you here? Have you heard anything from the Rangers?"

He nodded. "You need to come back to the ranch. It isn't safe."

"Other than a pest like Rollo Moore, whom I can handle quite easily, by the way. I'd say being in public is the best protection."

"Abby, your father was killed in this very store."

Like she could forget. "But his killer's in jail."

"I don't want to alarm you, but I rode out this morning, looking for clues beyond where the two bodies were found. Came across some ATV tracks. About that time, someone took a couple of potshots at me."

"No!" Had she come this close to losing Vince? And she hadn't known. Hadn't felt a flicker of premonition. Not a clue. She could've lost him before...before she had a chance...or even knew for sure, if she wanted to start up with him again.

"I don't know yet if their murders and your break-in were connected, but I want to keep you safe. I've warned my brothers and the ranch hands to keep an eye out. Full security. So you will be safe."

"But only if I stay with you. What will people say? I mean, this is still a small town."

"We could say we're engaged."

"Engaged."

"Yeah, that would work."

"Isn't it a little soon after your wife's death?"

"She's been gone nearly a year. If I grieved, at all, I'm over it."

"I don't know, Vince." She shook her head. An engagement of convenience. How romance novel-ish could you get?

"It wouldn't come as a shock to anyone." His tone was warm and seductive. "After all, we were an item years ago."

"An item? That sounds more like a shopping list." *Playing* at being engaged wasn't high on her list of desirable things to do. But actually being engaged—now that was something else again. "I'll have to pass on that. You've barely given me the time of day since I came back to the Valley. An engagement, even a faux one—" She broke off with a shake of her head. "Won't work. No one will buy it. I think I'll just go home this evening and clean up that mess."

"Abigail! That's exactly what you should *not* do."

Tired of being told what she should and shouldn't do, she gave a loud sigh. "Do *you* need a prescription filled?"

From the brief moment of confusion, her question had the desired effect of catching him off-guard. "What?"

"Even though there are no customers in the store," she said patiently, "I still have work to do. I'm going over my end-of-month accounts."

Clearly not happy with where the conversation was headed, Vince scowled. "Oh. So take a hike, cowboy. That's what you're saying."

"Yes. " She gave him her sweetest smile.

"Fine." He shifted his stance as if unsure whether to leave.

"I'll come out this evening to pick up my things and to thank Marti for putting up with me. And I really appreciate the effort you went to in order to see I was safe."

"You're welcome. Whatever...you want." Vince leaned forward, his gaze intense. "But I hope you will take some of my advice. Turn on that alarm. Keep a gun handy. Just in case you have a midnight visitor."

"If I do have such an unwelcome guest, I will be armed and dangerous. And I'll turn on the security system. Thank you very much."

"See that you do," he said, clenching his jaws.

She'd definitely riled him. Good. That was her intention.

He nodded, then left.

She waited until he'd cleared the store and let out a cry of frustration. "Men!"

Chapter Five

On his way to the office, Vince swore under his breath. "Women—was there even one of the creatures who knew what the hell she wanted?

He entered the Sheriff's department and nodded to Dorothy. She winked and nodded back. He walked into his old office. Will started to jump from his chair then seemed to remember *he* was the acting sheriff.

"Any news, Will?"

"Still waiting to hear on the autopsies. Your firearms from the house are all cleared. We'll release those back to you."

"Good. Now I can protect my ranch if the shooter comes back."

"Now, Boss, you know how procedures go."

"Yeah. But I don't have to like it."

"Cut me some slack. I don't like this either."

Vince kept his expression grim. "Thought maybe you were getting used to my office. Sitting at my desk. Acting Sheriff. More authority."

"No such thing," Will protested. "With you on administrative leave, we're a man short. This is my first murder case. It's not exactly fun times at Los Marcos High."

Time to cut his chief deputy some slack. For real.

Vince grinned. "Just yanking your chain."

"Thanks a lot. Say, can you be here at one? The polygrapher will be here then."

"I can and will. Now then, if I pass the poly, can I come off administrative leave and give you a hand?"

"That'll be up to the Rangers."

"Guess I'd better make nice with Ben." If all went well, he could be back on the job sooner rather than later.

Damned tired of waiting to hear of Vincent Tate's arrest. That's what he was. The sheriff's department was closing ranks. Protecting one of their own. Typical. Some things never changed.

Last night, certain events had contrived to keep him from searching the Fields house again. But tonight, the clouds would obscure the moon. He'd give it another go.

Vince nodded at the Ranger polygrapher and sat. It wasn't their first meeting. He'd played football with Bob Evanson at Texas A&M, but he didn't want to trade on their old friendship. While a polygraph was considered of questionable validity and unable to be admitted as evidence of guilt or innocence in court, his passing the test would lessen some of the heat he felt from above. He complied with the instructions while he was fitted up. Then they proceeded to the baseline questions.

Evanson began with, "Answer only yes or no. Is your name Vincent Tate?"

"Yes."

"Do you live at 9925 Los Marcos Highway?"

"Yes."

"Now I want you to lie in response to the next

question. Do you like pizza?"

"No."

"This time tell the truth. Do you like pizza?"

"Yes."

"Do you intend to lie on this test?"

"No."

"You were married to Elizabeth Tate?"

"Yes."

"Did you kill her?"

"No."

"Did you hire someone to kill her?"

"No."

"Did you kill Edward Barnes?"

"No."

"Did you hire someone to kill him?"

"No."

"Did you know your wife was having an affair?"

"Yes, I suspected she was."

"Did you know with whom she was having an affair?"

"No."

"Do you know how their bodies came to be on your ranch?"

He hesitated. His answer wasn't yes or no. He suspected. Mainly, he had a theory.

"Mr. Tate, do you know how their bodies came to be on your ranch?"

"Yes, I think so."

"Did you have anything to do with their bodies being discovered on your ranch?"

"No."

"Do you know who might have brought their bodies to your ranch?"

"No."

And so it went for another two and a half hours. Over

and over the same points. Finally, the polygrapher said, "That's it for now."

Vince unfastened the chest, bands, the arm cuff and removed the finger sensors. He couldn't resist asking, "Did I pass?" even though whether or not Evanson would tell him was debatable. "I'd like to get back to work."

"No major areas of concern," Evanson admitted. "Final word on when you officially resume your duties is up to the mayor and town council. I'll make the results available to the acting sheriff and Ranger Rasmussen, but the Rangers will remain in charge of this case."

"Understand." He nodded, then left the interview room to find Will. Maybe initial autopsy results would be available. Once again, he found his chief deputy ensconced in the sheriff's office. "Don't get too comfortable. I aced the poly."

Will gave him a sheepish grin, but then leaned back with his hands clasped behind this head. "This chair's damn comfortable. You sure I can't take it with me?"

"That's a big oh-hell-no." Vince laughed, feeling the tension leaching from his shoulders. Dark cloud over his head lifting. Blue skies in sight. "Anything back on the autopsies?"

"Matter of fact, I had a call from Ben. Seems they both were shot with the same nine mil. Barnes multiple times. Your wife, once, execution style." Will paused, then added, "Both had been tortured."

"Crap." No matter how their marriage had fallen apart, he never would've wish a death like that on her.

"Another interesting fact, due to the lack of decomp, the bodies had been kept on ice probably from the time they disappeared."

"The Rangers forensic team checked my freezer."

"Yes, they did. No human blood. Traces of bovine."

Vince nodded. "Texas ranch, figures."

"That's it for now. Toxicology pending."

"And still no sign of the bank's money? Find the money. Find our killer."

The phone rang. Will answered. All Vince could hear was one side of the conversation.

"Yes, sir. He's here now. Yes, sir." He handed the phone to Vince. "It's the mayor."

Vince smiled. He was about to get his administrative leave rescinded. "Yes, Mr. Mayor?"

"I hear good things about your polygraph."

"Yes. I aced it if I do say so myself."

"Then get back to work. Just stay hands-off with this case. Got it?"

"Got it." Smiling, he replaced the receiver on the phone. "Vacate that chair, Chief Deputy Rasmussen. Your backside has warmed it long enough."

Will grinned. "Great!" He jumped up. "It's all yours. Welcome back!"

Vince took possession of his desk, chair, badge, and service weapon. Will gave him an update of all things not related to the murder case. He would have enough paperwork to keep him busy for the rest of the week.

But sooner or later, he'd stop and see how Abby was coping. Crazy female. Had no business staying by herself with a burglar, who might be a killer, on the loose. One night with her at his place—enough to know he'd never gotten her out of his system. He wanted her there on a permanent basis. All he had to do was convince *her*.

Pesky trust issues would take longer to hash out.

It was almost eight when Abby unlocked the front door to her family home. Mid-summer twilight. An occasional firefly winked on and off. The air was fragrant, scented by the crape myrtle, heavy with pink blooms. Entering the code to stop the beeping, she then closed and locked the front door. After resetting the alarm, she left the motion detector off. No point in activating that until she went to bed.

When she'd gone to the ranch for her things, Vince had been nowhere in sight. Coward. Marti had tried to convince her to stay another night, but Abby wouldn't be dissuaded from returning home.

This was her house, and she'd be damned if she gave into fear and abandoned it. Tonight she'd taken precautions by using the security system. And don't forget the shotgun under her bed. All she had to do was make sure the dang thing was loaded. Vince would approved of that much anyway.

She couldn't help but wonder how his polygraph test went and if he were back on the job. Hopefully, he was. Otherwise, he would've come by to check on her. At least, she'd assumed he would since he'd seemed *so* concerned about her being alone in the house.

Dammit. Maybe she'd misread the signals. Maybe he didn't care that much, after all.

After a supper consisting of Diet Coke, microwave popcorn, and a handful of Hershey's Kisses, she decided to make an early night of it. Vince Tate could just go screw himself.

He waited until half past midnight. He planned to come in the back way, like he had the day before. Damn. He spied her car parked under the portico at the side of the house. She'd returned. He'd waited too long. Time was running out. He had to find that money and deed.

Time was running out for her, too. He'd just have her taken care of her like he had the others.

He eased to the back door, unlocking it easily with a pick.

He opened the door.

The piercing sound of the security alarm system woke Abby from a dead sleep. She covered her ears.

No. Get the shotgun. Thank heavens she'd taken time to load it before going to bed.

She sat up, swung her feet to the cool oak floor, and immediately went down on her knees to reach for the twelve gauge. She doubted the thing had ever been used, much less cleaned. Would it work or blow up in her face?

Still, it was better than meeting her intruder unarmed.

Her phone rang. Probably the alarm company checking to see if it was a false alarm. If she didn't answer, they would automatically notify the police department. At least they were supposed to. She could either hold the shotgun or answer the phone. Not much of a choice.

She moved swiftly to the door and locked it.

Hold on. The bathroom. It had a hall entrance as well as the one in her bedroom. She ran to the bathroom door and locked that one too.

Surely the very sound of the alarm would send the intruder scurrying away like the no-good rat he was.

Along with the blaring of the alarm, the pulse pounded in her ears. Her head might explode. Her heart hammered as if her ribs would break.

The door knob moved as if someone on the other side of the door was testing it.

She gasped. "Just so you know, I'm armed. There's a twelve gauge shotgun aimed at the door. I'll blast you if you try coming in."

She held her breath.

It was late. Far later than Vince had planned when he turned onto Elm, the street to Abby's house. The evening dispatcher come through the radio. "Code 459A at 501 Elm." That was the code for burglary alarm. Abby's address. "Unit one responding. I'm almost there." He hit the lights and siren then pressed the accelerator to the floor. He squealed to a stop in front of her house.

He jumped from the Tahoe, drawing his weapon. Safety off. Front door appeared secure. No lights on. He eased around to the portico where her Toyota Maxima was parked. That door also appeared secure. Now for the back. He poked his head around the corner. The screen door was ajar. He eased forward. Inner door open as well.

"Sheriff's Department," he called, entering the house. He quickly cleared the downstairs. "Abby!" he called and headed upstairs. The one thing that would really screw this up was if she mistook him for the intruder and shot him instead. "Abby. Sheriff's Department. No one downstairs. Are you all right?"

Just in case, he stood away from the door, tried the handle.

"Just so you know, I'm armed." He could hear the quivering in her voice. "There's a twelve-gauge shotgun aimed at the door. I'll blast you if you try coming in."

"Abby?" he said, louder this time to overcome the sound of the alarm.

He heard a long sigh. "Vince? Thank God. I'm unlocking the door now. Don't shoot me."

"I'm more worried you'll shoot me. Listen to me. Put the shotgun down, and *then* open the door."

"What if someone has a gun to your head? Why should I believe you?"

"Because I said so, dammit! Put down your gun and unlock the damn door." He didn't blame her for being cautious.

"All right. I'm laying the gun on the bed."

He waited, then heard the sound of the door being unlocked, then holstered his weapon. The door opened and Abby fell into his arms.

"Thank God, you're here."

Her body was soft and pliant against his, her arms snaking around his waist as she rested her head on his chest. His heartrate sped up. "I was just up the street when the call came in," he managed to get out. Her skin, smooth as satin and scented by a flowery lotion.... Oh, God. His senses overwhelmed, he buried his face in her hair and inhaled. Clean and citrusy.

He took a ragged breath. "You all right?"

He felt her nod against his chest. "Let's get this alarm turned off. Where's the keypad?"

She raised her head then glanced over her shoulder. "There's one beside the bed."

"Then enter your pass code and shut it off....please."

"Right." She moved away, reluctantly it seemed. He hid a smile.

The sudden cessation of sound made his ears feel full. "I need to call this in and shut off the lights. Then I'll check your back door."

"Thank you. Would you like some coffee?"

How considerate and thoughtful when she'd just been scared to death. "No. Don't go to any trouble."

"No trouble. I won't go back to sleep tonight. Not after all this excitement."

"Neither will I," he said. He left Abby's bedroom,

although it was tempting to stay and pull her into his arms again. She looked damn hot in her rock band sleep-shirt and tousled hair. He shook the image from his mind. *Focus*.

He went downstairs and left the house through the front door. Once inside the Tahoe, he called dispatch, reported in, then signed out for the night. "You can reach me on my cell."

He locked the SUV and checked the perimeter of the house and grounds. Wonder what she would think of him spending the night? No way would he let her stay alone. The intruder could be waiting in the shadows for him to leave.

Abby drew on a nylon robe over her Guns N' Roses sleep shirt. She hadn't meant to fall right into Vince's arms. Honestly, though, she'd almost kissed him for showing up so quickly. She smiled to herself. He'd been coming to check on her. He hadn't forgotten, after all.

Downstairs she quickly set a pot of coffee to brewing. She glanced at the backdoor and shivered. She walked over, pulled the screen door to, locked its flimsy lock, then the wood door. How had the intruder managed to open it? She'd locked it before going to bed.

The front door opened. She started at the sound, even as Vince walked back to the kitchen. "This is nice." he said, looking around. "The kitchen's changed a lot since you left for school."

"If I remember correctly, we had a lot of fun burning microwave popcorn," she said with a smile. Fond memories. The coffeemaker burbled and hummed. She stood and pulled a couple of cups from an upper cabinet. She poured two cups, handing one to Vince, she said, "The kitchen was all Mom's vision. She used to email me about the changes, asking my opinion on the best appliances and finishes. She had an interior designer, but Mom contended it would be mine someday so I might as well have a choice. We just didn't know how soon that would be." Her throat tightened. Her eyes stung with unshed tears. More than anything, she mourned her mother's loss. She'd never know her grandchildren. So many things.

Vince set his cup on the counter. "Sorry. Didn't mean to upset you."

"You didn't. Just sometimes. I wish I'd been closer when she needed me. "I never got to say good-bye...to either one of them." She sniffed. "They were both good people, and they deserved better. They should've lived long happy lives."

"No argument here." He walked around to her side of the island. "There's something I never told you about your father's death."

"What do you mean? What else was there to tell?"

"At the time, I didn't want to upset you, and there wasn't anything to connect it to. Your father was shot by a druggie, it's true. But what the department never revealed was he was tortured before he was shot. Now I have to consider if his killer was someone who was hired to obtain information or the location of whatever someone still thinks is hidden in your house."

"What could it be other than the deed?"

"And what about the deed?"

She quickly brought him up to speed about what she'd learned at the court house. "Right! There's a deed transfer is pending to a Macedonia Corporation. I handed a copy over to Dad's attorney, Samuel Dunaway—well, actually, I left the copy with his paralegal since he was out of the office. Didn't he graduate with your class?"

"Yeah. Sam and I played football and baseball together, too. He's a good man." He leaned back against the kitchen island. Every movement of his tall muscular body was casual but fluid. "Do you have another copy of the deed? Where's the property located?"

Abby shook her head. "I don't know. All I remember is some plot this or that number. I figure the lawyer can scope that out, as well as, what this Macedonia Corp. is."

"Not local. But I can look up the plot number for you."

"It just hit me." She flashed him a wide smile. "You must've passed the lie detector test."

He smiled, his sky blue eyes crinkling at the corners. "I did. Damn glad of it, too."

His gaze settled on her, warm and intense. Suddenly awkward, she pulled her robe together, making sure her breasts were covered. "I guess I'd better let you get on home. It's really late."

"Uh-uh." Vince shook his head. "I'm not going anywhere tonight."

"I'm sure he won't be back tonight." Her neck and cheeks grew warm at the thought of him staying. "Especially now that he knows my alarm is active."

"He certainly knew how to use a lock pick. It's no real stretch that he could know how to disarm your system."

She gasped, her hand going to her throat. "Really?" Before the first break-in, she'd always felt safe in Kenton Valley. She'd certainly never bothered with the security system, but her father had installed it for some reason. Now, she couldn't imagine not using it.

"Probably not, but I'd feel better if I stuck around here tonight. Then tomorrow, you can move back to the ranch and stay there until I catch this dude."

Moving back to the ranch. Somehow that sounded like a not-so-bad idea. "I still have to open the drugstore and all that entails," she protested somewhat feebly.

"You should be relatively safe in town during the daytime. You oughtn't work any nights."

She frowned, not wanting to appear to give in too easily. "I guess you're right. I'll call Darla tomorrow and explain why she's stuck with nights for a while."

"Sounds like a plan. Now why don't you go back to bed" His tone was tender and comforting. "No one's breaking in on you tonight."

"I have three other bedrooms," she offered. "Take your pick."

He gave her a shy smile. "You don't want to share?"

Her chin dropped, at his suggestion, but she recovered quickly. "I snore. That's the reason for my divorce." A playful fib, but a harmless one.

"Right." He rounded the island, closing the distance between them. "I don't plan on sleeping."

"Oh—" Her heart skipped into overdrive. She swallowed hard.

His expression grew teasing. "No—I mean I'm staying awake. I'll stay down here. Just in case."

An unexpected sense of disappointment wracked through her. She stood, crossing her arms over her breasts. "Well, then, I'll say Goodnight."

"Night, Abby. Sleep tight." He shot her a quick salute. "Thanks for the coffee."

"There's more in the pantry if you need it." She nodded at the door to the pantry. "I still wish you'd stay in one of the guest rooms."

"I'm fine," he assured her, his voice deep and resonant. "I don't sleep on the job. All I need is plenty of coffee."

She met his steady gaze with one of her own. "But this isn't your job. This is more personal." Yeah, more like a personal body guard than a lawman.

"I'd say so." His tone was playful, his mouth quirking upward in a half grin.

"Right." She ducked her head and headed for the stairs. How would she ever sleep knowing he was only steps away?

Vince watched the sway of her slim hips as she literally ran for the stairs. Her thin robe didn't do much to hide her slender curves. Fine with him. Very fine.

His lids grew heavy. He shook his head. Time for another cup.

He hid behind a hedge of wax myrtle. Damn her. She had a security system. His ears were still ringing. Why hadn't she been kind enough to place a sign in the yard like other folks? Half of those weren't connected anyway. And that sheriff. He must've been barely a half a block away. He'd come roaring in so fast with his lights and siren, leaving almost no time to take cover. Still, he'd managed to keep out of sight even when the lawman inspected the grounds. Surely he'd see everything was all right in the house and leave. But no. Lights stayed on in the kitchen. An hour later and the sheriff was still there. Might as well go home. He'd have to take his chances another night. Or maybe use another method.

Chapter Six

After a basically uneventful day at the drugstore, Abby was ready to leave. Not totally uneventful, though. Beth had come over from the Mercantile to gossip about Vince's having spent the night at Abby's.

"How did *you* know?" Abby demanded. Beth was only the fourth person to mention it.

Leaning her elbows on the counter, Beth smiled. "It's a small town, or have you forgotten? So, how was it? Was it as good as you remembered? Better?"

Abby gave her friend the old eye roll. "For what it's worth, there was an attempted break-in. He stayed to protect me. He didn't even use the guest room. He stayed downstairs and decimated my stash of Kona coffee."

"How disappointing." Beth batted her long dark lashes furiously like a silent movie star.

"No. Not really."

Beth gave a huff of disgust. "I mean disappointing for *me*. I thought I'd get to hear some juicy details. Get a vicarious thrill, don't you know."

"Out of here. Can't you see how busy I am," she said, shooing Beth back to the Mercantile.

After updating Darla, Abby headed out to her car. She'd packed quickly that morning. She texted Vince.

DOES MARTI KNOW I'M COMING?

YEP

THX. LEAVING NOW.

BE RIGHT BHIND U

The drive to the Tate ranch was a pleasant one. It was a typical Texas summer day. The wide sky was the bluest of blues. The cottonwoods and grew tall on one side of the hill and the other side of the road was carpeted with Indian Blanket. She rounded a curve ready to cross the bridge over a dry creek when a black SUV with darkened windows came up fast behind her and bumped her rear bumper.

What the devil!

The SUV started to pass, sideswiped her hard, metal screeching. The side airbags exploded as the Maxima careened through the guard rail. She held her breath and braced for the crash. Somehow, time seemed to slow and fast-forward at the same time.

Her head hit the steering wheel. Stars. Then black.

After answering Abby's text, Vince finished the last of his reports. Damn. He still needed to locate that plot number in question for Abby. As for the Macedonia Corporation, he'd not been able to locate it. Tomorrow, he'd assign one of the forensic IT guys to do a more thorough search. But he had a sneaking suspicion it was some kind of a shell company. But what kind of dealings would Abby's dad have had with one of those? Had he been involved in something illegal? Was that why he was killed?

He pulled up the Los Marcos County records and keyed in the plot number. The area covered by the deed, owned by Jerald Fields, Abby's father, was four-hundred acres, five miles north of town. Nothing much there but scrub oak and mesquite. And hills. What would could possibly be of interest to this Macedonia Corp? Guess that would depend on what the company's business was.

He printed out the information for Abby, slipped the printout into a folder and into his briefcase. She was already on her way to the ranch so they could review the land deed tonight after supper.

He was almost home when he came to the bridge that crossed Simon's Creek. Half the right guard rail was missing. He slowed. Stopped. Jumped out. Looked down.

His heart almost stopped. Abby's white Maxima was tipped onto the passenger side. He reached for his mic. Called for an ambulance.

Heart hammering like a bass drum, he skidded down through the creek side brush and rocks. "Abby!" He climbed on top and tried to force open the driver side door. "Abby!" He tugged to no avail, the damage too great.

He scrambled off the vehicle and picked up a rock. He'd have to bash one of the windows.

His feet on the ground, he struck the windshield. The safety glass shattered in a web, but didn't fracture through. He struck again, harder. Success! He took off his shirt, wrapped his hand and forced it through the opening, jerking the windshield from the frame. "Abby!"

She groaned. Alive, thank God. "Abby, I'm here. An ambulance is on the way." He sniffed. Gasoline. Leaking.

"M'all right."

"Can you unfasten your seatbelt?"

She grunted, then he heard a groan of frustration. "Can't get to it."

He pulled out his knife. Reaching through the aperture, he said, "Hold on. I'm going to cut it. Can you get your feet under you so you can get out?" He sawed through the seat belt, but held onto it to keep her from falling.

She wriggled around trying to get her feet out from under the steering column. "Give me your hands. I won't let you fall."

"Anything broken?"

"Don't think so." Her hand went to her forehead. Blood streamed freely from where she'd hit the steering wheel. "My head hurts like a you-know what. Actually, I hurt all over."

"I can imagine. You'll be all right. Got a whopper of a knot, though. "

"Not a lot of room to move around. The console's in the way." She brushed tiny slivers of glass from her chest.

"Wrap your arms around my neck. I'll pull you out."

"I see where this is going," she said. "Wrap my arms around your neck—uh huh, sure."

"You're not hurt too bad if you can joke."

She wrapped her arms around his neck all the same. "Are you sure you're strong enough? I'm kind of bottom heavy."

"Less talking and more assisting would be of help here."

"If you say so."

"I do."

He braced his stance, grimacing because he was probably going to hurt her, then dragged her from the wrecked Maxima.

"Ouch!"

"Would you rather stay inside until the Jaws of Life arrives? The fuel line is leaking."

She rubbed her knees, which had scraped over some retained safety glass. "I'll live."

He carried her up to the Tahoe, setting her down on the running board.

She brushed the hair away from her injury. "You know you probably should've waited for the EMTs to get here and put a collar around my neck."

Gently, he brushed glass slivers from her hair. "If I had one, I'd put it over your mouth. That might work better."

"Nothing wrong with my mouth," she muttered.

"That's for damn sure." But he knew she was right. True, he shouldn't have moved her, but he could still smell fuel, and he wasn't about to risk her being caught in an explosion.

"How did this happen? Looks like you were sideswiped." He kept his tone neutral, but just let him get his hands on the bastard who did this.

"Big black SUV, dark windows—just like in the movies. Bumped me then tried to pass on the bridge and knocked me through the guard rail." She smiled up at him, her green eyes sparkling. "Aren't you going to ask me if I got the license number?"

He shrugged. "No one ever gets the tag number."

"I got part of it. APR...something."

"That's a good start." He smiled. She was observant. "Now, how about the make or model of the SUV?"

She worried her bottom lip with her teeth. "Sorry. Big and black is about as specific as I can get."

"Figures." He shook his head.

"If you'd been right behind me as your text said, this might not've happened." She poked his chest with her finger.

"Wow. That's all the thanks I get for saving your life?" he teased back. God, if he'd lost her...

Resting her head on his shoulder, she reached to caress his cheek. "Thank you. Saving my life is getting to be a habit with you. Careful, I could get used to it." Her tone was soft, her breath warm against his neck.

"It's not a bad habit. Seems like someone is out to get you. But I'm going to get them first."

The wailing sound of an approaching ambulance rent

the air. "At last," she said, in that charming, teasing way of hers, "I'll get some decent medical care."

In spite of many protests, Abby eventually allowed herself to be tended to by the EMTs and loaded into the back of the ambulance. "No siren, please." She wagged her finger at the younger of the EMTs. "I already have a headache."

Vince remained behind, in order to deal with the accident report, assuring her he'd see her as soon as the accident scene was cleared.

Two hours later, after a seriously annoying CAT scan and the additional tender mercies of the ER nurses, she emerged from the Los Marcos Co. General hospital. Vince was just pulling up.

"Great timing," she told him as he opened the passenger side door.

"Figured you'd need a ride. Your Maxima is totaled."

"Are you sure? Oh—my cellphone's still in the car somewhere. I really need to call my insurance—"

"Already done. A rental car will be delivered to the ranch this evening. " He handed her the cell phone, then shut the door. "Seatbelt," he warned with a nod.

Complying, she smiled. "You really jump right in and take care of things, don't you. As an independent woman of the twenty-first century, I might call you on that."

"But you're not going to." He got in and fastened his own seatbelt.

"No. Because I'm afraid I really appreciate not having to deal with it right now. But you ought to be finding out who's trying to get rid of me. 'Cause I'm officially tired of this woman in jeopardy scenario."

He started the motor. "I have someone checking the

DMV right now." He faced her with a laser bright smile. "Listen, doll, I know how to delegate."

Doll. Now that's what he used to call her in high school. "Right. What do you say we delegate some dinner. Think maybe Marti's keeping it warm for us." Her stomach growled.

He chuckled. "I'm counting on it."

"Good. Because all I had for breakfast was coffee. Add a bag of chips for lunch. You could say I'm a tad hungry." Her stomach growled again.

"So I hear. Home, James. Forget the park."

She flashed him a wide smile. "Right."

When they drove up to the ranch, Abby spied Marti Mills, hands on hips, pacing on the front porch. "What on earth am I going to do with the two of you? Dead bodies. Shootings, Break-ins. And now, wrecks. If I weren't a hardy Texas woman, I'd take you and we'd skedaddle to New York City where it has to be less exciting than this place."

"And I'd go with you in a heartbeat," Abby said. "I hope we haven't ruined dinner by being so late."

"No indeed." Marti wiped her hands on her apron. "My pot roast wouldn't dare dry out. I have culinary secrets like you wouldn't believe. You'll see. It's a simple supper. Pot roast cooked with vegetables. Tender enough to fall off the fork. Hot buttermilk biscuits ready to come from the oven in the next five minutes. Chocolate cream pie for dessert."

Abby's mouth watered. "You had me at pot roast."

Guess that showed her. Now all he had to do was listen to the evening news to hear whether she was dead or merely injured. He drove past the Tate ranch to his own small spread where he kept this SUV hidden in one of the barns. He parked the SUV out of sight, closed the barn doors, and went inside his small house.

He turned grabbed a beer from the fridge, went into the living room, and turned on the television. Shouldn't take long. Sorely tempted to drive back into town and see what was happening at the scene of the hopefully tragic accident. Too big a risk. Wouldn't want to get stopped by law enforcement and have to answer their lame questions.

After doing entirely too much justice to Marti's fine dinner, Abby spread the plot map Vince had brought over his desk. She smoothed out the wrinkled edges. "I don't understand why my father bought this parcel of land. It's all scrub. And I don't understand why his lawyer didn't know anything about it. Very curious."

"I thought the same. Where do you think he got the money for it? Could this Macedonia Corporation have used him as a front man to make the purchase?"

"I can't think where else the money could've come from. They'd just done the first floor reno, and I've seen those receipts. It was a *major* expense." Vince came up behind her, his body oh-so-close. How was she supposed to focus, much less think? But she persevered. "What if something like oil or rich mineral deposits had been discovered? These Macedonia folks didn't want to let on, so they—like you said—used my dad as a front man to make the purchase. But why would they have him killed before the transfer went through?"

"Maybe the two aren't related, after all." His hands rested on her shoulders, lightly massaging her sore muscles. His hands on her body. She wanted to melt into his arms.

But no.

"But he was tortured. Why—?" She stopped short. She could really get used to having Vince around. "What if along the way, he discovered that something wasn't on the up and up, so he balked and refused to allow the transfer."

"That's certainly plausible." He turned her around to face him. His gaze was warm and inviting.

Honestly, the man was sucking all the air from the room. She dragged in a ragged breath. "But then, what does all this have to do with the murder of your wife and the banker?" she managed to ask, but being so close to him was turning her knees to Jello. She placed her hand on his upper arm to steady herself.

"The deeper we dig," he said, "the more complex the situation becomes. I still don't believe in coincidence. The tip on the bodies and the break-in at your house on the same day—it's too much. But we're missing something. That's for sure."

"Maybe the Rangers know something we don't," Abby suggested, more and more aware of Vince's presence. So drawn to him. Just like years ago.

"Maybe they do, doll." His tone was low and intimate. "But *I* know one thing they don't."

"Really?" Her heart pounded in her ears. Heat flashed through her body and pooled between her thighs.

"They don't know I'm going to kiss you right now." He dipped his head and covered her mouth with his. Her arms circled his neck. She clung for dear life as he explored her mouth. In danger of losing herself, she gasped for air.

A quick knock sounded. They jumped apart. Her head spinning, Abby grabbed the desk for support. Getting caught necking. Like being back in high school. Her cheeks must be on fire like the rest of her body.

"Whoa! Sorry. Forget I was here." Chase Tate said,

then spun to leave.

"What do you need, little brother?" Vince's tone was a growl.

"Damn, if I can't remember now." Chase's tan cheeks flushed. "Oh, Marti said to ask if y'all wanted some fresh coffee."

"She did, did she?"

Chase nodded, backing toward the door. "Yep. Sure did."

"That's done. Mission accomplished. Get the heck outta here."

"I'm going." He waved both hands. "I'm gone. As in Chance and I are heading out to the Branding Iron. Friday night, you know."

By the time, Chase made his escape, her breathing had returned to some resemblance of normal. Her legs were no longer Jello. "Maybe we should take a break and have some of that fresh coffee."

Vince heaved a sigh. "I reckon we ought, at that."

Still unsure whether to be disappointed or relieved, Abby ambled into the kitchen, Vince sticking by her side.

"You're too good to us, Marti," Abby said. "Let me help with something."

"No ma'am, Miss Abigail Fields. You've had a concussion or something thereabouts. You're not lending a hand in my kitchen. Not tonight." She pulled out a chair. "Now sit yourself down and take a breather."

Abby sat.

Marti reached into an upper cabinet and removed a bottle of NSAIDs. "Need a little something for your headache?" She set the pill bottle in front of Abby. "I know it's bound to be hurting." She stopped long enough to turn to Vince, wagging her finger. "Young man, you need to take better care of this li'l gal. And that's the truth."

"Yes, ma'am. I'm doing my best, but she's on the stubborn side."

"That's called spirit and spunk. Mighty highly desired attributes in a young woman."

"Yes, ma'am." Vince nodded, pulling out a chair and sitting.

No doubt who the real boss in the household was. Abby smiled. "You tell him, Marti. He seems to think I should hide away here at the ranch until *he* finds the bad man."

"Men. Especially Texans. They're all like that. But this time, you might want to consider doing just that."

"You'll get no argument from me," Abby agreed with a wide smile up at Vince.

"Ganging up on me, are you? It's really not fair," Vince said. "Women. Especially Texans."

"That's the way it's always been." Marti nodded for emphasis. "And will always be."

Marti untied and removed her apron, then folded it. "Now I'm a-going let you young folks have the kitchen to yourselves. My favorite TV show is coming on."

Abby's interest perked. "What's your favorite?"

"What else but *Scandal*? Best nighttime soap there is. Oh, that fast-talking Olivia and that sexy President Grant. I just can't get enough of all that sex and political skullduggery." Marti smiled. "I know it's on hiatus, right now, but I can't bear to miss seeing what they're up to again. Plum scary when you think about it. But I suspect we're not supposed to think too hard, are we?" Marti gave a little cackle. With that she scuttled from the kitchen.

Abby smiled. "She's a treasure. I could get used to having Marti around. Careful I don't steal her away."

"The only way you're going to have Marti fulltime is if you—"

"If I *what?*"

"If you move in full time." He reached across the table, covering her hand with his large one. "I wouldn't mind that one bit."

"Oh, I'm sure Marti has her hands full seeing after you and your brothers."

"You're not much trouble."

"*Not much*," she scoffed. "Seems like I've been a lot of trouble lately." She eased her hand from his. Things with Vince were getting a little too comfortable. Or maybe she wasn't ready to jump into another relationship. But the way he made her feel, omigod.

She gave herself a mental shake. "I guess I'd better head off to bed." More than reluctant to leave the warm coziness of the kitchen, she rose.

"Long day." His tone was understanding, but his gaze seemed to beg her to stay.

"For both of us. I still need to open the drugstore first thing in the morning. I'd better get some rest."

And think. I need time to think.

He stood. "Ma'am, may I walk you to your room?"

Abby chuckled. "Sure." She took two of the NSAIDs and swallowed them down with her coffee.

Vince walked beside her upstairs, his hand placed in the small of her back. He always knew how to treat a woman, even when they were in high school. Never crass or in-your-face raunchy like some of the jocks were. Always polite. Somehow, even his politeness was so sexy.

They stopped at the door to the guest room. His gaze was warm, tender even. "You know I'm just down the hall...if you need anything."

"I know." She shut the door and dope-slapped herself. What the heck was the matter with her anyway? Did she or did she not want a closer relationship with Vince? Of course, she did, but—

But was it just old feelings resurfacing? Was Vince drawn to her just because she was there and convenient? Or was this the beginning of something new. Something more lasting than hot sex in the bed of a pickup.

No. All this togetherness was too much. She still didn't trust him. They just had too much history to let this go on any further. They were just never meant to be. He'd gone off to college while she was still in high school. He'd made promises. She'd made them too.

Then a month after school started, his brother Chance told her all about his big brother's exploits in at Texas A. & M. The frat parties. Wild and willing coeds. That had been the final straw. The bone deep hurt was the real reason she'd chosen the University of Georgia's pharmacy program instead of going to school in Austin as they'd planned.

Abby softly shut the door to her room. Vince could've groaned in frustration—or he would've if he weren't in danger of being overheard. Granted, Marti was immersed in her TV show in the back of the house, and his brothers had left for the Branding Iron Bar for their Friday night blow-out.

He walked to his room and shut the door behind him. Dammit. Too many people lived in this house. Somehow, he had to get Abby away from the ranch if they were ever going to take things to the next level. Not that he was sure that was what she wanted. But it, sure as hell, was what *he* wanted.

It was what he'd been afraid of all along. Rekindling the old fire that burned between them so steadily when they were not much more than kids.

When he'd gone to college and left her behind, she'd sworn she'd be faithful. He'd buckled down and studied hard to keep his football scholarship. Then came the emails from his brother Chance, telling him how much fun Abby was having without him, dating two of her fellow classmates at the same time. Guys that had been friends of his.

But now, time to face the truth. No matter how badly she'd treated him in the past, he was still in love with her.

He had to wait until the ten o'clock news to hear the first word about the accident. "Driver taken to hospital with non-life-threatening injuries." Indeed. He'd just have to do better next time. Nothing was turning out like he'd planned.

Nothing!

Chapter Seven

At six, Vince walked into the kitchen. "Abby up yet?"

"She's already *gone.*" Marti handed him a steaming cup of coffee. "Ran out of here with a cup of coffee in one hand and one of my cinnamon buns in the other." She shook her head. "I don't know what to think about her. She doesn't eat enough to keep a bird alive."

Vince nodded his agreement, then took a sip of the hot brew. The drugstore didn't open until seven. Was she avoiding him? He'd have to find out, one way or another.

"I'm out of here," he said with a wave.

"Well, I never!"

He didn't respond, but he'd bet dollars to donuts, the housekeeper's hands were on her hips.

The sun was just up over the northern hills. Dew glistened on the grass as Vince got into the SUV. He liked being up early with only the sun in his line of sight. More test results should be back from the autopsies this morning. Now that he'd been cleared, Ranger Ben Rasmussen should have no problem sharing all he'd learned.

***

Vince drove past the drugstore. Still closed. Abby's rental car nowhere in sight. Damn. At the next block, he took a left, drove another two blocks, then turned down Elm. Sure enough. Her rental car was parked under the portico. What the hell was she doing back in her house? He'd be sure to find out when he saw her again.

Crazy woman had a death wish. Fine. Let her call him again. See how fast he'd respond.

Still in a temper over Abby's foolhardiness, he picked up the phone to call the Rangers when Ben Rasmussen walked into his office. Today he was dressed more casually, in starched, pressed jeans, a Sig-Sauer P226 pistol strapped to his side. Vince stood and shook hands with his friend. Ben tipped back his white cowboy hat and straddled a chair.

Vince set aside the phone. "What do you know that I don't?"

"No drugs in their systems except caffeine and alcohol," Ben said. "They'd eaten recently. Dinner according to the stomach contents. Salad and chicken for Liz Tate. Steak and potatoes for Ed Barnes. Both had wine."

"So they were killed by someone they trusted or, at least, felt comfortable with."

Ben nodded. "Perhaps, someone who was complicit in the bank embezzlement, as well."

Vince rubbed his chin, considering whether or not to reveal his additional concerns. "I have to wonder if there's some connection between the break-ins at Abigail Fields's house. She had another close call yesterday, a more serious one. Thoughts?"

"Since you're asking, it's kind of a stretch. How do you

figure?"

"I know this is a wild hunch. What if it goes even further back than the bodies and the break-ins? Her father's death could fit in there, somewhere. It was obvious whoever broke into Abby's house was looking for something. So we took her father's papers back to the ranch to go through them. She discovered a check to the county court clerk. When she went to the courthouse, it was for a land deed that was in the process of being transferred from her father to a Macedonia Corporation."

He unrolled the plot map and spread it across his desk. "Right there," he said, indicating the section of land. "For all intents and purposes, this company appears to be a shell company out of New Jersey. Why else would they buy 400 acres of scrub land" Neither she or her father's lawyer knew anything about it."

"Missing money. Dead bodies. Shell company out of New Jersey. Sounds mob related."

"Another reason for combining Fields's murder with the rest is he was tortured. Could've been a murder for hire."

"Sounding more and more mob-related."

"But Jerald Fields, the local pharmacist and the mob?" Vince shook his head. "I never would've thought it. Don't know what Abby is going to think if that's even close to the truth."

"She won't like it."

"No. She idolized both her parents. Her father's murder coming so close after her mother's death was a real blow."

"Sounds like you know her pretty well," Ben said with a skeptical expression.

"We—uh, hung out in school. And I investigated her father's murder. Yeah, you could say I know her pretty well."

Ben stood, adjusting his cowboy hat to level. "Careful your priorities don't get out of whack."

Vince nodded. "This is your jurisdiction. Just keep me in the loop."

The Ranger ambled from Vince's office.

Now. Time to find out what Abby's up to.

Abby glanced at the clock on her phone. Almost seven. Time to open the drugstore. With a groan, she got up off her knees and brushed her hands on her slacks. In spite of all her soreness from the accident, she'd managed to straighten the living room and kitchen in the space of an hour. The furniture was upright in its usual position. The cushions were in place, but all the upholstery would have to be replaced. Nothing else would suffice.

The phone vibrated then rang. She noted Vince's private number. "Hey. What's up?"

"You left awful damn early this morning. Anything up with you? You sound a little breathless."

"I decided I'd left this house in a mess long enough. I needed to straighten things. Take some measurements for the upholsterer. That sort of thing."

"You're at the house. Alone?"

"Yes. And I've decided I'm not going to let a burglar scare me off."

"Drawing a line in the sand. You're not worried about someone breaking in again?"

"I am, but I'll take precautions. I still have that twelve-gauge shotgun."

"Are you sure you could—"

"Look. I hate to be rude, but I've got to get to the drugstore." She disconnected, wincing as she did so. Now he'd be pissed off, but too bad. She was tired of his over-protective act. As for why he was, she didn't know or want to guess.

She washed her hands in the kitchen sink, dried them, and then grabbed a clean white lab jacket from the downstairs closet. She'd have to hurry or she'd be late. And she was never late.

Slowly, he drove by the Fields house on Elm. Strange car in the drive. Uh-huh. Probably a rental. He was pretty sure he'd totaled her Maxima. His big mistake was not taking time to stop and finish her off. Still, it was one of the busier roads in the county, since it led to the next town. The risk had been too great. But his business partners wouldn't be happy. They wanted the money. Money and the deed they'd waited nearly a year to get their hands on. But more important than the money was the land deal still in limbo. Damn Fields for his last-minute pangs of conscience. They'd gotten him killed.

No wonder his partners were getting impatient. And when *they* became impatient...

He shivered at the thought. It was time he stepped it up.

No more mistakes or half-efforts.

Abby closed down the pharmacy computer for lunch. There hadn't been anything in the house, so she'd head over to the Mercantile for lunch then pick up a few items for the fridge. Either Beth or Lola should be free for a quick chat before her lunch hour was over.

She walked to the front of the store. "Ellen, I'm taking lunch. I'll be at the Mercantile if there's anything urgent.

Just text me."

Nodding, Ellen never bothered to look up from her iPhone. "Sure thing."

Abby wasn't a slave driver, by any means, but she couldn't resist suggesting, "Aisle four needs restocking...if you're not too busy." She wasn't normally passive aggressive, either, but Ellen seemed to bring it out.

About to cross the street, she glanced to her left. Vince's Tahoe pulled up and parked in front of the store. She steeled her determination. Might as well get it over with.

His long legs emerged from the SUV. She held back the sigh that built within her chest. He had absolutely no business being so ruggedly handsome. His gaze was fixed on her as he closed the distance between them. Her mouth grew dry. "Good morning, Sheriff."

He tipped his hat. "Mornin', Abby. You left awful early this morning."

He'd invaded her personal space. She took a step back so she wouldn't have to crane her neck. "We already covered that ground on the phone."

Keep talking. Maybe he'll move on. "The intruder made such a mess. I couldn't put it off any longer. The furniture needs recovering, so that's another thing to take care of."

Did she imagine it, or had he just given her an eye roll? "You're not concerned about him trying again?"

She shrugged. "I look at it like this. He's made two attempts at the house without success. I'll be careful, but I'm not going to let him run me out of my home."

She turned to walk away, but Vince grabbed her wrist. "You're fooling yourself if you think he won't come back. I've been shot at. *You've* been run off the road. What does it take to get through your thick head that you're in danger?"

Her chin dropped in disbelief. "My thick head? Did you *really* just say that?" Another comment like that and she'd have to smack him upside the head.

"I did. Furthermore, if you won't stay at the ranch where you can be looked after, then I'm going to move in with you until I catch 'im."

She planted her feet apart and raised her chin. "You're *what*?"

"You heard me. If you won't look out after yourself, I will."

She pulled herself to her full five feet, three inches. "I am *not* some child or delicate flower that has to be rescued," she said, trying to keep her voice low. But she was mad. And no other man could make her so freaking mad.

"You've been doing a damn good imitation of it. So far."

A wave of righteous anger flashed through her. "Of all the high-handed—" She sputtered, "A-and you're going way above the call of duty."

"Guilty on both charges. Duty has nothing to do with it. I care about you, Abigail Fields. I'll never understand you. I thought we were getting to a good place. If not already there, then on the way."

"Under your thumb? Under your control? Is that what you call a *good place*?" In spite of her efforts at self-control, her voice rose.

"It's not a matter of control. It's a matter of your safety. As for the good place, I was referring to us. The personal us. You and me. I've enjoyed getting close to you again. I thought it was mutual. Reckon I was mistaken."

Abby glanced over her shoulder as someone walked by them. She dropped her voice. "Do you realize we're on the sidewalk right in front of my store? Everyone in town will hear about this discussion before the sun goes down."

Another eye roll. Damn, how dare he!

"They can already hear you. Come sit in the SUV with me."

"I'm on my way to lunch." She turned and struck off across the street.

He followed. "Abigail."

Ignoring his dogged presence on her tail, Abby entered the Mercantile. Why couldn't he simply take the hint and disappear? She walked into the cafe section.

Lola Wheaton looked up from the counter and smiled. She and her sister Bethany were polar opposites. Lola was a brunette with blue eyes, while Beth was a blonde with brown eyes. "Abby and Vince. Why it's like old times." She handed them two menus.

Giving a tiny shake of her head, Abby scowled.

"Not Abby *and* Vince then," she said with a puzzled expression. "Two tables for one?"

"Yes," Abby replied with a snap.

"One table for two," Vince said at the same time. "Will you please join me for lunch, Ms. Fields?"

Abby glared and clenched her jaw. "Fine."

She sat, opened the menu, then glanced over her shoulder at the blackboard for the daily special. "Reubens. Yum."

Vince sat across from her. "Abby, I don't understand what changed. We were comfortable together at the ranch."

"Too comfortable if you ask me," she said quietly. "So we dated when we were in high school. We're not kids anymore." She unwrapped her eating utensils. She loved the fact that the Mercantile didn't use plastic tableware.

"No, and as adults, we should be able to have a discussion without you getting all het up. You make me feel like I've broken some unwritten rule. A rule, I might add, I have no idea what it is."

"For example, I've been back home an entire six months, and until the break-in, you ignored me."

"Hold on. Didn't I investigate your father's murder? I certainly didn't ignore you then."

"You treated me like a *stranger*."

"I acted in a professional manner. You can't fault me for that. It's my job after all."

"So moving into my house without any regard to my wishes is part of your job. Is that professional?"

"I thought we'd gone beyond that. My mistake." He stood. "Have a nice sandwich."

"I will." She turned to Lola. "I'll take a Reuben, easy on the dressing, and fries."

"Well, that was certainly exciting. What's up with the two of you? I heard you were staying out at the Tate ranch...since the break-ins. But you didn't look too cozy to me."

"Is he gone?" Abby asked, unwilling to turn around and be caught watching him.

"Oh, yeah. He's gone. From the look of him, maybe *forever*."

"Things were getting a little too cozy, if you know what I mean."

Lola slid into the booth across from Abby. She leaned forward, her eyes bright with interest. "No, I don't. But you'll tell me—right?"

"Not until you put my order in. I'm *hungry*."

"Right." Lola jumped up and put in the order.

Thankfully, another two more diners came into the cafe, leaving Abby to herself.

Small towns were the worst for everyone knowing everyone's business. Kenton Valley had to be the worst of the worst.

Never had he felt more like taking Abigail Fields across his knee and spanking her. He wasn't totally against the old adage, spare the rod and spoil the child. That's exactly how she was acting.

Stubborn. Reckless. And—dammit, he couldn't think of another negative to describe her. Infuriating, yeah!

That's the third. Damned infuriating.

She got to him in more ways than he could count. A real bona fide button pusher—that's what she was. At least where his buttons were concerned.

Whether she believed it or not, she was in danger. And he *would* spend the night at her house if he had to unroll a sleeping bag on her front porch.

Let the town gossips chew on that.

There'd been many naysayers when he'd been appointed sheriff by the town council to fill out his father's term. Too young. Too immature. But he'd been re-elected at the end of that term.

"Whoa! What's up, brother?"

His brother Chance was coming into the Mercantile as Vince was coming out. "Almost had lunch with Abby, but she's in a mood. So I didn't."

"Now what have you done to piss off our houseguest?" Chance grinned. "Must've been bad."

"She's not our house guest anymore. She moved back home."

"Something really bad," he said with a pleased grin. "Guess I'd better go inside and apologize for you being a horse's behind."

"Suit yourself."

Vince crossed the street. If he wasn't mistaken, his

little brother had a crush on Abby. Always had, even in high school. For all the good it did him. Abby belonged to him, and he'd give his little brother a smack upside the head if he wasn't careful.

Abby was ready to bite into her Reuben, when she heard, "Abby, fancy meeting you here." She glanced over her shoulder and smiled. "Hey, Chance." She patted the side of the table Vince had vacated not a minute before. "Join me."

A smile lit up the young man's face as he slid into the booth. "Just met my big brother. Storming out of here, looking like a storm cloud, too. Y'all have words?"

"Maybe," she admitted, not willing to go into details. Anything between Vince and her was private, so she changed the subject. "So what are you up to? Not enough to keep you busy at the ranch?"

"Oh, there's plenty to do there. I came into town for supplies. Marti gave me a long list. And given that she's the one responsible for feeding us, I'm more than happy to give her a hand. She's the best damn home cook around."

"After a couple of dinners at the ranch, I can believe it."

He scooted from the booth. "Guess I'd better get busy. It sure was nice running into you."

"Same here."

Cheeks flushed, he tipped his hat and strode from the cafe.

Both the Tate boys—yes, she still thought of the twins as boys—were strikingly handsome. But Vince, the eldest of the three, was a man. He was more than handsome. He had an air of danger about him. Maybe it was because he was a lawman. Maybe it was because she'd known heartbreak at his hands. But she'd loved him for a long time. And that hadn't changed.

Back in the pharmacy, Abby noticed the line for the pharmacist's voice mail was blinking. Instead of the call being from a doctor's office, as she'd anticipated, it was a message from Rollo Moore wanting to meet with her about a business proposition.

A business proposition? What business? He was a real estate broker. The only real estate she had was her home and the drugstore. And she wasn't in the market to sell either.

No. Wait. What about the 400 acres of scrub land that was in limbo. Did the land belong to her or not?

Rather than return Rollo's call right away, she placed one to her lawyer, Sam Dunaway. He'd know.

The attorney's A.A. put Abby through quickly.

"So what's the situation on the land?" she asked, cutting to the chase.

"As things stand, the land belongs to you until that deed transfer is completed. In laymen's terms that means the purchasing party or their representative must come forward with their copy of the deed as proof of purchase."

More and more curious. "Do you have any idea why my father was handling this instead of going through you?" What on earth had her dad been up to? Her mouth grew dry.

"I can only assume he wanted to handle the transaction himself."

"And the basic reason someone would do that?" Waiting for his response, she held her breath.

"Privacy, obviously. Skirting some legal issues. I hate to guess. I doubt the latter would be the issue in your father's case. His death was unexpected, therefore, the transfer wasn't completed. But I hasten to add, it still could be."

Abby thanked him and hung up the phone. She began pacing. So many questions. Had her father been acting as a front man or some kind of go-between for this Macedonia Corp? If so, why hadn't it gone through? And had her father been killed because he stopped the transfer or had his death merely screwed up the transfer?

Now, to return Rollo's call.

But first, she checked the fax machine. A whopping six prescriptions to refill. Rollo could definitely wait.

Chapter Eight

Abby never found a spare moment to return Rollo's call. Too busy. Not that she really wanted to talk to him anyway. More likely, he was just looking for another opportunity to try it on with her.

After a quick stop at the Mercantile for groceries, she turned onto her street. Oh no, Rollo's black BMW was parked in front of her house. Too late to drive on by. He'd seen her.

Nothing to do but face him and tell him to take a hike. She pulled into her driveway and parked. She got out, picked up the tote bags, and unlocked the side entrance. Once inside, she set the groceries on the counter and started removing the items.

The doorbell rang.

Of course. Rollo, just waiting for his chance.

She opened the door. "What is it? I'm in the middle of something."

"If you'll spare me a few moments and let me in, I'll tell you."

"You'll have to talk while I finish putting away groceries." She turned toward the kitchen. He followed on her heels like a lost puppy. She continued her task as if he weren't there, setting two porterhouse stakes in the fridge's meat drawer.

"I'll cut to the chase. I have someone who's interested in buying your house."

"It's not for sale." She pulled out salad fixings and set them in the veg drawer. Five microwave dinners ought to do her for a few evenings. Into the freezer. Nothing like Marti's sumptuous cooking, for sure.

"He's offering $900,000."

Now, that got her attention. She faced him. "In this market. In this area. That's absurd. The house isn't worth anything like that much."

"That's how serious the buyer is."

She shook her head. "No way. This house has been in the family for four generations. It's going to stay that way."

"But it's ridiculous to turn down that amount of money. It's just a house, Abby. You could build yourself a mansion."

"Not with the history and memories this one has." She smacked the countertop with her hand.

"He'll pay cash up front for immediate possession. He wants it just like it is."

She got in his face. "Just tell me, how does he know what it's like inside? Who is he? Is he the one who broke in and tried to choke me?"

"Oh, no. Surely not." Rollo backed up, then smiled. "But I've been inside. I've described it to his satisfaction."

"No. The answer is still No. Now you can leave."

"But, Abby—"

"Right now, or I'm calling the sheriff." She picked up her cell phone, ready to tap the number.

He just wouldn't give up. "One million dollars. Cash. Abby, cash."

She picked up a stalk of celery and brandished it. "No. Get out."

"I'm going. I'm going." He turned to leave and

muttered, "Stupid bitch."

"What did you call me!" Celery stalk still in hand, she drew it back. "Get your skinny behind out of my house. Now!"

She followed him to the door, locked it behind him, and set the security alarm.

Of all the nerve.

Furious, she flew back to the kitchen and finished putting away her groceries in what had to be record time.

She leaned on the island and wondered. What was in her house that someone would break in twice and then offer to pay a million dollars cash up front?

It was about time she had another look-around herself. She hadn't been in the attic since before she left for college. Maybe that would be a good place to start.

She headed for the stairs, but stopped. Someone had just stepped onto the porch.

Better not be Rollo Moore, again. She ran to the door ready to give him a piece of her mind.

She whipped it open.

"Vince."

"Abby."

"What do you want?" Her manners had suffered due to Rollo's visit. *Calm down. This is Vince. It's not his fault Rollo pissed you off.*

"You're scowling and her cheeks are flushed. Has something happened?"

"It's just—" She opened the screened door. "Might as well come on in. I just had a disagreement with Rollo Moore. I'm surprised you didn't see him."

"Tell me." He stepped inside, following her into the kitchen.

She climbed onto one of the stools around the island. "He tried to get me to sell the house. Said he had a client who would pay up to a million dollars cash."

"Whoa." He rubbed his chin and nodded. "In normal times, I'd say that's a better-than-nice offer."

"But these aren't normal times. Someone—Rollo or whoever—wants something he thinks is in my house."

"That's my thinking."

"And I mean to find it. Starting with the attic." Anxious to implement the search, she jumped off the stool, ready to head for the stairs.

"Hold on." He pulled her into his arms. She meant to struggle, but somewhere along the way, she lost the will. Being in his arms felt so safe. So right.

"I meant what I said about spending the night here until I find whoever's responsible for the break-ins and the rest."

Without meaning to, she let a small sigh escape. "Maybe we could talk about it tonight."

"You're not going to fight me?"

"What's the point?" She lay her head on his chest, the sound of his heartbeat so comforting. She didn't want to give up the feeling. "Come for dinner. I'll fix something. It won't be up to Marti's standards, but I promise not to poison you."

"Don't think I've ever had such a charming dinner invitation before." He kissed the top of her head. "I have to go, but tonight after dinner, I'll help you search. Old houses like this are bound to have lots of secret hiding places."

"Dinner will be around seven. Will that fit into your schedule?"

"It should. If something comes up, I'll call you."

"I'll keep it simple."

"Meat," he said with a smile. "That's all I require."

Abby returned his smile. "You'll be glad to know the

Mercantile had their steaks on sale this weekend."

Vince beamed. "You know me too well, Abigail."

"I don't know about that, but I know Texas men and their appetite for all things beef."

"You're guilty of generalizing, but I'll let that statement pass."

"Chicken was on sale too," she said, teasing him. "I do a mighty fine grilled chicken."

He grimaced. "That's all right. Steak's perfect."

"Then I'll see you around seven. And we'll talk."

"Yes, you will, and yes, we *will* talk."

She closed the door behind him and engaged the security system. Yes, they would talk. Before they could forge a future, they had to put the past to rest. Maybe it was ridiculous to cling to past hurts. But still they needed to be aired.

Away from the ranch and all the spying eyes and big ears, they could speak openly. Possibly even take the friendship to a new level. Maybe her move back home was a subconscious desire to have some space to themselves.

Just like buying those steaks today. She never cooked steak for just herself. Microwave dinners and take-out were more her speed. Funny how she had picked up the perfect ingredients for a simple dinner...for two. Grilled Steaks. Salad. Baked potatoes.

Now, no interruptions. No brothers popping in to say *hi*. No Marti—bless her good heart—offering fresh coffee.

But first, the attic.

Abby stared at the door to the attic, holding her breath. The attic had always been her mother's space, while her dad preferred the confines of the basement for his home office and man cave.

Finally, she took another breath, gathered her courage, and unlocked the door. She reached inside and turned on the light. It would've been stifling had it not been for the whole house fan that pulled out the worst of the summer's heat. It remained plenty warm.

She took one step inside. Then another. Most people's attics were probably a jumble, but not this one. Her mother had been an organizer from the get-go. Old pieces of furniture were stacked neatly along the back wall of the attic. Boxes full of Christmas decorations took up the front wall, each piece put away with all her mother's tender loving care just like she'd left them after her last Christmas. The odor of mothballs reached her nose from two old oriental carpets rolled over to the side. Before the big remodel, they graced the living and dining rooms. The smell had to be coming from them.

Whatever the intruder was looking for, he hadn't made it to the attic. Too neat. A portable wardrobe, standing on her left contained winter coats. She unzipped the opening. More mothballs. She closed the zipper, then stepped away from the pungent odor.

She shook her head. The attic was a waste of time. Still, not wanting to overlook anything, she went around the perimeter of the space, tapping on the walls for the sound of hollow spaces. She eyeballed the floor as she walked back and forth, listening for creaks or loose boards.

No. Nothing. Maybe Vince would have more ideas about where to find any secret hiding spaces.

In the meantime, he was coming for dinner. So it would soon be time to fire up the grill and place a couple of potatoes in the oven. But first, what was she going to wear?

After shutting the attic door, she scooted back to her bedroom. She pulled out a flowered halter top and the pale green skirt that went with it. Strappy sandals. She didn't want to appear to be trying too hard.

Now for a shower.

Vince strode back into his office in the Sheriff's Department. He nodded at the dispatcher. "Anything?"

"You need to call Ranger Ben," the dispatcher said. "I would've radioed you, but he said it could wait a bit."

"Thanks." He removed his cowboy hat and sat to make the call.

"You have some new information?"

"The forensic accountants have traced the Macedonia Corporation even farther back to the original shell company called Los Marcos Fulfillment. I believe the names of the owners will surprise you."

"Give it to me, man."

"Two of the three owners are lying in our morgue. But there's a silent partner who's still running the supposed company. We know that because the registration has been renewed since they disappeared."

"My wife and Barnes?" When did his good-times-loving wife find the time or money to form a shell company with her lover Barnes?

"None other. And since they were local, it's not too far off the mark to consider that the third partner is a local."

"Could Jerald Fields have been the third? He died the end of January."

"No. The registration was renewed in May, this year."

"So that leaves Fields as a go-between for the shell company?"

"I'd say so, but it's still early days in the investigation."

He thanked Ben for the update and set the phone back on the charger. As much as he hated to suspect the mild-mannered and well-respected pharmacist of double-dealing, Vince had to wonder if drugs or extortion were involved.

Time to take a run out to the 400 acres of scrub land. He glanced at the clock. He'd have plenty of time to make it to Abby's by seven. Just the same, better give her a head's up.

"I'm heading out to that property for a look around," he told her. "I'll text you when I'm on my way back."

"Good," she said, sounding a little breathless. "I'll wait for your text to put the steaks on the grill."

"Everything okay?"

"I'm fine. After you left, I checked the attic, but I didn't find anything, though. I was hot and dusty, so I took a shower. Just got out when the phone rang."

"I'll see you later." He disconnected, feeling—dare he admit it to himself—warm and cozy like part of a real couple. With a real future. Maybe.

Vince stared at the plot. Viewing four hundred acres could better be done by air. Maybe next time, he'd inveigle the Rangers into using one of their choppers. Plain to see, a trail of vehicle tracks led onto the property.

And two signs posted. Private Property.

He shrugged. Might as well see what's so private about this piece of land.

His phone rang. He glanced at the Caller ID. One of his local henchmen. "What now?"

"The sheriff's snooping around on your property. Thought you'd like to know"

Snooping on *my* property. "Take care of him then."

"As in take care of him permanently?"

"Dammit yes! Something needs to go right for a change." Enraged, he threw his phone across the room, smashing it against the wall.

Abby washed the romaine under a rush of cold water, then tore it into pieces for the salad. She found herself humming. How long had it been since she'd been this happy? Really happy?

Too long.

It was as if some of the dark cloud leftover from her parents' deaths had dissipated.

It's too soon to be thinking about a future with Vince.

True, there was still a lot to talk out. The old hurts to be aired then gently folded and put away like an old quilt. A giddiness threatened to overwhelm her. Vince's thoughtful call warmed her as if he'd placed his arms around her and pulled her close.

The hot Texas sun beat down. Yellow Texas dust hung in a haze behind him as Vince followed the vehicle tracks for three quarters of a mile. The tracks ended at what twenty years ago might've been a nice RV, but was now pretty decrepit. There was no record of anyone in residence on the land. Had to be a squatter. He climbed from the SUV, unsnapped his holster, and walked over to the ramshackle RV. Rust around the windows. After wiping away a thick film of dust, he peered inside. From the dirty dishes and overall general mess, it appeared someone was definitely living there.

A flash of light sparked in his peripheral vision, his only warning. He hit the ground. Just in time. A shot whizzed over his head and struck the RV. It came from the hill to his right. He scooted along on his elbows aiming for cover. If he could just make it to the Tahoe, placing it between him and the shooter.

He pulled out his weapon. The hill was half a mile away, an easy shot for someone with a high-powered rifle and a scope. An easy shot for someone who knew what he was doing. And this one did.

Too far for his service weapon to reach.

He hunkered for a second behind a rusted barrel. Another shot straight through the barrel, just above his head. Bunching his muscles, he sprang for the shelter of his SUV.

Once he'd reached cover, he eased his hand up to open the door. If he could get to his rifle... A second shot blew out the glass. Passenger and driver sides both. Damn!

He ducked again, his heart ratcheting like an AK47.

He reached for his radio. "Shots fired. Pinned down. Send backup." He gave the approximate location.

Another shot hit a tire on the passenger side. Another shot ditto.

Damn good shot. He'd managed to disable Vince's vehicle with two shots. With two flat tires, he wasn't going anywhere.

Chapter Nine

The grandfather clock in the hallway chimed at the half hour. Seven-thirty and Vince still hadn't texted. Something was wrong. She could feel it in the crawling-ants sensation up and down her arms. She rubbed her upper arms to banish the feeling, but it didn't help. Unable to sit still, she paced.

Enough of this. She grabbed her cell phone and called the sheriff's department. The dispatcher hemmed and hawed, refusing to give a straight answer.

"Something's happened, hasn't it? Tell me!" Abby demanded.

"I'm sure it's nothing serious." Dorothy paused. "But he did call for backup."

"Backup. That definitely means trouble." She punched the disconnect icon.

Now what? Wring her hands? She wasn't the type.

No. Action was called for.

She covered the salad, turned off the oven, and put the steaks back in the fridge. With her phone and purse in one hand, she set the security system, then ran to her rental car.

She headed down Main and out of town. True, she only had a vague idea where the plot of land was, but Vince had called for backup. All the patrol cars in the county would be on site. She should have no trouble finding it.

Better have another go at reaching his rifle. Keeping his head down, Vince crawled, then reached up to open the rear door. His rifle was secured in a customized hidden compartment under the back seat. He unlatched the mechanism and removed the semi-automatic AR-15 along with two magazines.

Now see how the shooter liked having the odds evened.

Vince only had a vague idea of the shooter's location. Nor did he know if the shooter had changed position.

The shooter had the advantage. He knew exactly where Vince was.

He maneuvered his position in the dust and sharp rocks, avoiding the tires. Two of 'em had already been shot. He needed to get a fix on the shooter's location. He picked up a rock and threw it toward the rusty barrel.

A shot rang out.

He darted up for a second look. Good. Shooter still under cover of scrub oak.

He aimed and fired with a hail of bullets over the area.

Ducked down. Waited.

In the distance, the welcome sound of a siren. Make that two sirens.

He blew out a sigh, then checked his watch. Less than three minutes to respond. Seemed longer, though.

"Sheriff?" The call came crackling through his radio.

He grabbed the mic. "One shooter on the hillside. High-powered rifle."

"Got it," Will Rasmussen responded.

From his position, Vince couldn't see, but he could hear. His deputies left their vehicles, using them as cover, no doubt.

He waited for the sound of more gunfire.

Nothing. Had the shooter given up, or was he waiting to draw the deputies out and then fire?

The sound of a motorcycle revving.

"He's getting away!" Vince emerged from cover. Brushing the dirt from his clothes, he said, "The scrub oak's too dense to follow, except on a motorcycle. I got one round of shots off. Check for any sign I hit him. Might get some DNA."

Will nodded. "Sure, Boss."

"Get a wrecker out here. I'm gonna need a ride."

He hopped into Will's vehicle. What a fiasco. The shooter had gotten clean away. No closer to figuring out who was trying to kill him than before. Now if forensics could just find some DNA and connect someone to the scene.

As expected, just two miles out of town, Abby spied flashing blue lights and a deputy waving her around. Instead of driving by, she pulled over to the side of the road and parked.

The deputy walking over to her vehicle turned out to be Darby Longworth, who'd graduated a couple of years after she had. He was tall, with dark blond hair, brown eyes, and a killer body.

She lowered her window. "Darby?"

He nodded. "You need to go on, Ms. Fields. There's nothing to see here."

"Don't you dare give me that tired old song and dance. I know something's going on. Vince was coming to my house for dinner after he checked on something out here. I also happen to know he called for backup, so what's wrong? Is he hurt?"

"Far as I know, the sheriff's fine, ma'am."

She held back a growl of frustration. "*What* happened?"

"Since you know so much, you ought to know I'm not going to give a member of the public any details on an open investigation."

"But—"

"No buts. If you won't move along, then stay in your vehicle and keep your doors locked." He turned as if to return to his post, then stopped. "Better yet, go home. I'm sure the sheriff will let you know as soon as he's free."

She clenched her jaw in frustration, then called after the deputy. "Are you *sure* he's all right?"

"Yes, ma'am. Go home."

It wasn't Darby's fault. He'd been perfectly professional and within his rights to tell her to go home. But she didn't have to like it one bit. Not one bit.

A wrecker drove up and was waved into the property. Vince's Tahoe was wrecked? Her heart nearly came out of her chest. Darby had said Vince was fine. But was he? Really?

So she should just go home and wait patiently for his call or text.

Deep down she knew there wouldn't be a call or text. *Something* had happened. Even if he wasn't injured, there would be reports to fill out.

Lots of missed dinners. Broken dates. And the gut-wrenching fear when something went wrong. That's how it was when you were involved with a lawman. She'd either learn to live with it or move on. Obviously, his late wife had found someone else. Liz Kellen had never struck Abby as housewife material. Maybe Liz hadn't been cut out to be a lawman's wife, either.

Taking a lot for granted, aren't you, Abby-girl?

Their new relationship or whatever you wanted to call it was simply too new to know where it was going. Yes, the old chemistry was still there. Magnified by a thousand. That single interrupted kiss out at the ranch had nearly rocked her world.

But there wouldn't be any kiss—interrupted or otherwise—tonight.

Back in his office, Vince filed reports on the incident, as well as the paperwork necessary for getting his vehicle repaired. Nothing would happen before tomorrow.

Will Rasmussen knocked on Vince's door.

Vince looked up and motioned for him to enter. "We located some fresh blood in the scrub oak. It wasn't a lot. Looks like you winged him. "

"Good. Put out a BOLO to the local doctors' clinics and the hospital about anyone coming in with a gunshot wound."

"Already done," Will said. "The DNA results will depend on the Rangers' backlog in Austin."

"Appreciate the quick response out there this evening."

"Anytime, Boss." He turned to leave then stopped. "Thought you ought to know, Abby Fields showed up this evening. Longworth said she was pretty upset.

His hands went to his head as he swore. "We were supposed to have dinner tonight." He placed the reports into a folder and shoved the folder into a drawer. "I'm through for the night. Give me a ride over to her place?"

"Sure thing." Will's mouth quirked up in a half smile. "Good to see you moving on."

Vince cut Will a sideways glance that was meant to shut him up.

But not Will, who blithely continued, “I know you just found out your wife was dead, but she’s been gone and dead a good while.”

“Will... Enough.”

“Yes, sir, Sheriff, sir.” He gave Vince a cheeky salute. “Meet you in the parking lot.”

Vince stood. “I’m behind you.”

He watched the sheriff climb into one of the deputy’s vehicles. Damnation! He was tired of unsuccessful half measures. No more ordering incompetents to do his bidding. He’d already ordered his incompetent henchman to take a hike, recommending another state even. He’d take care of this himself. He followed the deputy’s vehicle from a respectable distance. Instead of heading out of town, the deputy turned onto Elm. Excellent.

The sheriff climbed out of the vehicle, and the deputy left.

Even better.

Maybe he could kill two annoying birds with one proverbial stone.

All he had to do was wait.

Vince rode with Will. Neither saying much. As far as Vince was concerned, Will had said plenty back at the office. The SUV turned onto Elm. He’d always admired the Fields’ house. It stood for stability. It was the perfect house to raise children in.

Will stopped and Vince hopped out. “Thanks for the ride.”

His deputy nodded. “Anytime, Boss.”

He strode up the walkway. The downstairs lights had

just gone off, but the porch light came on. Abby opened the front door before he could knock. The security alarm started beeping. He smiled at her through the screened door. "Glad to see you're taking my advice about using the alarm."

"Don't I *always* take your advice," she teased, while reaching to disable the alarm.

"This has to be the *first* time."

She looked around him. "Where's your bedroll?"

"What bedroll?"

"Yeah, you said you were going to camp on my front porch."

Smiling, he cocked his head to one side. "But you're not gonna make me do that."

She seemed very pleased with herself. She folded her arms across her perky breasts, telling him cheekily, "I will if you don't tell me what happened tonight."

"That's the price of admission?"

"Indeed it is."

"Okay." He let out an exaggerated sigh. "I'll talk. But I surely could use a cup of coffee."

"That could be arranged." She opened the screened door. "Come on in." He followed her into the kitchen. "Pull up a stool," she said. "I'll put the coffee on. And *you* spill."

He watched her prepare the coffee. Her halter top didn't hide much. Not that he minded one damn bit. She brought two cups of coffee, set one before him, then pulled up a stool next to his.

The coziness sharing coffee and conversation in the late evening pleased him beyond words, as did her head resting on his shoulder.

"Are you sure you're all right?"

"I am." He took a swallow of his coffee. "Now I'm better."

"You could've been killed." She gazed into his eyes, her emotions unreadable and oh-so mysterious. He couldn't help wondering if she felt anything like he did. An easy comfort mixed with a whopping dose of desire. And gut-wrenching need. "That's part of the job, Abby."

"I know," she murmured, giving him ideas he had no business having. "Any idea who it was?"

"No," Vince said, shaking his head. "He fled the scene on a motorcycle."

"Lots of those around here."

Just being with her, here in her kitchen, a sense of warmth and ease enveloped his entire body. "Sounded like a hog." He set his cup down, covered her hand with his larger one. "One that needed a new set of plugs." Such a mundane conversation but so perfect. Because Abby was perfect for him. Always had been.

"I'm glad you're all right," she said.

"You might've mentioned that once or twice," he said. "You were getting ready to go to bed, weren't you?" His voice deepened with emotion. Dammit, he wanted her.

"I was, but I don't mind the company, especially yours. If you're hungry, I could still fire up the grill."

Who needed sleep when the sexy, desirable woman he'd always loved was so close. "Not necessary. You go to bed. I'll sack out on your couch." His eyes grew heavy. He didn't really want to spend the night on her sofa.

Her eyes welled with tears. "I was so worried when they said you'd called for backup."

He took both her small, capable hands in his. "I don't want you to worry. We'll catch this guy. Now—just so there's no misunderstanding—by *we,* I mean my fellow law enforcement officers."

"But he's targeted me too."

"That's beside the point. You're not law enforcement.

You're a pharmacist, for Pete's sake. Promise me, you'll keep you head down and take precautions when I'm not around."

His no-nonsense attitude didn't faze her a bit. She had to protest like he knew she would. "I know what I am and what I can do."

"Go to bed, Abby." He leaned forward and kissed the top of her head. Her sleek black hair had a citrusy scent, so clean and fresh like the woman herself. "Get some rest."

She slipped her arms around his neck, causing his heart rate to skyrocket. "Come with me, Vince. Let me love your cares away."

"Oh, Abby, if only you could." The gruff huskiness in his voice had returned. Nothing else could give away his true feelings so quickly.

"I'll do my best." She lay her head on his chest. He wondered if she could hear the rapid beat of his heart.

"I know. That's what I'm afraid of."

"Afraid of me?"

"No, afraid of *me*. That I'll hurt you. That you won't be able to put up with the life I live."

"If you say so." She slid off the stool, kicked off her sandals, and walked toward the stairs. Looking back over her shoulder, she gave him a definite *come hither* stare. Then she slipped off her halter top, letting it fall to the floor. All that was left was a lacy strapless bra. With one foot on the stairs, she stopped and shimmied out of her skirt, letting it fall, revealing a pair of panties that were no more than scrap of lace. Halfway up the stairs, she unfastened the bra and let it drop. "Coming with me?"

Abby had driven him crazy just being in the same room, but now this...this striptease, for want of a better word. "Hell, yeah." He watched the trail of clothes she left behind, and with each garment that fell, he grew harder until he thought he'd burst. He bounded up the stairs behind her. At the top, he caught her around the waist and pulled her to him, her small, but perfect breasts pressing against his chest. He groaned with frustration. "Tempting me are you? Playing games? Two can play those games."

"I was counting on it." She smiled up at him, her green eyes glittering with desire.

Abby slipped from his arms and ran for the bedroom. She wanted nothing more than to make love with him. Vince. Her brief marriage aside, the man she'd always loved.

When she'd just reached the bed, he caught her wrist. "Oh no, you don't. You're not getting away from me this time." He brought her hand to his mouth and kissed it, his lips warm and tender against her skin.

"I didn't run far, did I?" she teased, gazing into his sky blue eyes. Eyes that would, if they could, devour her. Her heart raced, her breathing quickened.

He placed a light kiss on her neck, in that oh-so sensitive spot below her ear. "You didn't run too fast, either."

"No." Her arms snaked around his neck. "A psychologist might say I wanted to be caught." Their bodies were so close she could feel his hard-on jutting against her thigh.

"To hell with the psychologist," he said, sounding almost as breathless as she felt. "What do *you* say?"

"I say the psychologist knew his business. I absolutely wanted you to catch me." She smiled up at him, the heat building in her belly and pooling between her thighs. "Always have. Ever since third grade."

He let out a bark of laughter. "That long, huh?" He

lowered his head and claimed her mouth with his. She opened to him, longing for more. Much more. She moaned his name.

He lifted her onto the bed then pulled down her bikini panties. "God, you're beautiful. More than ever."

"And *you're* still dressed."

"I'll fix that. Right now." He tore off his uniform shirt, then sat on the edge of the bed to pull off his boots. Then the jeans came off.

From her spot on the bed, she watched his perfect chiseled body emerge. First, his broad shoulders, just right, perfect even. Powerful, muscled thighs from years of horseback riding. Hands, strong but gentle. But it was his face, especially his intelligent, expressive eyes glittering with desire that she loved most.

He skimmed off his briefs. His manhood...now that was for her and her alone.

"Come here," she said, patting the bed beside her. "Make love to me."

He paused with one knee on the bed. "You talk too much." Then he was covering her body with his. His kisses blazed a trail from her neck to her breasts. He grasped one nipple between his teeth, pulling tenderly.

She moaned as her nipples budded into exquisite points of delight. Her inner muscles pulsed with anticipation. Her hands kneaded the muscles of his back. She arched toward him. He abandoned her breasts, laving his way to her belly. Gently he spread her thighs, and licked her clit. Then sucked.

She grasped the sheets and arched her back, moaning with pleasure. Then he entered her. Her legs circled his waist as he plunged her inner depths, his hunger seeming as fierce as hers. The earth-shattering orgasm took her by surprise. Unprepared, she gasped his name.

His climax came seconds later, his body shuddering and collapsing to the side of hers, but maintaining their connection. “Sorry, I was so quick. This is *not* all there is.”

A merry peal of laughter emerged from her throat. “I should hope not because I’m definitely not through with you.” She snuggled into his arms.

“Glad to hear it.”

After a while they made love again, this time longer and slower, with even greater intensity. Soaring at the apex of emotion and passion, they came as one.

Chapter Ten

Awakening in a strange bed, Vince smiled. Yeah, he was in Abby's bed. But something wasn't right. He raised his head, sniffed the air, then levered onto his elbow. Nudging Abby, he asked, "Do you smell smoke?"

Beside him, Abby stretched and yawned. "The smoke alarm isn't going off."

He sat up in the bed and swung his feet to the floor. "I *know* I smell smoke."

Abby rubbed the sleep from her eyes and yawned. "I'll go see."

He was out of the bed and at the door before Abby's feet could hit the floor. He laid his hand against the door. Cool. Meaning he could safely open the door. But before he could do so, he noted a wisp of smoke seep under the door.

Adrenaline slammed through him. His heart quickened. His breathing increased. "There *is* a fire. There's smoke. Come on. We gotta get out."

Abby's eyes widened. She shot to her feet. "I've got to get dressed."

"Now!" He held out his hand.

"All right!" Abby yanked the sheet and light blanket from the bed. Rushing to his side, she handed him the sheet with trembling hands. "Here." Her voice was raspy with fear. "You're nekkid."

He whipped the sheet around his waist, then cautiously opened the door. The smoke was heavy. From what he could tell, it was the front of the house that was involved.

They made their way downstairs quickly, his hand holding fast to hers.

"I have a fire extinguisher under the sink," Abby said, heading to the kitchen. She tore open the cabinet door and pulled the extinguisher from the cupboard.

He took it from her, yanked the ring, and ran to the living room. The drapes and a couch were in flames, with thick, dark acrid smoke billowing from them. His breath caught in his throat, knowing furniture often put off poisonous gases. "The fumes," he choked out. "Out the back. Front hall's blocked."

He grabbed her wrist, pulling her toward the back of the house. He unlocked and tried to open it. He shoved his shoulder against the door. "Something's blocking it from the outside."

Abby ran to the side door and tried it. "Same here." He detected the note of rising panic in her voice.

They had only a minute, possibly less to get the hell out. Battling his own terror, he forced himself to say calmly, "We'll break out a window. Climb out that way." He picked up one of the kitchen stools and launched it through the window over the sink. He wrapped his hand with the sheet and cleared the glass shards as best he could, then boosted Abby onto the counter. "Careful."

She nimbly slipped through the window as if she did it every day. He followed, nothing graceful about it, scraping his back. Compared to burning alive, not a big deal.

His feet hit the ground. He glanced around. Where was Abby?

Surely she hadn't gone back inside. Before he could panic, Abby out of breath ran to his side. "I knocked on the neighbors' door," she gasped. "They already called 911."

Seconds later, screaming sirens filled the night air. He pulled her trembling body closer. "It's going to be all right."

Her eyes full of disbelief, she said, "Someone really wants us dead."

"Looks that way." And with each attempt, they were getting closer to succeeding.

Sometime around four-thirty in the morning, the sky had just starting to lighten. The fire chief came over to the ambulance where Abby and Vince were sitting drinking bottled water.

"Sheriff," the fire chief said.

"Chief," Vince responded. "What can you tell us?"

"The fire's contained mostly to the front of the house. Smoke and water damage throughout the first two stories. It appears an incendiary device was thrown through a living room window. The arson investigator will check into everything as this is clearly an arson. Your exits were barred. The perpetrator intended for y'all to perish in that fire. We'll keep an eye out for hot spots through the rest of the night and morning."

In spite of the warm summer early morning, she shivered. "I don't understand why my smoke alarms didn't go off."

"Your batteries must've been dead," the fire chief suggested.

"No. They couldn't be," Abby said. "I replaced them when time changed in the spring."

"The investigator will look into that as well." The fire chief smiled. "Do you have somewhere to go?"

"Would it be safe to go back inside for some clothes first?"

"I'll go with you." This time the chief smirked.

Vince cleared his throat. "We *both* need our clothes."

"Of course, Sheriff." He clapped Vince's shoulder. "Follow me."

Once back inside the house, Abby groaned. It was a disaster. Or so it seemed. The major fire damage was in the living room and hallway. The draperies and furniture were lost. The window frames charred. Elsewhere the walls and ceilings were intact, but still dripping water. The kitchen cabinets were rimmed with black smoke. The stairway was solid, thankfully. She gripped Vince's hand. He squeezed back.

"All things considered," the chief said, "it's not so bad. This house was well built. Your insurance will pay for the damage. Another month or so, and you won't know the fire ever happened."

"If you say so." She opened the bedroom door. Not likely she'd ever forget this night. Her feet squelched in the water-soaked Oriental rug. "I think we can manage from here, Chief," she said with a faux smile.

He cleared his throat. "Certainly. I'll wait outside."

Abby shut the door behind the fire chief. "For a minute, I thought he was going to stay in here and watch us get dressed."

"He deserves *some* kind of reward for saving your house," Vince said with a snicker.

"As if..." She opened the closet and sniffed. "It all smells of smoke." Wrinkling her nose, she pulled out a red T-shirt, jeans, and undies from the chest of drawers, then dressed quickly. "This'll have to do for now." She groaned.

"I can't believe I have to open the drugstore in less than three hours."

He pulled up his jeans, zipping and snapping the closure. He pulled on his uniform shirt and buttoned it. "I need to shower and change before I go on duty. Call in your relief pharmacist. I'll take you back to the ranch."

She walked over to his side, slipped her arms around his waist, and gazed up at him, her heart filling with gratitude and love. "Would you? That sounds like heaven."

A knock on the door sounded. "You folks all right in there?"

"Yes, we're coming out," Abby called, then covered her mouth with her hand to keep from laughing.

Vince grabbed her hand. "Let's get out of here."

Back downstairs the fire damage seemed even worse than it had initially. The front windows had blown out. The massive oak door was deeply charred on the inside. Shaking her head, Abby heaved a deep sigh. "This will never be the same."

Vince hugged her. His beard was scratchy against her cheek, but comforting all the same. "Don't worry. All we have to do is hire one of those companies who deal with fire damage restoration. The chief's right. It'll be good as new."

We. He'd used the word *we*. The thought of having to see to the all the repairs needed was still daunting. But she wasn't alone in the world. Not anymore.

Along with the few clothes, Abby had retrieved her purse, car keys, and iPhone. She inserted the key into the ignition. The engine purred to life as she pulled away from her home. "At least this rental car wasn't damaged. I had visions of the fire getting to it and KA-BOOM!" She motioned the explosion with her hands widespread.

"Hands on the steering wheel, ma'am," Vince teased in his most officious voice.

"Yes, Sheriff. You'll see both of my hands are on the steering wheel." She shot him a quick smile. Truth be told, she felt a little giddy. Whether it was the effect of smoke inhalation, Vince's presence, or the memory of how passionately they'd made love, she wasn't sure. "How did they manage that feat?"

"One of the firemen put it into neutral and let it coast down the driveway to the street. Now, eyes on the road."

She pulled over and stopped. "You need to drive."

"Just kidding. But you were a little unsteady."

"No, I'm serious. Look at my hands." She held out her hands; they trembled as if palsied. "It's the after-effects of an adrenaline rush."

"All right. That'd be my diagnosis."

"You're a lawman," she scoffed. "Not a doctor."

"And in my capacity as a lawman, I've seen and experienced many an adrenaline rush. You'll be fine."

She opened the door and got out so they could switch places. He did the same. They met in front of the Toyota. He put his arms around her. She snuggled close to his chest. "Thank you for remaining so calm. If I'd been alone, I probably would've freaked out."

"You're not the freaking out type, Abby. Not at all. That said, I'm glad you weren't alone either." He nuzzled the top of her head. He chuckled, then said, "You're hair smells like smoke too."

"Look who's talking."

A car passed, slowed, then sped up.

"Let's go on to the ranch," she said, "instead of giving the entire town a peep show."

He released her, reluctantly it seemed. "If you say so. I

suspect your reputation is already ruined. Anyone who saw us wrapped in the sheets and blankets will have no illusions about what were we up to last night."

"Not that I care."

Back inside the car, Abby leaned back, shut her eyes, and promptly fell asleep.

He drove by what had to be the two luckiest individuals in the world. Another failure! What did he have to do to get rid of those two? The next time there could be no mistakes. None. What he needed was a pro.

Like last time.

When they reached the ranch, Vince opened the passenger side door and picked Abby up. He carried her into the house, cursing because the front door wasn't even locked. That was about to change. He carried her still asleep upstairs into the guest bedroom she'd vacated only the day before.

Carefully, he undressed her. He smiled. Her slender body was as perfect as an ivory statue. Pure ivory except for her small dark nipples and the patch of black at the apex of her thighs. After a rummage in one of the chests, he found her something to sleep in, free of smoke. Then he slipped the cotton sleep shirt over her head. Still asleep, she murmured his name. How he loved caressing every inch of her body. He pulled a sheet over her, but couldn't resist touching her one more time, the curve of her hip proving irresistible.

Reluctantly, he let her sleep.

He picked up her smoky clothes and opened the bedroom door.

"What's going on?' Marti asked, her hands on hips.

"There was a fire at Abby's house. These are clean, but they still smell of smoke."

She held out her hands. "Hand 'em over. I'll get 'em in the wash." She sniffed, wrinkling her nose. "Looks like you could use a shower yourself. And a shave." She shook her head. "Don't know what you young folks get up to. Fires, it is now. Someone sure has a hate-on for you two."

"Yes, ma'am, sure does." He frowned. "And speaking of security, the front door was unlocked when I brought Abby in. I'll speak to the men, but I'm leaving you responsible for security in the house, and I want the doors locked at all times."

"Yes, sir. I thought—" She stopped. "No excuses. The doors will be locked at all times. You're all grown men. You have keys. You'll just have to use 'em." She gave an I-mean-business nod.

"I'm not angry. I just need to keep everybody safe, at least until we know who's out to get us."

Marti nodded her agreement, turned to go to the laundry, then turned back. "Any ideas on that?"

"One or two. Nothing definite." He scratched his chin. "I'm hitting the shower. Any chance I can get a cup of coffee once I'm clean enough to sit in your kitchen."

"You mean *your* kitchen." Marti grinned. "I'd say your chances are pretty good."

Vince smiled. "I'll be ten minutes." He bounded up the stairs. Marti was a treasure. The phrase "worth her weight in gold" came to mind. Whatever. If it ever came to that, he'd fight to keep her. But as long as she didn't know exactly how much he valued her, he could still afford her.

After a brief sit-rep with his chief deputy, Vince spent

the early part of his morning ignoring the knowing "looks." Being a small town and a small sheriff's department meant that absolutely everyone from the dispatcher to the cleaning lady knew about his spending the night with Abby...and the fire. As for the fire, he combed through the last five years of records on the lookout for any fire-related incidents. So far, nothing.

His phone beeped. He answered, "Sheriff Tate."

"The arson investigator's here to see you, Sheriff."

"Send him in."

Vince rose to greet Rafe Dawson. The arson investigator was in his mid-thirties and the female deputies always seemed to be enamored by his good looks since. Once again, they were jockeying for the best vantage point. In Vince's book, Rafe's looks didn't matter. He was a hell of an investigator and bass fisherman. Now those were things that *did* matter.

He listened intently as Rafe laid out the particulars. "Whoever he was, he meant business. There's evidence of two incendiary devices, Molotov cocktails, if you will. Both lobbed through the living room windows. All three exits were blocked with pine planks nailed over the doors. I'm surprise you didn't hear the hammering."

"Something woke me," Vince said, rubbing his chin. "At the time, I assumed it was the smell of smoke, but it could've been a noise. What about the smoke alarms? Abby swears she changed the batteries in March."

Rafe shook his head. "She must be mistaken. *No* batteries in any of the smoke alarms."

"A couple of days before the fire, she had a break-in. Judging from the manner the house was torn up, he was searching for something. The batteries could've been removed then. During the past week, we've had several attempts on our lives. I've been shot at twice. In addition to the break-in, Abby was run off the road."

"Forensics will remove the alarms and check them for fingerprints." The investigator frowned. "You and Ms. Fields need to watch your backs. Someone this determined isn't giving up."

"I know. We need to put a name to him. And fast."

Rafe stood. "I'll instruct forensics to remove the alarms right away. It's a stretch. He probably wore gloves."

Vince rose, extending his hand. "Thanks for everything. You're going out to the ranch?"

"Yes. That'll be my next stop."

"I'll give her a head's up then."

Rafe nodded.

He reached for the phone. Abby would appreciate the head's up. Hopefully, she'd slept late. Thoughts of the night they'd spent together, before the fire, brought a smile to his mouth. Their lovemaking had been smoking hot, but the too-real fire had dampened the mood.

Chapter Eleven

Abby opened her eyes and yawned. The sun was well and truly over the horizon. She sat up and stretched. Glancing down at the cotton sleep shirt she was wearing, she smiled. Vince must've changed her clothes without ever waking her.

A light *tap-tap* at the door.

She slipped out of bed and opened the door.

Smiling, Marti handed her a pile of freshly washed clothes. "Here ya go, darlin'. I've washed these. No more smoke."

Abby threw her arms around the tiny housekeeper. "Oh, Marti! You're a wonder. Thank you!"

"Vince said to tell you that he's gone to the Sheriff's Department, and that the arson investigator will be here to interview you sometime before lunch." Marti stopped long enough to take a breath. "And he also instructed me to tell you to stay here until he comes home." She winced as if not quite sure how that particular instruction would go over.

"Oh, he did. *Did* he?" Abby let out a huff, then smiled. "After what we went through last night, I'm inclined to follow your boss's imperious instructions."

Marti heaved a small sigh. "Glad you see it that way. I told him I was afraid you'd take my head off and then come after his."

"A week ago I would've taken *his* head off."

A sly smile crept to Marti's mouth. "Reckon a lot can change in a week."

"Surely has. Now I'm going to take a shower and get the smell of smoke out of my hair. Thank you so much for doing my laundry. But however long I'm here, I'll keep up with my laundry. I don't expect you to do it. You have enough to do, riding herd on the three Tate brothers."

"I appreciate you wanting to be a help, but you have enough on your mind. You don't need to be worrying about doing laundry or cooking. One additional person, such as yourself, doesn't add to the load. Besides, I enjoy having some more estrogen influence around the place. Helps to balance out all that *testostyerone*." Marti rolled her eyes with her mispronunciation.

Abby nodded with a smile. "All right, if you say so." Honestly, it felt good to be around the housekeeper. She missed the loving relationship she'd had with her mother. While no one could ever fill the gaping hole left in Abby's heart by her mother's death, experiencing Marti's warm and generous nature eased the ache a bit.

After a long, hot shower, Abby remembered the arson investigator was on his way and was probably, at that very moment, sitting downstairs waiting. She dressed quickly in the freshly washed clothes Marti had provided. Just a red T-shirt with a local band logo, and a pair of jeans, but the clean fresh scent was heavenly after smelling of smoke for what seemed like forever. She slipped her feet into a pair of sandals and skipped down the stairs.

As soon as she walked into the kitchen, Marti handed her a cup of coffee. Abby took the cup, sipped, and breathed, "Thanks. I really needed this."

Marti glanced out the side window. "If I'm not mistaken, that's the arson fella who just drove up."

Abby ran to the front door and peeked through the window. "It's a fire department vehicle, so you're right on the money." She opened the door and watched a tall, gorgeous man carrying a briefcase climb out of the truck. Rafe Dawson. OMG! He'd been several years ahead of her in school. But if anyone in Kenton Valley could've gone on to a career in Hollywood, she'd have placed her money on him. His classic handsome features were almost too perfect. It was reputed that his deep brown eyes could melt any woman who dared gaze into them long enough. Hair black as night with what she could just make out was a streak of silver at the temples.

Still, as gorgeous as Rafe was, she'd always been drawn to Vince. Only he could make *her* melt.

"Ms. Fields."

She acknowledged she was and showed him inside. "Coffee?"

"Thank you, no. Already had my quota for the day," he replied with an easy smile.

She reminded herself to breathe. "Where do you..." She glanced around, trying to think of an appropriate place to take him.

"Anywhere you feel comfortable."

"Let's talk in Vince's office." She led the way back to the cozy room that served as the ranch office and man cave. She took a seat on the sofa. Setting down his briefcase, he pulled out the desk chair, swiveled it around, and sat facing her.

She leaned forward. "What can you tell me?"

He opened his briefcase on his knees, then pulled out a sheaf of papers. "Two incendiary devices. Both through the front windows. The doors had been blocked with planks nailed. You didn't hear any hammering?"

Abby felt her neck and cheeks flush. "No. I was sound asleep—" she paused. "I didn't know anything until Vince woke me, saying he smelled smoke."

"About your smoke alarms."

"Yes, I know I replaced those batteries in April when I turned the clocks forward."

"There were no batteries whatsoever in your smoke detectors."

Her hands went to her throat. "None."

"None. Now Vince told me about the attempts you've had made on your lives. You have any idea what it's all about?"

"Maybe something to do with a deed on some property my father owned outside town. Whoever broke in tore up the entire first floor. He must've removed the batteries while he was at it. But I don't know why anyone would do such a thing."

"He was trying to kill you, Ms. Fields. This is a very serious matter, as you must realize."

"Of course I do." She stood and started pacing. "I just don't know what to do about it. Some nut job has it in for both of us."

"You're certainly safer here with people around than you would be at your home."

"But my presence is a risk to everyone who lives here."

"But there's safety in numbers," he countered.

"What do you think? Should I leave town? I have a business to run. I don't see how I can just up and leave."

"There's always a chance, if you leave, he'll lay low, wait for your return, then renew his efforts."

"So I might as well stay here. I do feel safer out here on the ranch."

"That's what I would advise. Sooner or later, the

arsonist will make a mistake. And that will be that." He placed the paperwork inside his briefcase. "Is there anyone you can think of who might want to harm both you and the sheriff?"

"The only person I've had a run-in with—if you can call it that—is Rollo Moore. "

Setting the briefcase on the floor, he leaned forward. "Tell me about it."

"He made an outrageously high offer on the house. Said he had a client who wanted to buy it. I refused. He was pretty angry when he left. I had to insist he leave."

"I'll follow up on that. Now have you notified your insurance agent? I'll be filing my initial report this afternoon. You should be able to get started on renovations, as soon as I complete the report."

"I'll notify him as soon as we're through here."

"Is there anyone else who has a beef with you?"

"No. Just wondering if this has something to do with the murder investigation. You know they found two bodies on Vince's property, his wife and the bank VP everyone thought had run away. That money's still missing."

"Yeah, I heard about that." Rafe frowned. "That's something to keep in mind." He stood. "I'll be going. Appreciate your help. And be careful."

"I will," she said with a nod.

She watched Rafe leave. He walked with just the tiniest bit of a swagger. No wonder. Even she found it difficult to think coherently when he was around.

"Abby?"

Startled, she whirled. "Chance, you scared me. I didn't know you were standing there."

"Vince told me to keep a close watch on you. You didn't hear me come up. Don't tell me you're as google-eyed over Rafe Dawson as all the other women around town. He's not worth it."

Hm. Just a hint of jealousy in his voice, wasn't there. "Keeping a close watch on me doesn't include sneaking up behind me." She wasn't able to keep the pique from her tone, so she smiled to soften the edge.

"Sorry. I care about you, Abby. Always have. I'm not sure Vince deserves you after the way he treated you before."

Abby took a step back. Chance was definitely in her personal space. "Let me worry about whether or not Vince deserves me."

Chance's gaze narrowed. He flushed darkly under his tanned cheeks. "Excuse the hell out of me."

"Just back off. Okay?"

He raised his hands. "This is me backing off. 'Sides, I've got chores to do." He spun and strode out the back door, allowing it to slam. The noise only serves to jar her already jumpy nerves.

"Dang." Abby ran her hand through her hair. "What was that about?" After all, this was one of Vince's brothers. Still, she couldn't help but wonder if he'd always been a little on the jealous side and she'd just never noticed.

Remembering what Rafe had said about her insurance, she pulled her cell phone from her jeans pocket and brought up her contact list. Might as well call her insurance agent while it was still on her mind.

He just hoped the contact number was till the same. He had to search his desk for a good half hour before he found it. Really should've thrown it away. Never really expected to need it again, after having Liz Tate and Ed Barnes taken care of.

But finally, there it was. Crumpled up and stuck in the

bottom of a file folder. The phone number for the Houston mob hitman.

He pulled out a burner phone and punched in the number.

It rang. A man answered, "Speak."

"This is—uh," He faltered then gave the code name he'd used before. "I have another job for you."

"How many?"

"Like before. Two. Same terms as before?"

"Rates have gone up. Add fifty percent and we have a deal."

He hesitated, wondering if he should haggle, then decided against it. "Deal."

After talking with her insurance agent, Abby called her relief pharmacist.

"Darla, I know this is a great imposition, but they want me to stay away from town. We'll have to cut the pharmacy hours the pharmacy until this is resolved. There's no way you can work sixteen-hour days seven days a week."

"No argument there. Just so you know, you're absolutely ruining my love life. What the heck is going on?"

"I wish I knew enough to tell you. All I know is I've been broken into, had my car forced off a bridge, and my house set on fire. And that's just what's happened to me. Vince has been shot at twice and nearly burned to death with me last night."

"Mm. That sheriff sure is tasty. So's his deputy, by the way, but tasty or not, I'm not sure I'd want to hang around him with all that going on. Anyway, as soon as I heard about the fire this morning, I knew I'd have to open for you."

"It was on the news?"

"Let's say I have an inside source."

"That sounds interesting," Abby said. "You can tell me when you're ready."

"I will. Not yet though. Too new."

They discussed what the new hours would be, then Abby terminated the call.

One thing taken care of—no, counting the insurance agent, that made two things.

Now what? Marti didn't want help with the cooking or cleaning. Abby wasn't used to being idle. Surely Vince didn't expect her to stay cooped up in the house twenty-four hours a day.

She walked into the kitchen where Marti was covering a bowl with a tea towel. "Rolls need to rise," she said by way of explanation.

"Any chance I could go for a ride? I'll go crazy if I have to stay inside all the time."

"Considering Vince has already been shot at, I think you'd better stay inside or at least close to the house." Marti secured a rubber band around the edges of the mixing bowl, then set it the proving drawer.

More of Marti's fabulous yeast rolls. Abby held back a sigh. Truly, she'd be two hundred pounds if she stayed at the ranch much longer. "How about a swim? Surely I can go for a swim. The pool looks so refreshing. I'd love to do some laps. Relieve the stress, y'know?" As well as burn some calories."

"I reckon that'd be okay. I'll call one of the boys to keep a lookout."

"Please don't. No need to pull them away from their work. I don't suppose you have a swimsuit I could wear?"

"Hon, mine would fall right off you," Marti said with a chuckle. "Maybe there's an old one of Liz's around here... somewhere."

Abby wrinkled her nose. "That would be too weird." She scratched her head, thinking. "Maybe a pair of cutoffs and a T-shirt—a dark one," she suggested since she didn't have a conventional swim top.

Marti's mouth twisted to the side. "There might be something in the attic. Let me see what I can find."

A few minutes later, Marti returned. "These look like something one of the boys might've worn when they were teenagers." She handed Abby a pair of cutoffs and a dark blue T-shirt with the number twenty-one across the back.

Abby smiled. "This was Vince's. I remember his number."

She took the garments upstairs and changed, pulling the T-shirt over her head. The cutoffs were a little loose around the waist. She rolled up the legs, then looked around for something to use as a belt. She poked into one of the drawers and found a yellow scarf.

That would work. She ran the scarf through the belt loops and tied it.

Perfect.

She ran downstairs and outside onto the patio. Taking a flying leap, she dived into the inviting turquoise water of the pool. The coolness of the water shocked her, but in a good way.

She swam along the bottom of the pool until her lungs screamed for air, then kicked to the surface, emerging for a quick breath. Slowly at first, she began swimming laps, then gradually picked up speed, sliding through the water like silk.

"Looks like *you're* having a good time." Chance's voice pulled her from the *zone*. Dammit. She stopped and began to tread water. "Yeah, it's great. Great for stress relief."

"There's better ways to relive stress," he said lazily, one foot propped on a lounge.

"Whatever." Ignoring his adolescent attempt at a double entendre, she began to swim laps again. Maybe he would take the hint and leave her alone.

"I could join you," he called. "I could keep an eye on you better."

She slowed, took a breath. "Not necessary." Then she kicked her feet and increased her strokes.

But he wasn't going away. "Got to keep an eye on you. That's what Marti said. And we always do what Marti says."

She stopped at the far end of the pool and boosted herself onto the edge. Shaking the water from her hair, she twisted the tail of the T-shirt to wring out the excess water.

"You must be sentimental, wearing Vince's old shirt for swimming."

"This is just what Marti brought me from the attic. Sentiment had nothing to do with it."

"*Excuse me.* Don't know what's got you so testy."

"I don't know either. Maybe the break-ins, wrecks, and fires are getting to me. Ya think?" She got to her feet and started walking toward the house. Why hadn't she thought to bring a towel? Where was her brain?

"Do you think you could bring me a towel, Chance? I don't want to track water all over Marti's clean floors."

"Trying to get rid of me, darlin'?" He stood feet spread apart, hands on his hips.

"No. I just need a towel."

"Reckon that's all I'm good for. Towel boy. Too bad we don't have a cabana. I'd make a real good cabana boy."

Abby gave him an eye roll and added with some attitude, "I think you would at that."

Marti strode onto the patio. "Chance Tate, don't give our houseguest any more guff. Get Abby a towel."

"Yes, ma'am." He left muttering to himself.

"Thanks. I don't know what's gotten into him. We used

to be friends in school, but now he's—I don't know—smarmy, smug, or something." Whatever was wrong with him, he made her a little uncomfortable.

"Just between you and me, darlin', I think he's a little green-eyed."

"Jealous? Of whom?"

"Here I go. I'm speaking out of turn. I adore all the Tate boys, but Chance is a little difficult sometimes." Marti waved her hands. "I've said enough."

"I guess Vince is a lot to live up to."

Marti pointed at Abby. "You got it in a nutshell." She glanced over her shoulder. "Guess he's forgotten 'bout that towel."

"I'm sorry for all the fuss. It's my fault. I should've brought one with me."

"Yes, you should've." Chance emerged from the house with a towel which he presented with a flourish and a theatrical bow. "Does madam require anything else?"

"Thank you, Chance." She dried her legs and feet, hopping from one to another, then wrapped the towel around her wet clothes. "Now that you mention it, I'm going to have to go shopping to fill out my wardrobe. And I need to stop by the house. I can take some of those clothes to the cleaners. May I borrow one of the ranch vehicles?"

"Only if I tag along," Chance said, his expression glum. "Vince's instructions were very specific. You're not going anywhere without me."

"Fine. But you really need to get over yourself."

"Well, Miss La-di-dah, maybe *you* need to get over *yourself*."

Abby was ready to snap back, but Marti stepped forward. "All right. I can see I'm going to have to separate you two. Since you can't seem to mind your manners, I'll ask Chase to escort Abby."

"He's busy on the north range," Chance argued. "It'll have to be me, or you can wait until my big brother comes home."

Better to wait? No. "I'll go change. I won't take long." No point in making the situation more ridiculous.

Chance nodded, his expression not improving.

No way would she let his surly mood ruin her day or keep her from accomplishing another task on her to-do list.

An hour ago, Dot had handed Vince the figures for the next year's budget. If there was anything he hated more than working on the budget, he couldn't think what.

Ranger Ben Rasmussen knocked on Vince's door and stuck his head inside. "Got a minute?"

"Sure." Vince shoved the budget aside. "Got more than one if you need it."

Ben took a chair. "Ballistics are back on the—uh, bodies found on your ranch."

"Why don't you go on and say it—my wife's and Barnes's bodies. What's the result?"

"We got a hit in NIBIN. The 9mm weapon used to kill your wife and Barnes has been used in contract kills all over the US, but primarily in the south and southwest. Fourteen documented kills, using the same weapon. He must really love that gun. I'd give my eyeteeth to take down this s.o.b. If we ever find the gun, we'll have him."

NIBIN was the National Integrated Ballistic Information Network and contained digital images of ballistic evidence.

"So someone *here* in Kenton Valley put out a hit on my wife and Barnes. What on earth were they into that brought a pro into the situation?" Vince leaned back in his chair. "What about the two attempts on me? I'm sure both of those involved a rifle."

"As for the second shooting, the one that took place outside town, that one was from something like an AR15, not in the database. As for the shooting that took place on your ranch, the ballistics don't match the second."

"So two shooters...or one shooter, two guns."

Ben frowned. "Whoever shot at you on your ranch used one of your rifles."

Vince straightened. "What?" Unbelievable. He tried to absorb the information. "Someone who had access to the ranch and to one of our rifles took a pot shot at me?"

"It was the spare rifle kept in the tack room. It'd been wiped down."

"Could've been anyone." His stomach plummeted. Someone he knew and trusted had tried to kill him.

And Abby was at the ranch. Dammit. She wasn't any safer there than she'd been at home.

Abby climbed into Chance's truck. "I appreciate this, Chance. I know it's a hassle."

Without looking at her, he asked, "Where do you wanna go first?"

"The house. I'll pack some clothes that can go in the washing machine, and then pull out a few things that can go to the cleaners. Then, if you'll run me by the Mercantile, I'll check in with Beth and Lola. Plus, I need to run over to the drugstore–just to see how things are there. Shouldn't take too much time."

"Women getting together gabbin'. That could take all afternoon," he grumbled.

"I'll try to hurry." Anything to ameliorate his bad mood.

They rode along in silence. Not a comfortable one

either. Maybe she should just ask him outright what in the hell was the matter with him. Glancing over at his set jaw and frown—eh, maybe not.

Finally they reached the outskirts of town and a minute later, he pulled up in front of the house. “Looks like a real mess. Sure it’s safe to go inside?”

“Yeah, the basic bones of the house are sturdy. I won’t be long.”

“Nah. I’m keeping an eye on you.”

Great. “Suit yourself.”

He followed her inside and up to her bedroom. He glanced over at the bed and raised an eyebrow.

Flushing at the memories of how her bedroom got in such a state, she pulled a carryall from the closet, unzipped it, and dumped in a collection of underwear, T-shirts, jeans, and a swim suit. From the closet, she grabbed a pair of running shoes, as well as a pair of boots. Didn’t hurt to be prepared.

Leaning against the doorjamb, Chance said, “I kinda liked you in the T-shirt.”

Oh brother. She flashed him a quick, if insincere, smile. “That should do it,” she said, ignoring his *kinda* compliment.

He took the carryall. “You said something about stuff for the cleaners?”

“Right.” Frankly she just wanted to get the hell out of there. She ran to the closet and pulled out three sundresses and a suit. “Let’s go.”

The cleaners was located next door to the Mercantile. “Wait here,” she told Chance after emerging from the cleaners. I won’t be long.” Hopefully, Chance would take the hint and wait outside the store.

"Sorry, Miss Daisy, I'm still keeping an eye on you. Go ahead. I'll just poke around the store while you girls *chat*."

Only by clenching her jaw was she able to refrain from giving him a piece of her mind.

She found blond Beth hard at work in her office.

Beth stood and hugged her. "How are you? We heard about the fire. Do you want to stay with us?" Beth and Lola lived in a spacious apartment over the Mercantile.

"I'm fine. I just wanted to let you guys know I'm back at the ranch with Vince. As you can imagine, the house is a mess, and there's no way I can live there. Besides, Vince insists I shouldn't stay there by myself, anyway."

Looking over Abby's shoulder, Beth smiled, "So you have a hunky bodyguard."

"No. What I have is a surly, pissed-off bodyguard."

Beth gave an eye roll. "Nothing new about that. He's always had a bit of an attitude, if you know what I mean."

"I'm afraid I do. And it hasn't improved with age."

"He always had a thing for you. But you never could see it for Vince. He was always the one for you." Beth gave a knowing smile. "And it appears he still is."

Abby allowed a smile to creep to her lips. "Yeah. He's still the one."

Beth's eyes widened. "Oh, girl. You've done the deed. Haven't you?" She twitched her shoulders. "I figured you had since everyone said he was wearing a sheet the night of the fire."

"Maybe." She glanced around to see where Chance was. "I don't have time to elaborate. I still need to check in on Darla to see if anyone is having a problem with the reduced pharmacy hours. I just hope she doesn't quit on me before all this crap is straightened out."

"Omigod. What would you do if she did?"

What *would* she do? She shrugged. "I'm afraid I'll have

to worry about that *if* it happens."

"Okay, Scarlett O'Hara."

"Later." With a quick wave, Abby hurried away before Beth could dig for further details."

Vince picked up the phone and called Abby's cell. "Where are you?"

"I'm across the street from you. I just finished checking in with Darla. What's up?"

Whatever happened to her staying at the ranch? "You're not alone are you?

"No. Chance is with me."

"Good. Why don't you all come over here? I need to talk to Chance."

"Oh, you don't want to talk to *me*?" Her tone was playful.

"Of course, but I need to update him about something—security-wise."

"That doesn't sound good. Okay. I'm through here. See you in a couple of minutes."

He blew out a sigh of relief. So far, so good.

Unable to sit still, he stood and began to pace. The damn budget would have to wait until tomorrow.

He stopped as soon as he spotted her trim figure crossing the lobby to his office. Even dressed in jeans and a knit shirt, the sight of her was as refreshing as an ice-cold beer on a hot day. Her nose was pink as if she'd had some sun. Ah, the pool.

Trim as she was, she filled out her jeans just right. As for the rest, she was perfect. His heart lifted, and suddenly, everything was all right in his world.

He opened the door to let her in and nearly shut it in his brother's face, forgetting for a second his existence. He chuckled. “Sorry. I was just so glad to see Abby’s all right that I didn’t see you.”

“Impressive, brother. Well, I’m right here, and Abby’s safe due in no small part to me keeping an eye on her. As instructed.”

Not caring for his brother’s tone, Vince frowned, focusing his gaze on Chance. “What’s with the attitude? I thought you an Abby were buds from way back.”

“We *are*,” Abby interjected. “You know how I am. I can be a real pill at times. Poor Chance. He’s not used to running all over town with me. He’d rather be doing manly things like—I don’t know—calf-roping or branding.”

Vince noticed the puzzled expression Chance shot Abby. What was going on with these two?

“Yeah. Abby’s got it right. She’s a real pill...sometimes.” Chance’s shoulders seemed to relax, and he let out a strained chuckle. “Yeah. We’re fine. Don’t worry. I’m not gonna let anyone get to her.”

“Y’all sit down. I’ve received some rather unpleasant news.”

Chance pulled up a chair for Abby. Good sign. Then he sat. “What gives?”

“The ballistic reports are back.”

Chance leaned forward. “And?”

“There’s bad news and then really bad news.”

Chance swore then added, “Come on, Vince. Spill it.”

Abby’s eyes widened. “He’s right. Just tell us.”

“Ballistics tie the weapon used to kill Liz and Barnes to fourteen confirmed hits.”

Abby sucked in a breath. “That’s the really bad news, right?”

“Ballistic report from the shooting outside town, is an unknown high-powered rifle like an AR15. That one isn’t on NIDIM. That’s the national database law enforcement uses for recovered ballistic material. An entirely different rifle was responsible for those potshots taken at me on the ranch. They came from the rifle kept in the ranch's tack room. No prints. That's the really bad news. Someone I know and trust tried to kill me. Abby, you're no safer on the ranch than you were at home."

Chance swore again, and Abby was sorely tempted. "Then what am I supposed to do? I'm not safe at home. And now, I'm not safe at the ranch. Where do I go?"

"There's an old cabin back in the hills," Chance suggested. "We used it when we were kids. There's even an artesian spring where we used to play."

Vince shook his head. "It's still on the ranch. Everyone on the ranch knows about it." Dammit. Not being able to trust the men on his ranch sucked. "I'll call Ranger Rasmussen. The Rangers can set you up in a safe house until this situation is resolved."

"A safe house?" she almost wailed. "What about you? You're in danger as well."

"Nothing new about that. All part of the job."

The pro from Houston pulled into the parking lot of a truck stop off I-10. To blend in, he drove a semi, just like the others. But his only cargo was a black Dodge SUV, as generic as they came. Making sure his cowboy hat covered the majority of his face, he checked into the motel alongside the truck stop. He gave a generic name, Tom Duncan, to the dumpy blonde at the registration desk. "You have a package for me?"

"Yes, sir."

Tom took the package and his room key. He wouldn't be here long, but the low-rent motel provided him with a base of operations several miles away from Kenton Valley where he could prepare the next phase of his assignment.

Once in his room, he opened the package. It contained all the information he needed. Addresses. Photos. The sheriff and a woman. She had chin-length dark hair, intelligent eyes. She reminded him of his sister. He could have some fun with this one.

He'd already been paid half his fee by wire to his Caymans account. The other half would be paid once he provided proof of the kills. Normal procedure.

Another private disposal. No torture this time. Too bad. He really enjoyed tormenting his victims to their limits before terminating them. Taking out a lawman was a trickier proposition and could bring a lot of heat. In addition to the higher fee.

Yes. Private disposal suited him just fine.

Chapter Twelve

Tom drove through town just to get the lay of the land. He swung by the house his employer had unsuccessfully tried to burn down. Fire. Always tricky. Never certain. Too many variables.

Unlike a bullet to the base of the skull.

Following the directions on the provided map, he drove by the Tate ranch. Gated. Probably never used until his employer's futile attempts. Armed ranch hand in sight. Better to get them out in the open.

Back to town. Now to check out female mark's pharmacy. He parked in the side parking lot.

Might as well, buy something small and unmemorable to check out the store. He took note of the reduction in hours taped to the entrance. That told him she might be sticking close to the ranch. He strolled down the aisles and picked up a box of sinus medication and some antacids. He cast a glance at the pharmacist. No, not his mark.

Now *that* gave him an idea.

Abby sat across the desk from Vince, trying to pay attention to the Ranger's instructions. Not having much success. She tried to read Vince's expression, but not having any success at that, either.

"You'll have an armed escort to a safe house situated two counties away. You'll have a Ranger with you at all times until we catch whoever's making these attempts on your life. It'll be like Wit-Sec. Witness Protection. Same rules apply. Tell no one where you're going. You'll stay inside the safe house at all times, away from the windows. No telephone or Internet contact. Might as well hand me your cell phone now." He held out his hand.

"But—" She couldn't do without her phone. Really. At the very least, she needed to keep in contact with Darla at the drugstore.

"That's the way it has to be."

"What about Vince?" She glanced over at him. "He'll know where I am, won't he?" Reluctantly, she handed him her smart phone. Her life was on that phone. Talk about cutting the connection.

"No. That's for your safety."

"That's silly. He isn't the one after me."

"If Vince doesn't know, he can't be tortured to reveal your whereabouts."

Tortured. She sucked in a quick breath. "Would someone actually do that?" She clenched her fists at her sides to keep them from shaking.

"Sure. Someone desperate enough," the Ranger said. "And if we're dealing with a pro, definitely."

Vince's expression was stern. Uncompromising.

"Is this what you want me to do?"

Vince cleared his throat. "Yes."

She turned to the Ranger, pleading, "But how long can this go on? Not indefinitely."

"Until law enforcement is certain you're safe."

So matter of fact. As if going to a safe house were an everyday occurrence. "I guess it's a good thing I have some clothes in the car. They need washing...because of the fire. But I just left some others at the cleaners."

Vince shot her a glance that said, *You're worried about your cleaning? Really?* But what he said was, "They're not going anywhere."

"All right, then." Standing, she held her hands up in a gesture of surrender. "I'm all yours." She bit her bottom lip. "If I could have a minute or two to say Goodbye?"

"Two minutes." The Ranger nodded. "We'll leave via the rear exit."

The thought of leaving Vince's protection for that of the Rangers brought tears to her eyes. "I don't want to go. I'm afraid I'll never see you again."

He chuckled. "Don't worry. You can't get rid of me that easily." He stood and walked around the desk, then scooped her into his arms.

She rested her head against his chest. "We're just getting close again. By the time you all find whoever's trying to kill us, you may have forgotten all about me."

"Or you could fall in love with your bodyguard."

Gazing into his eyes, she sniffed. "Don't be silly."

"No sillier than me forgetting about you." He held her tightly, as if he didn't want to let her go. "Do what the Rangers tell you, Abby. You'll be fine and back in my arms before you know it." He kissed the top of her head. "Let law enforcement do the heavy lifting."

She closed her eyes, wishing the moment could go on forever. Then she felt his warm lips cover hers. The kiss was long, first tender, then intense. Then tender.

A sigh escaped without her willing it. "Please be careful. Don't let anything happen to you while I'm away."

"Count on it, doll."

Ranger Rasmussen knocked on the door, then stuck his head inside. "Let's go."

Vince released his hold on her body, but not on her heart. She could still feel the pull between them. "Behave," he said softly.

"I will," she promised. What choice did she have? None.

Once again, Vince tried to concentrate on the annual budget. He worked steadily on the figures for a couple of hours. "That's enough of that." He stood, stretched, and was ready to scavenge a cup of coffee, when his phone chimed.

"Ms. Fields has reached the safe house," Rasmussen said. "No problems along the way. You can rest easy. She's safe."

Vince heaved a sigh of relief. "Thanks. I know this was a personal favor."

"Something had to be done. The perpetrator was getting more and more determined."

"Have your forensic accountants discovered what the Macedonia Corporation was going to do with that land?"

"We may never know until we find out who's trying to have the two of you killed."

Vince leaned back, hands linked behind his head. "I'm thinking some kind of building project. Commercial probably."

"Not exactly the prime location for a strip mall."

"Or a dude ranch."

"Like I said..."

"You're sure Abby will be all right?"

"If she remains in protective custody and follows the rules. She'll be fine."

"You don't know Abby." But he did know Abby, and he was sure she was already plotting how to get out of protective custody.

Tom waited until the drugstore closed at six. The pharmacist came out along with the cashier and got in a white Ford Escape. He followed her until she reached a condominium development, Green Arbor Villas. He drove past just slow enough to see her enter a first floor rear condo. He took note of the position of the security cameras.

Now all he had to do was wait until dark. In the meantime, he might as well have a bowl of chili at the truck stop.

Vince spent a restless night at the ranch, tossing and turning, worrying about Abby and whether or not she was truly safe. He rose at six, showered, dressed, and grabbed a cup of coffee from the never-complaining Marti as he headed out the door.

Will Rasmussen came on duty not long after Vince arrived. "You look like crap." He handed Vince a fresh cup of coffee."

"Thanks, Will, I'll make a note of that."

"Heard anything from the Rangers?"

"Only that Abby made it to the safe house without any problems."

They discussed the evening call outs. Nothing pressing.

At nine, the dispatcher called, "Sheriff, we have a phone call from the cashier at the drugstore. She says the pharmacist, Darla Murray, is late and isn't answering her phone."

"We'll do a do a welfare check." He turned to Will. "I don't like this."

"A welfare check? Maybe she just overslept," Will suggested quickly. "You really think it might have something to do with everything else that's been going on?"

"I don't like coincidences, so yeah." He keyed Darla's name into the computer, making note of her address and car tag number. "Let's go."

As they walked out, Vince told the dispatcher to have the condo manager meet them.

He and Will drove to the outskirts of town where the Green Arbor Villas had been built two years ago.

"There's her car." Will nodded toward the Ford Escape. "She should be home."

As requested, the manager was waiting with a key and a concerned expression.

"Sheriff Tate," he said. "And you are?"

"Avery Wilson," she said. "I've been the manager here for the last year. Ms. Murray has never given us any trouble."

"Let's hope she's not in trouble now," he said. He knocked on unit 111's door. "Sheriff's Department. Ms. Murray?"

No response.

An uneasy feeling centered in Vince's gut. He took the key from the manager. "Stand back."

She nodded, stepping back and giving them a wide berth.

He unlocked the door and walked inside the neat condo. Nothing appeared out of place in the living/dining room or the kitchen. But that uneasy feeling hadn't gone away.

He walked down the short hallway and knocked on the bedroom door. "Ms. Murray? Sheriff's Department."

When there was no response, he turned the door knob, opening the door.

And wished he hadn't.

Darla Murray lay face down, naked, hands and feet bound. Blood at the base of the skull.

Pulling a pair of Latex gloves from his hip pocket, Vince swallowed. There were cigarette burns all along her arms, back, and buttocks. Dear heaven. Torture. He steeled himself not to remember the vivacious young pharmacist who handed out prescriptions often with a smile and a joke or two.

Vince heard a ragged gasp from his deputy. He turned and eyeballed his deputy. Poor kid sagged against the wall.

"Not what I expected to see first thing this morning," Will said, his voice had a wavering emotional quality. And he was pale and looked as if he might get sick.

"Get outside if you're going to throw up. Don't contaminate the scene. We need forensics. Are you up to this?"

Will shook his head. "I think it's a case for the Rangers." His hands trembled as he tried to pull on his Latex gloves.

"I agree." His chief deputy was usually made of sterner stuff. "It's a rough scene," Vince acknowledged. "Your first?"

"You could say that." Will took a shuddering breath. "There's something you need to know." Will's voice broke. "Darla and I were seeing each other. Just the last month or so."

Vince swore. Another LEO-involved murder. "Get out of here. Call the Rangers."

At first glance, it looked like some garden variety, sick son of a bitch had stalked and murdered Abby's employee. But in his gut, Vince knew this was a pro. A pro who was a lot more than your basic sick son of a bitch.

***

The safe house turned out to be a nondescript three bedroom/two bath ranch. Located in an anonymous subdivision, it was on a large lot, set back from the street. Must've been built in the seventies because the interior decor and furnishings screamed seventies.

Abby spent a restless night, dreaming about making love with a Vince who morphed into a faceless boogeyman.

"At least let me watch TV," she begged after breakfast. Her guard was Bob Randal. The Ranger appeared to be in his mid-forties, and, in addition, cooked a mean Southwestern omelet.

"What can it hurt, Ranger Bob? I don't have a phone. There's no internet access. The books are geared to hunting and fishing, neither of which I'm interested in. Please, just let me watch the local news and Good Morning Hill Country." She fluttered her lashes, hoping it would melt his heart.

"Fine." Ranger Bob looked up from doing the breakfast dishes. "Turn on the TV. Anything is better than listening to you whine."

"Thank you," she said, awarding him with her sweetest smile. She picked up her cup of coffee and settled down on the sofa. Good. The local news was on.

She leaned forward. There was a reporter doing an on-scene report. Over the reporter's shoulder, Abby could see Vince in the background.

"We're coming to you from a murder scene in Kenton Valley. A young woman was found murdered earlier this morning. Her identify hasn't been released yet, pending official notification of the family.

"Right now, the Los Marcos County Sheriff Vince Tate is about to make a statement."

The camera swung to Vince. At least he was all right.

"We have a twenty-nine year-old woman who didn't show up for work this morning. When my chief deputy and I performed the requested welfare check, we discovered her body. We are treating this as a suspicious death. That's all I have for now."

The camera focused back on the reporter. "From a confidential source, it's our understanding the young woman was found bound and gagged. She's a young professional who worked irregular hours but according to her neighbors was always quiet and respectable. Another neighbor mentioned that the victim of this horrible crime had been dating someone in law enforcement."

A nagging memory buzzed in the back of Abby's mind. Darla had dropped a hint or two about her tasty new boyfriend. "Bob, have you seen this? There's been a murder in Los Marcos County. I know those condos. That's where my relief pharmacist lives. Oh my God!" She sprang from the sofa. "I have to know if she's all right. Give me a phone. I have to check with the drugstore."

"No can do."

"Then call the drugstore and ask for the pharmacist. I have to know. Can you do that? Please."

"Sit down," he said, his tone gruff. "I'll make a call."

He went to the small utility room off the kitchen to make his call. Could she hear a single word? Hell no!

She paced until he returned, his expression solemn. "No answer at the drugstore."

"There *has* to be someone there. You should've at least gotten voice mail." She held out her hand. "Give me the phone."

He took a step back. "Not going to happen, ma'am." He blew out a breath. "I called Ranger Rasmussen. He's at the crime scene. The drugstore doesn't answer because it's closed. That's all I can tell you."

Her knees weakened. She grabbed the back of the sofa for support. "You just told me my friend, my employee, Darla Murray, is the victim. Otherwise the drugstore would be open and taking calls."

"I'm sorry. That's all I can say."

She recognized pity in his gaze. Stiffening her spine and squaring her shoulders, she shot him her most no-nonsense expression. "I *have* to leave."

"No."

"You can't keep me here.

"I can."

"No!" She glanced around wildly for something to throw. Something to break. Anything to relieve the anguish wracking through her body.

The Ranger shook his head. "If you break something, it'll come out of my salary."

His response, so mundane, so normal, shocked her from the frenzy threatening to overwhelm her. She sank onto the arm of the sofa. "Really?"

He lifted his broad shoulders in a shrug, "Probably not."

Abby raised her gaze to meet Bob's knowing one. "Technically, I'm not a prisoner. I haven't broken any laws, have I?"

"No. Neither one." He heaved a sigh as if he knew her argument before she could make it.

"Then you *can't* keep me here. I *have* to go back to the Valley." She picked up her bag. "I am hereby assuming responsibility for my life. I need to see Darla's parents. I need to make arrangements for my cashiers so they won't be targets. Whoever killed Darla wanted to draw me out into the open. So be it. I don't want anyone else killed because I'm holed up safe and comfy two counties away. I can run the drugstore on the new schedule Darla and I set up."

"You're signing your own death warrant."

"That's better than losing one more person because someone has a hate-on for me. I'm ready for this to be over with. Take me home, Bob. Just take me home."

"You killed the wrong pharmacist!" Tom's contractor screamed into his ear. Tom leaned back and grabbed the TV remote.

"No. I didn't. This 'un was a freebie. Chalk it down to necessary collateral damage. Very simple. The mark'll have to come out of hiding to run her drugstore." *Amateurs.* Dealing with them was the pits.

"I guess that makes sense in some sort of twisted way. What's your plan for the sheriff?"

"Let me worry about him. He's my problem. Stop calling me, or *you're* going to be another problem I have to take care of." He terminated the call.

Now then, time for some porn.

Chapter Thirteen

Nightmare. Absolute freaking nightmare.

Vince leaned back in his chair and rubbed his temples. His chief deputy wasn't the only one who hadn't seen a crime scene like that one before. And Will was a basket case. After handing over Will's service weapon, Vince had released him from duties, but asked him to remain available for an interview. Ranger Rasmussen was none too pleased to be investigating yet another LEO related death, especially since this time the LEO involved was his younger brother. Forensic techs were still at the crime scene.

The main thing was to get Will's service weapon cleared. While Vince wasn't thrilled to have a hitman running around willy-nilly in Los Marcos County, if the ballistics matched the hitman's weapon, it would go a long way toward clearing Will of any involvement in Darla Murray's murder.

No doubt in Vince's mind that his chief deputy was innocent. Even if he hadn't known Will all his life, no one who'd observed the deputy's reaction on seeing her body would've believed him guilty.

No one.

Still, the *Is* had to be dotted and the *Ts* crossed. Procedure was procedure.

At least, Abby was safe. That was the one thing Vince

could count on.

Or so he thought. For about ten minutes.

His office door opened and Abby walked in. For a second, the onslaught of her physical presence overcame practical considerations. Memories of their lovemaking had him shifting in his seat. He knew every inch of her slender body. Every dip. Every dimple. The sleek muscles in her firm thighs. The softness of her breasts against his chest. The warm touch of her hands on—

He stood, leaning forward, his hands on the desk. All the better to keep from wringing her pretty neck. "Dammit all to hell!" He sucked in a breath, his face heated as anger roiled. "What in the Sam hill are you doing here?"

"I'm here to notify you that I have no intention of sitting safe and sound two counties away while everyone I know is being murdered or in danger of it."

Her absolute air of calm and sensibility really pissed him off. "How did you find out?"

"Ever heard of the television, Vince?" She braced her hands on his desk, staring him down. "The Ranger took away my phone, but he couldn't take away my eyes and ears."

"Just calm down. I know you're upset about Darla, but risking your life by coming back to town is plain stupid."

"I'm calm. Or I *was* until you call me stupid. Stupid, really?" Her face flushed a pretty pink.

He tried to backtrack. No sense in both of 'em being pissed off. "Not stupid—wrong word—unwise."

She straightened, folding her arms across her chest. "I don't care how you spin it. I'm here to stay."

"Fine. As soon as I'm through here, I'll take you to the ranch. I've already doubled security since this morning. I knew you'd come home if you found out."

"Oh no." She shook her head. "I have to see Darla's

parents, assuming you've already notified them. Then tomorrow, I'm going to re-open the drugstore and run it by myself. No point in risking any other lives."

More than anything, he wanted to give her a good shaking, as if that would actually shake some sense into her. He sucked in a deep breath. Might as well speak his mind, no matter how she'd react. "Now that *is* stupid—not the parents thing but re-opening the store."

"Well..." She pouted. God, that kissable mouth. "If you wanted to post one of your hands to keep me company, I wouldn't object. Three quarters of the town uses my drugstore. I can't just hand over the business my father worked so hard to build to the chain store. And that's what would happen if I completely closed. I'd never get those customers back."

"From a business sense, you're right. But I'd feel a hell of a lot better if you went to the ranch and stayed there."

"I can't do it. I just can't. Is there any way my cashiers, Ellen and Kay, can be protected? I don't want them drawn into this mess."

"Ellen has already gone to visit her aunt in Houston. The last time I spoke with Kay, she was making plans, too. I'll check to make sure she makes herself scarce." At least Abby's employees had more sense than their boss.

"Good."

"I'm going to send Will with you to the Murrays. Come to find out—"

"They were seeing each other. I didn't know. She'd hinted, but I was too blind to see it."

"They were. He's pretty messed up. He was with me when we found her body."

"Oh, no."

"It was the worst crime scene *I've* ever attended, and I've seen some bad ones." He walked around the desk and took her in his arms. "I won't let this SOB get ahold of you."

He felt the dam give way. Whatever self-control she had shattered. He held her until her sobs subsided. "I'll keep you safe if it's the last thing I do."

She sniffed. "I'm all right now. I've got to hold it together for her mom and dad."

"You shouldn't have to go through this."

"At least, I'm still alive." Her body started to shake.

"It's all right. We'll get through this together."

Finally depleted of tears, she nodded against his chest. "I can do it now. I'm all right."

He watched her leave. His hands fisted at his sides. More than anything, he wanted his words to be true. But even more than that, he wanted to kill the bastard who'd tortured and killed an innocent young woman.

Abby drove Will's SUV over to the Murrays' house. Poor guy. All he did was stare out the window. Darla's parents lived in a recently-built gated community that catered to retirees, but even those gates couldn't keep out the gaggle of TV news crews and reporters that already lined the street. En masse they turned in her direction as she pulled into the paved drive and parked behind the Murrays' Land Rover.

"Don't engage," Will said. "Just keep your head down and head for the front door."

At least he'd snapped out of his lethargy. "I won't. I'm just here to see her parents. They must hate me. This is all my fault."

"No, it isn't. No one could've predicted..."

Abby opened her door and slid from the SUV. Will came around, taking her by the arm and shepherding her through the crowd of reporters.

"Who are you?"

Someone answered for her. "She owns the drugstore."

Another reported pushed toward Abby, shoving his microphone in her face. "How does it feel to have one of your employees murdered?"

She glared at the reporter. Yes, he had a job to do, but it sure was a scummy one. "How the hell do you think it feels? How would *you* feel if one of your fellow reporters was murdered?"

Will's grip on her arm tightened. "That's enough." He pulled her toward the front door.

The door opened. Darla's father let them inside the condo. He was a tall distinguished man in his fifties. His clear blue eyes were red, but his body was tense, more angry than sad. Heartbreak would come later. Darla's mother sat on the sofa staring at nothing, her eyes red and nearly swollen shut from crying.

Abby extended her hand "I'm so sorry for your loss, Mr. Murray. I can't believe she's gone." Not just *gone*. Murdered.

"Call me Fred." His tone was calm, deadly calm. "Darla really liked you. Loved working at the drugstore."

Will mumbled his condolences and almost broke down.

"I know, son. Just tell me you're going to find this bastard who killed my girl."

"We're doing our best, sir. The Rangers are on it."

Fred nodded. "The Rangers will get him. No doubt about that." Indeed, the Texas Rangers was a premier law enforcement agency, as internationally renowned as the Royal Canadian Mounted Police or Interpol.

Abby crossed the room to stand beside Mrs. Murray. "I'm so sorry. I don't know what else to say."

Mrs. Murray's face flushed, her eyes widened. She straightened. "What is there to say? It's *your* fault. Having her work crazy hours. All it did was make her a target."

Darla's father crossed the room and sat beside his wife. "Now, Mama, you know that's not true. You can't blame Abby. "

Mrs. Murray rose, somewhat shakily, pointing at Will. "And you! Where were you last night when someone was torturing and killing my baby girl? Some lawman. You're supposed to be protecting honest folks. Where were *you*?"

"On duty, ma'am." He barely choked out the words. "I was on duty."

"Then I'd say you failed in your duty." She rushed from the room. A door slammed.

Fred Murray turned to face them. "It's the grief. She doesn't mean any of what she said. She's just overcome with the loss."

Abby swallowed. Mrs. Murray's words had stung, mainly because they were true. "Should I call your doctor for some light sedation?"

"If you'd be so kind." His rigid posture seemed to weaken as if he were in danger of shrinking. "Dr. Reyes—he's our family doctor."

Abby made the call, explaining the situation. "Thank you, Doctor." She terminated the call, then turned to Mr. Murray. "Dr. Reyes will be here shortly. He'll give her something that'll help her calm down and get some rest."

He gave her a sad smile. "Thank you. I'd better see to my wife."

"We'll let ourselves out." Will took Abby's arm. "Again, I'm so sorry. Maybe if I'd been there..."

"It's all right, son. I don't blame you."

Poor Will was about to break down. "Let's go. We've got to get through a passel of reporters." Abby tugged on

Will's hand. "Come on."

Vince took a bite of the greasy burger, grimaced, then threw the rest in the waste basket. He took a sip of his coffee. Gross! Cold. He stood ready to get a refill when his phone rang. He glanced at the caller I.D. and sat. "Give me some good news, Ben."

"Again, I have good news and bad news. Will's service weapon is cleared. And our hitman is definitely on the hook for the Murray woman. Ballistics report is a one hundred percent match to the other fourteen. All we need is to find the man and his favorite gun."

"So he's in town. Right now." Could matters get any worse?

"I doubt he'll leave without taking out his primary target or targets."

"So Darla Murray's killing was a device to bring Abby out into the open."

"Yeah. I'd say, just watching the evening news, his plan worked."

"The news?" What now? Had confidential information been leaked?

"Reporters and a TV crew were at the Murrays' residence when Abby and my brother arrived. There was a *brief* exchange of words."

"Abby. Of course. They made her mad?"

"You could say that. But that's not all."

"What?"

"That was going in. On her way out, she took a moment to challenge the killer."

His heart sank. "No!"

"Yeah."

"Oh God."

"I'm sending you a video of said memorable moment. I'll see you in a few minutes, but I knew you needed to see this."

Heart racing, Vince waited for the video to load on his phone.

And suddenly, there it was.

Dread gathering in his gut, he watched Abby and Will emerge from the Murrays'. The reporters shouted questions at Will first. "Are you the law enforcement officer involved with the murder victim?" Stone-faced, Will ignored them. Smart.

"Ms. Fields, how are the victim's parents taking it?"

Vince watched her bristle at the intrusive question. Will's hands fisted at his sides. Abby tried to pull him toward the SUV.

Another question. "We heard she was tortured. Can you elaborate?"

Will took a swing, but Abby grabbed his arm and kept the swing from connecting. Good girl. The last thing the sheriff's department needed was being slapped with a lawsuit by a reporter.

Then Abby turned to the reporters. "I'd like to make a statement."

Oh no, don't.

Then the camera was right in her face for a close up. Now, it seemed Will was trying to pull her to the SUV.

"I have a statement for whoever murdered my friend and employee, Darla Murray—that's her name. The *victim* has a name, folks. All right, now that we have that clear. Leave my friends alone. You want me, buddy. Come and get me. Just to make it easier for you, the drugstore will remain open—on reduced hours, it's true—but I'll be there. You can't scare me away. I have a job to do, and I don't intend to let the people of Kenton Valley down. If you want me, I repeat. Come and get me!"

Then the camera cut to the TV reporter. "Local pharmacist Abby Fields just issued a challenge to Darla Murray's killer."

Vince sank back in his chair. What had she done? Painted a target on her backside. That's what.

He called Will's cell phone. "You and Abby, in my office now. *Right now.*"

Vince drummed his fingers against the desktop. What was taking Ben so long?

No sooner had the thought passed through his mind than the Ranger strolled into Vince's office.

He leaned forward, anxious for the Ranger's debrief. "What else do you have? Give me something, Ben. Do we have anything to go on so we can ID this guy?"

"Be patient." Ben straddled a chair.

"Hard to be patient when lives are at stake." Frankly, he wanted to throttle Abby for her shenanigans, but since he couldn't...

"Apparently, he cased the area in advance. Minimal exposure on the security cameras. He strolled in on foot through the breezeway between units, and entered through the back, using her patio door. Kept his face covered by a ski mask. Height approximately five-ten to six feet. Wore gloves. Unable to determine his race. Vehicle must've been parked at a distance. He left the same way he came, on foot."

More nothing. This hitman could be anyone. "What about the condo's security tapes for the last couple of days? Any unknown vehicles?"

"All vehicles identified, except for one black Dodge SUV. Appeared to have followed her after she left the drugstore. Plates covered with mud."

The hitman was a pro, no doubt about it. "Let's pull the tapes from the drugstore. I bet he did a recon there as well."

"Those tapes are being viewed as we speak."

"What about DNA?" *Please let there be some DNA.*

"Bastard used a condom, but we may have lucked out. It appears he removed his mask while he was in her condo. We recovered several short dark hairs from her body. If there's a root, we may be able to identify him...if he's in CODIS. The M.E. is still going over her body and the rest of the evidence. Considering how hot it was, he may find traces of his perspiration on her body. Or his skin cells on the gag he used to keep her quiet. It'll take time."

Of course he used a condom, many thanks to a certain long-running TV franchise. "Long shot."

"But if any of his DNA can be retrieved, it's the best clue we could have. He could be in in the CODIS database related to something minor."

"What about DNA related to the previous cases where the same weapon was used?"

"No. He's been careful. But those were hits. In. Out. This time, he stuck around and had his twisted version of fun with Ms. Murray."

"I really, really want to get this guy for what he did to her. I want to kill him myself. I want to hear him beg for mercy the same way she must have." Vince leaned back, sucked a deep breath.

"But you won't." Ben shook his head. "You're a lawman. No matter how much he deserves it, you won't cross that line."

"Don't be too sure. I'll do whatever the situation calls for in order to keep Abby safe."

Ben nodded. "Would expect nothing less."

On the drive back to town, Abby turned to Will. "How pissed off do you think Vince will be?"

Will let out a chuckle. "On a scale of one to ten, I reckon he'll hit a twenty."

"That bad."

"*Don't engage*. What part of that didn't you get?"

"Stop it! I don't need you yelling at me. Vince will be more than happy to do his share. The reporters just got to me."

"That's what they do, Abby. That's their job. If they can goad you into saying something stupid—"

"That was pretty stupid."

"Off the charts."

Of course it was. Anger had propelled her response to the TV and news crews. But now, the adrenaline surge had bottomed out, her insides quivering like an earthquake—maybe ten on the Richter scale. "I should've kept my mouth shut."

"No argument here."

"Well, we're here." Abby pulled into the parking lot for Sheriff Department vehicles.

"Stay put." Will opened his door and scanned the area.

"What are you looking for?"

"I'm looking for anyone with a high-powered rifle who might be waiting to take you out."

"Seriously?"

"Serious as a heart attack."

He got back inside, grabbed the mic. "Deputy Rasmussen here. Need an escort to get the package inside the building."

"*Package*, am I?"

"It's code in case someone's listening on a police

scanner."

"Oh." Still not a very flattering term.

Two deputies emerged from the building wearing bullet proof vests. One of them carried a third vest.

"I take it that one's for me."

"You're real smart *sometimes*."

She stuck her tongue out. "I guess I ought to say thanks."

"All in a day's work." He shook his head. "And in case you're not aware of it, you've just made our jobs a lot harder."

Oh, yeah, she had.

Leaning back on his bed in the motel, Tom watched the pharmacist mouthing off for the TV news cameras. His mouth curled into a smile.

Nothing like making it easy for me, bitch.

How he would love to give her the same treatment he'd administered to her friend. But he'd been paid to take her out and that was it. But he mustn't forget the sheriff. As for the pharmacist, she'd be well protected. So while all that attention was focused on the pharmacist, he'd take out the sheriff.

Piece of cake.

Chapter Fourteen

With more than a little trepidation, Abby tapped on the door to Vince's office. She was the one who'd screwed up, and he had every right to be pissed off. As for her stupidity in challenging a killer to *come and get her*, she really ought to be locked up somewhere with padded walls.

"Come in."

Crap. Vince's tone was anything but loving and romantic. Yeah, he was totally pissed. She glanced over her shoulder at Will.

He gave her a gentle nudge. "Go on."

The door opened before she could open it herself. Will Rasmussen's studly older brother motioned for the two of them to enter.

Instead of his normal easy-going expression, Vince scowled, his face red with anger. "Deputy Rasmussen, you were supposed to keep her out of trouble."

Will squared his shoulders. "I tried, Boss. Short of gagging her..." He shrugged.

"You didn't acquit yourself very well, little brother." Ben shook his head disapprovingly. "If it wasn't for Ms. Fields, you would've hit that reporter. She did a better job looking out for you than you did for her."

"You're right. And no, I didn't. But she—"

"*She* can speak for herself." She leaned forward on

Vince's desk, challenging him. "Don't blame Will. He warned me not to engage with the reporters. But dammit, that reporter made me mad."

Vince stared right back, his blue eyes sparking with anger. He appeared to be considering his next words carefully. After what seemed like an eon, he spoke. "Your big mouth just made my job and the jobs of everyone in this department ten times—hell, a hundred times—harder. Setting yourself up as a target. News flash: You're already a target.

"The reporter made you mad? Yeah, that's a hell of a reason to challenge a professional hitman, one we have no clue who he is. Insane, that's what. You're certifiable."

Abby's cheeks grew hot under his scrutiny, but he wasn't saying anything she hadn't already said to herself. Time to pull up her big girl panties. "I know. You're right."

But Vince wasn't through. No. He was just getting warmed up. "By insisting on keeping the drugstore open, you'll need who knows how many of my deputies guarding you. To a man, they've all volunteered to keep you safe. Good men. And your selfishness is endangering their lives. Yes, it's their job, but do you want to live with one or more of their deaths on your conscience? Just so you don't lose your customer base. Men you've known your entire life. You went to school with most of 'em. You know their families. Their children."

Overcome by the shame of her unthinking recklessness, she swallowed the hard lump that had formed in her throat. "I won't re-open the drugstore until this is all resolved."

"Thank, God." Vince let out a loud sigh. He got to his feet. Rushing around the desk, he scooped her into his arms. "When I saw that news video, you took ten years off my life. I'll keep you safe, Abby, but you have to help me."

Relief that Vince still cared and didn't hate her for her stupidity, swept through her. "I'm so sorry. I was thoughtless and stupid."

"No argument here, doll."

"Now *that's* settled, what am I going to do? I don't want to go back into the Rangers' protection." She glanced at Ben. "As much as I appreciate it, I believe the killer will just lay low until he either finds me or I come out of hiding."

Ben nodded. "She has a valid point."

"Then what? Where?" Anywhere she went, she would put other lives at risk.

"Where's easy, doll. You're coming back to the ranch."

"No. Because..."

"Until I come up with a better plan, it's the ranch." He kissed the top of her head. "No matter how good he is, I'm not going to let that SOB get ahold of you."

"But I'm still placing the lives of everyone on the ranch in danger."

"It's not the same. Keeping the drugstore open was an unnecessary risk for you and my deputies. On the ranch, every precaution will be taken. We'll limit access—we already have. The main compound is gated. *You* will follow the rules and take every precaution. You'll keep out of sight. We'll put the word on the street—"

She snorted. "The *word on the street*? You act like we're in Houston or Dallas."

Ignoring her bout of pettishness, he continued, "This town's gossip mill works a treat. Everyone knows everyone else's business. We'll spread the word that you've decided to go back into the Rangers' protection, after all. He's bound to discover it's a ruse."

"Then what?"

"We wait. He'll make his move or a mistake."

"What about Marti?" Abby gazed upward, pleading. "I don't want her dragged into this."

"She's a problem," Vince admitted. "She refuses to leave the ranch. Says she feels safer there than anywhere else."

"No! You have to make her go for her own safety."

"Easier said than done. I reminded her that I pay her salary, but she turned around and said that didn't give me the right to make her leave unless I out and out fired her. I offered to send her to a spa. She just laughed."

"Let's go home, Vince." She rested her head against his strong chest. "I've had enough."

Ben spoke. "I'm taking one of our female Rangers as a decoy. That'll make it look like you're going into protection."

"I hate putting her at risk."

"She's a top notch Ranger. And she can handle herself. Don't worry."

Abby cut her gaze from Ben to Vince. "Do you all realize I'm attending Darla's funeral. Whatever's required, I *have* to go."

Vince groaned and ran his hands through his hair. "I was afraid of that. Ben?"

"The Rangers will form a protection detail. We won't allow you to come to harm."

"That's when he'll make his move," Vince said. "When she's out in the open."

Ben shook his head. "The more I learn about this shooter, it's less likely he'll shoot from a distance. He loves that nine mil. Likes to get up close and personal."

"That's what I'm afraid of." The words came out so quietly, she wasn't sure if she'd said them aloud at all.

Vince's arms tightened around her. "He's not about to get up close and personal with you. I'll die before that happens."

A small sigh escaped without her volition. "Always the hero. *My* hero."

"Damn straight." He picked up his cowboy hat. "Let's get you disguised and out of here." He nodded to Ben. "You do your thing. I'm taking her home... to the ranch."

A warm, cozy feeling suffused her body. Home and ranch. Both were quickly becoming one and the same.

The aroma of grilled steak reached Abby's nose the second she walked into the house. Her stomach growled. "I'm famished. I don't think I've eaten since breakfast." Breakfast? Had it only been this morning? It seemed as if a week had passed since she'd seen the news about Darla. With that thought, all hunger left her, replaced with a feeling of loss.

Vince flashed a wide smile. "Marti grills a mean steak, all right. I'm guessing she'll have salad and baked potatoes. A word of warning, that's what constitutes a light meal in Marti's culinary repertoire."

During dinner, Abby tried to make small talk. She picked at her food, barely managing to swallow a quarter of what must have been a delicious meal. Her mouth was so dry it was like trying to swallow sawdust.

When Marti brought out chocolate pie topped with meringue, Abby rose, scooting back her chair. "I'm sorry. I can't do this wonderful meal justice. I'm going to bed. If it's all right?"

"Of course, darlin'. You go on to bed." Marti's words and gentle tone were a balm on Abby's soul.

Upstairs, Abby showered and then readied for bed.

She slipped between the cool sheets, but sleep wouldn't come. No. Images of Darla's last moments filled Abby's mind.

Distraction came with a light tapping on her door. "Are you all right?"

"I'm fine. Come on in."

Vince expression was grave, seen in the light streaming from the hallway. He wore only a pair of jeans, his hair damp from his recent shower. "Earlier, you said you were hungry, but you didn't eat much."

"I was. And then I wasn't. Too much has happened. I can't get the images out of my mind." Her eyes welled with tears. She blinked them back, not wanting to break down and blubber like a baby.

"Need a cuddle?"

"Always." She patted the mattress. "Tonight, I'd rather cuddle than—you know."

"Then cuddle it is." He unfastened his jeans then stepped out of them, leaving him in a pair of briefs.

"What about your family? Will they be shocked if you spend the night in here?"

"Chance, who knows where the hell he is. Chase has guard duty tonight. Marti is in her quarters with the TV on max volume. I think her hearing is starting to go."

He slipped into the bed beside her. She turned away from him so they could spoon. His hands ran over her shoulders, caressing her ever so gently. "You're tense. No wonder. It's been a hell of a day."

"It boggles my mind that someone would kill and torture another human being, much less someone I know."

"Evil exists. Don't believe for a moment it doesn't."

"It's so horrible. I keep imagining... If only I could've been there. Done something."

"You couldn't have stopped him. He would've killed

you too. And he would've enjoyed it, the sick bastard." His arms encircled her body. "I won't let anything happen to you, Abby. Please know that. Believe it."

"I do." And she truly did believe down to every cell of her body that he would protect her with every fiber of his being. From the warmth of his embrace to the coiled strength of his body molded to hers, he would keep her from harm.

The next morning, Tom drove by the drugstore, parked, and checked the notice on the door for the new hours. Instead he read, *Closed until further notice.*

The bitch! He clenched his jaw to keep from screaming his rage. So she was going to hide from him after all. Her house was uninhabitable. Where else would she go? The sheriff's ranch. As for getting inside the heavily guarded compound... A challenge, right up his alley.

Leaving Abby still asleep hadn't been easy, but she needed the rest. And he needed to get back on the job.

After grabbing a thermos of fresh coffee—bless Marti—he jumped into the Tahoe and headed toward the gate. "I'm leaving," he radioed the guard. No point in having to wait for the guard to open it.

With one hand he unscrewed the thermos and took a long drink of coffee. Nothing better to get his motor started. He drove through the open gate and turned onto the road to town. He reached for the radio and turned it on. Country music filled the cab of the SUV. Then he ran over something in the road. He wrestled the steering wheel for control.

Damn! Spike strip or something. The SUV careened

down the embankment, flipped and rolled over.

Once. Twice. Stopped.

The vehicle still rocking, he tried the seatbelt release. No use. Son of a bitch! He rummaged for the belt cutter he had stowed into the armrest console and cut the belt.

He tried the door.

Jammed.

He pulled the baton from his duty belt and gave his window a whack. The subcap he'd added made the baton perfect for just this situation.

The tempered glass shattered into tiny bits. He brushed the glass from his hair and face and then crawled from the wrecked vehicle. He clambered up the embankment, scrabbling through the rocky undergrowth.

A homemade spike strip made of steel pipe and nails lay in the road where he'd run over it. His distraction with the coffee and radio had been a huge mistake. He pulled his phone from his pocket, snapped a photo of the tire shredder then picked it up and tossed it into the ditch.

That twitchy feeling, the one you get when there's a gun aimed at you, centered between his shoulders. He ducked.

A shot whizzed over his head. Abby wasn't the only target. Good to know.

He hit the dirt, rolled, then scrambled for cover. Another shot ricocheted just over his shoulder.

Too damn close.

Where was the shooter? These shots were hitting with greater accuracy than the previous attempts. A *lot* closer. The Houston hitman. The one who liked his nine mil. Hmph. He reached for his comm. unit. "Shots fired." He gave his location. Without raising his head from cover he scanned the horizon. His gaze drew toward a grove of cottonwood. Figured. There was an access road from an old mine in the hills behind the trees.

Hell, the shooter was still in sidearm range. Must be he was using his trusty nine mm, after all.

He leaned forward to lay down some fire, then ducked back.

Not soon enough.

He felt the telltale burn in his left shoulder. His left arm went numb. He thanked his lucky stars it wasn't his strong side.

Still, he was losing blood. He shook himself to steady his aim. Fired.

Passed out.

Abby turned over, feeling around for Vince. Not finding him, she yawned. What time was it anyway? She glanced at her phone on the nightstand. Ten. Really?

She shot from the bed, quickly dressing in jeans, a T-shirt, and running shoes. She flew downstairs, even though she knew it was way too late to catch him.

"Good morning, Sleeping Beauty," Chance called as she walked by the ranch office.

Her response was a grunt. Surely no one, not even Chance, could expect civility before she'd had her morning coffee.

On entering the kitchen, the aroma of coffee hit her nose. "Morning, Marti. Tell me there's some coffee left, please."

"Indeed there is." Marti handed her a cup. "Freshly brewed."

Abby yawned, "Thank you" and sat at the table. "I don't know why I slept so late."

"You don't?" Marti grinned, but wisely said nothing else. "What would you like for breakfast?"

"Oh, nothing. Thank you, but I never eat breakfast."

"Then I suppose you're not interested in these cinnamon rolls I'm getting ready to pull from the oven?" Marti smiled, then opened the oven door.

The spicy smell of cinnamon wafted through the air. Abby's mouth watered. She swallowed. "Maybe just one."

"They're kinda small."

"Okay—two."

Abby reached for the pan of rolls.

Marti chuckled. "Careful. You'll burn your fingers."

"I can't wait. I'm starving."

She plucked the first hot roll and popped it into her mouth, then moaned with pleasure from the spicy sweetness. "Just one more," she said and repeated the process. Licking the icing from her fingers, she said, "I can't believe you don't run a restaurant or bakery. If the Tates ever let you go, I'll hire you. Just so you know."

Marti opened her mouth, probably to make a quick reply, but the phone rang. "Probably the boss checking on you," she said with a wide smile. "Tate Ranch."

Abby watched the wide smile change into a frown.

"I'll tell her. Can't you tell us anything else? Where did it happen?"

An uneasy felling centered in Abby's belly. Something was wrong. Very wrong. "What's happened?"

Marti held up a hand for her to quieten. "All right." She hung up and sighed.

"Tell me!" Abby pleaded.

"The boss has been shot. He's at County General. It's not too bad. He caught one in his shoulder. And *you're* to stay put."

"Stay put? Like hell I will." Abby sprang from her seat, ready to grab her bag and go.

Marti jumped in front of Abby. "Sit yourself down. You

will stay put, missy, if I have to get my shotgun. His deputy said Vince wasn't more'n a mile from here when he got shot."

Abby sucked in a deep breath. "That close?" Her heart rate soared.

"Yes. That close. Now the deputy said the shot was a clean-through, and the doc is going to release him in another couple of hours. So there's no need for you to rush out of here like a bat outta hell. No point at all. He'll be home 'fore too long."

"You're *sure* he's going to be all right." She couldn't lose Vince now. Not after all that had happened. She focused her gaze on Marti. "You sure you're not holding anything back?"

"Honest to God, I'm not holding anything back. Except you." Marti flashed Abby a wry smile. "Have another cinnamon roll."

Abby sat. For some reason, another sweet roll was the last thing she wanted or needed. Vince. Yes, his strong arms around her was all she wanted and needed. And the sooner, the better.

But who would protect him?

Vince eased from Will's SUV, wincing as he jarred his shoulder. "Thanks for the ride.

"Anytime. I'll get a vehicle sorted for you to drive. Have one of the deputies drop it off. Going to the funeral tomorrow?"

"Of course. Besides, Abby's determined to attend."

Will nodded. "Yeah, she should have protection."

Vince thought for a minute, then said, "I'm sorry for your loss, Will. I didn't know you and Darla were seeing each other. Anyway just wanted to say I'm sorry."

"Thanks." Will swallowed. "It was new, but we'd gotten real close in a short time."

Vince slammed the door, giving his deputy a nod.

He walked onto the porch, winching with every step. Who knew an injured shoulder could hurt so damn much. Every time he took a breath, the muscles cramped. Reckon he'd have some use for those pain pills the doc had insisted on.

The door opened before he had a chance to open it. "You're home!" Abby rushed toward him then stopped short. "Does it hurt a lot?"

"Yeah." He stepped inside. "I could use a glass of water. Think I'll take one of these pills." He rattled the pill bottle. "They filled it at the hospital since the drugstore's closed."

"They don't usually do that, you know." She darted to the kitchen and returned in a flash. "Marti says come into the kitchen and have a seat. Do you need to lie down?"

"No. Just need one of these pills." He read the label, "One every 4-6 hours."

"First dose, you can take two. That'll get the therapeutic level up."

"You sure about that?"

She gave him a definite stink eye. "Of course, I am."

"Right. You're a pharmacist."

"Right." She smiled prettily. "So in this situation, I'm the boss."

God, she was beautiful when she smiled. "You can be my boss anytime."

She handed him the glass of water. "I know you don't mean that, but I'll pretend you do."

He tossed the two pain pills down with a water chaser. He stood. "Think I'll rest a spell in the recliner."

"Good idea. Marti and I are preparing a light lunch, in

case you're hungry."

"Sounds good." He ambled into the family den and claimed his piece of real estate, a man-sized Lazy Boy. He eased into the soft leather recesses and shut his eyes. For just a minute.

The sheriff hadn't died. Tom had failed. Surrounded by incompetents. The bosses in Houston were on his ass. To say they weren't very understanding was an understatement. He grabbed the burner. "You failed. You're the pro. What happened?"

"He ducked," Tom said, as if screwing up a hit was no big deal.

My head might just explode. "Do I have to do everything myself?"

"Hold on. Your record ain't so great."

"Our bosses need a result. They're coming down hard on me. I'm passing the favor on."

"The sheriff might still die."

Might? "The corollary to that is he *might not.*"

"I don't know shit about his arteries. I know I plugged him good. Just not as good as I planned."

"His *arteries*?" Then realization dawned. He almost sniggered, but given he was dealing with a psychopathic hitman...better not.

Chapter Fifteen

The day of Darla Murray's funeral dawned like most Texas summer days.

Hot as Hades. Humid as all get-out.

Vince pulled into the parking lot at the Kenton Valley Methodist Church. He put the SUV in gear and turned off the motor. Wishing Abby had stayed home was a waste of time. Stubborn had to be her middle name. No, she was here to honor her friend and to support the Murrays. "You ready?"

Abby tugged at the neck of her body armor. "I can't stand this thing. I don't see how any of y'all can stand to wear one in this heat."

"Necessary part of the job. Since you're going to be away from the ranch, you'd best learn to tolerate it. Better the body armor than this." He jerked his head at his left arm in a sling. "Or worse."

"Really?" she scoffed. "I think a helmet would serve me better, given his M.O."

He glanced in her direction, one dark brow arched. "Now how would that go with your suit?"

"Make fun all you want." She smoothed her dark silky hair. "I think I could rock one."

"All fun aside, if he gets close enough, neither one will

keep him from doing his worst. And I've seen his worst. That's why we're here today."

"I *know.*"

"Wait here." He exited the SUV, then ran around and opened her door. "Stay close. Stay alert. I'll have my eye on everyone there."

She eased her way out of the vehicle, pausing long enough to smooth the wrinkles from her black suit. Tugging at the neck of the body armor, she grimaced.

"You look very nice," he said, trying to take her attention away from the body armor. Actually, she was beautiful. Always. Her dark hair was glossy, her skin so pale, a sugaring of freckles showed through her light makeup. Only the lingering redness of her eyes marred her appearance. Enough. They were about to attend a funeral, not go on a date.

He would've given anything to wipe away the pain and the guilt she felt. But his reasons for attending the funeral, aside from the obvious, were to scout the mourners for anyone who stood out for any reason. A stranger. Darla Murray's killer. Someone who was overemotional from guilt.

The killer often attended his victim's funeral. But Kenton Valley was a relatively small town. A stranger would be noticed by everyone. His other reason was to keep Abby safe, and he didn't trust anyone to do that but himself.

He ushered her inside the church, his hand in the small of her back to steady her. She gazed up at him, her eyes pools of green. "Thank you." Her voice was a barely heard murmur.

It took a moment for his eyes to adjust to the church's somber lighting. The cloying fragrance of lilies filled his nostrils. Organ music filled the air. He glanced at Abby.

Tears had already begun to stream down her cheeks. He reached into his jacket pocket for his handkerchief and handed it to her without a word.

She sniffed. "Thanks."

They sat two rows behind the Murrays. He would've preferred a position in the rear where he'd have a better view of the congregation, but Abby needed him. Normally, he would've assigned Will to watch his six, but his deputy was in mourning as well. He sat beside the Murrays.

The choir began to sing. Abby's shoulders shook with her sobbing. Vince placed his arm around her, giving her the comfort of his touch. And, he hoped, some of his strength.

Reverend Darwin began to speak, then pray, then preach. Vince didn't attend worship services very often. If today's performance was typical, he didn't care at all for the Rev's florid, high-flying manner of preaching. Today, he was in fine form, eulogizing the victim and condemning the heinous crime over and over, enough to put Vince to sleep, if he hadn't been here to protect and support Abby.

When the Rev asked if anyone had anything to say, Abby started to rise. Vince shook his head and held onto the bottom of her jacket. Her gaze widened, but then she appeared to accept the reason behind his action and settled back against the pew.

Finally, after what seemed like an eon, Reverend Darwin completed his sermon. Abby had never heard such an abundance of overblown adjectives and adverbs in all her life. He'd really outdone himself. Weird. Most of his sermons were more low-key and a little on the boring side.

Outside the church, Vince took her elbow and guided her toward his replacement SUV. She balked. "I want to go to the burial."

"No way. No wide open spaces for you." He jerked his head toward his left shoulder, his arm still in a sling. "Been there. Done that."

"Then I need to speak to the Murrays before we leave. Okay?"

"As long as I'm by your side. Just don't take too long."

She nodded, then wove her way through the crowd of mourners toward the Murrays. "Again, I'm so sorry for your loss."

Mr. Murray hugged her. "Appreciate that. Darla thought a lot of you."

But Darla's mother still seemed fragile, brittle even, as if the wrong word would shatter her composure. "I still blame you," she muttered into Abby's ear.

"I'm so sorry," Abby said, deciding to leave it at that. Mrs. Murray would have to grieve in her own way, and if she needed someone to blame, then so be it. God knew Abby blamed herself too.

Backing away, she felt Vince's warm hand squeeze hers, comforting her. Always.

"I don't want to attend the bereavement dinner. I'd rather not upset her any more than she already is."

"Hadn't planned on you goin'," Vince said. "Come on. The sooner I get you back to the ranch, the better. And the safer you'll be."

On the way back to the ranch, Vince received a call. "Put it on speaker, Abby. I've only the one hand to drive with." She removed the phone from his belt clip.

"Vince. Ben here. We finally got a partial print ID off a shell casing from your first shooting—the one with one of the ranch's guns."

"Yeah? Whose was it?"

"Hm, well..."

"Spit it out, man."

"Your brother Chance. His print."

"You're saying my *brother* shot at me?" What the hell!

"Evidence doesn't lie."

"What about yesterday's shooting?" He kept his eyes on the road, hoping to avoid another accident. "Did my brother have another go?"

"That was courtesy of our pro. Ballistics matched."

Figures. "And we still don't know who the hell the hitman is."

"Nope. Say, how was the funeral? Was Will okay?"

"Yeah, he got through it. I kept a lookout. Didn't see anyone who didn't belong. No strangers."

"Just proves our killer was smart enough to stay away."

"Or he's left the area."

"You don't believe that."

"No. I don't." A muscle cramped in Vince's shoulder. He tensed, making the pain worse than before.

Abby broke in. "So what you're saying is we're still in his sights?"

"Reckon so, Ms. Fields."

"But what about Chance?" Abby sighed. "I can't believe he'd do something so stupid. "

"Come to think of it," Vince said, "that time the shooter wasn't aiming all that close. More like he wanted to piss me off." Damn straight, he'd succeeded.

"Any idea why he'd want to do that."

"I don't know," Abby said. "But he's been acting kind of weird since I've been staying out at the ranch. Flirty. Smug."

Vince shook his head. "I'll have that boy's ass."

"Well, figured you'd want a head's up."

"Yeah. Sounds like time for a Come-to-Jesus meeting."

"Let me know if you want me to handle it."

"I'll handle my brother. Yeah, I will."

"My superiors may not let it go."

"I understand. Whatever they decide, Chance will have to deal with the consequences."

Ben terminated the call. Vince turned to Abby. "Okay, what's Chance done...weird, you say? In what way?"

She let out a small sigh. "I really hated to say anything, but he's been a little creepy. Maybe I was being over sensitive with everything that's going on. But yeah, almost stalker-ish."

"You shouldn't have to put up with behavior like that."

"But he's your brother. And I'm a house guest."

"I'll kick his ass for him. You don't have to put up with him harassing you."

"It was more a matter of his attitude. I'm not putting this very well, but he just made me uncomfortable. I'm sorry I mentioned it."

"Good thing you did." He set his jaw. At times, his brother had too high an opinion of himself. Time to take him down a notch or two.

They made it back to the ranch without incident. *Thank heaven for small favors.* Vince sent Chance a text to meet him in the office, ASAP. "I'd rather handle this alone," he told Abby.

Frowning, she worried her bottom lip. What he wouldn't give to nibble it himself.

Focus.

"All right." She nodded. "If you think that's the way to go."

Vince paced in the office while he waited for his brother to appear. What the hell had he been thinking? Time to give him a new attitudc.

Chance wandered in with his usual bored expression. "You texted, bro?"

"Yeah. Where the hell do you get off taking potshots at me?"

"Don't blow it out of proportion, big brother." Chance took a step back, holding up his hands in surrender. "It was just a joke. I wasn't trying to kill you."

Vince took a step forward. "Then what the hell were you trying to prove?"

Jutting his chin, Chance planted his feet wide apart. "Wanted to rattle your cage a bit. I'm sick of being treated like a ranch hand when a third of this ranch belongs to me."

"I'll buy you out right now. I want you out of the house and off the ranch. Pack your shit."

"Vince, come on. It was just a joke."

"Then why didn't you own up to it from the first, instead of wasting up tax payers' money and the Rangers time while they investigated. Did you actually think you wouldn't get caught?"

"You're worried 'bout the tax payers' money. I'm sick of your high-falutin' treatment. Worry 'bout this instead." Chance drew back and slugged Vince in the jaw.

The blow didn't knock Vince down, but dodging the main force of the blow rattled his shoulder. He staggered back a step. He rubbed his jaw. "That's it. I'll write you a check so you can get started. We'll handle this through our lawyer to come up with a fair settlement." He turned to the desk and pulled the checkbook from the drawer. "And wherever you end up, you need to stay away from Abby."

"Abby? That bitch. What kind of lies has she been

telling you?"

"You know what you've been doing. Cut it out."

"You'll never be happy with her. She'll dump you like she did when you were at college. She's as big a slut as your wife was. I ought to know. I slept with both of 'em."

Vince stopped writing. He straightened and, with his one good hand, gave his brother a punch in the gut, followed by an uppercut to his chin. Chance fell flat on his ass, knocking over a chair has he fell. "Now get out."

Chance scrambled to his feet. A little unsteady, he held out his hand. "The check."

Vince finished writing the check and signed it. "It's enough for a fresh start somewhere else. Texas is a big state, but don't let that limit you." He handed it to his brother, sick at heart that matters had come to this.

"It'll do for now," Chance said with a sneer. "But you'll be hearing from my lawyer."

"Consider yourself lucky you if you don't hear from the Rangers."

"Piss on the Rangers." He jammed the check in his jeans pocket. "And fuck you!"

Vince watched his brother slam out of the house. How could it be that twins, who were supposed to be so alike, could be so different? Chase was as laid-back as Chance was high strung. As for his brother's remark about having slept with both Vince's late wife *and* Abby. He wouldn't put anything past Liz, but Abby? Some room for doubt. After all, Chance was the one who'd sewn those seeds of doubt after Vince had gone off to college. Had Chance been the one of the ones she'd supposedly been sleeping with? Or had his brother lied about everything?

From the guestroom, Abby heard the commotion

downstairs in the office. Raised voices. Furniture knocked over. More loud voices.

Vince was injured and had no business fighting with his brother. She rushed from the guestroom and was halfway downstairs when she heard the sound of a slammed door.

She skidded the rest of the way downstairs then ran to the office. Vince sat at the desk rubbing his jaw.

"What happened?"

He shot her a wry smile. "We had a difference of opinion. Chance should be packing right about now. I threw him off the ranch."

Oh, no. This was all her fault. "I heard y'all fighting. You don't have any business fighting." She sank down on the sofa. "Are you all right."

Vince shrugged. "He got in a lucky punch. I'm fine."

"You could've reinjured your shoulder." She stood and tried to inspect his bandage. "Let me see."

He shook his head. "It's fine."

"What did he have to say about shooting at you?" She sat, leaning forward, her knees almost touching his. In spite of his insistence that he was fine, she wasn't sure. His face was pale beneath his usual tan.

"Said it was a joke. He wasn't trying to hit me, which is probably true. He didn't come all *that* close."

"But *why*?"

"He gave me a bunch of BS reasons," he said with a shrug. "Said he was tired of playing second fiddle at the ranch and such. So I wrote him a check. Told him to get out and that we'd settle the rest with our lawyers. The Rangers may still arrest him. Told him that too."

"I'm so sorry. This is all my fault." She'd never planned to come between Vince and his brother.

"No, it's been building for a long time. He said some

other stuff. That he'd slept with Liz."

Sensing an unspoken question in Vince's tone made her ask, "Did he say he slept with me too?"

"Why? Did he?"

"No!"

"Not even in high school after I left for college."

"No! I didn't date anyone after you left for college."

His gaze widened. "You didn't?"

"No. *You* were the one who was off playing the big man on campus. "

"Hmph!" Vince scoffed. "I suppose Chance was the one who told you that?"

"Yes. Why do you think I switched schools at the last minute? You broke my heart."

"Chance lied to both of us," They said, in unison.

"I never should've believed him. But Chance was my friend. I never thought he'd lie to me."

"Just like I never thought my *brother* would lie to me."

The decisions she'd made...all due to Chance's lies. Changing schools. A hasty marriage to the wrong man. Ten years of her life wasted when she could've been with Vince. So many things to regret.

His forlorn expression told her he was having similar thoughts.

"We blew it," she said.

"Yeah, we did." He leaned forward, as if to kiss her, then winced with pain.

"Your shoulder?"

"Yeah."

"I still feel responsible."

"No. Chance set this particular ball in motion a long time ago."

"What will happen to him with the Rangers, I mean?"

"I don't have to press charges, but they'll probably

pursue obstruction charges because of the time and expenses they incurred. Ballistics tests. Fingerprinting everyone on the ranch. He's the one who has to suffer the consequences for his actions. I say, let 'im."

"Do you think it's possible your brother had anything to do with Liz's and Ed Barnes's murders?"

"If he had, he wouldn't have been stupid enough to bury their bodies on the ranch."

"He might if he wanted to implicate you in their murders."

"I've already been cleared."

"We know that now, but he couldn't have known you'd be cleared so quickly."

"But what would he have to do with the break-in or the attack at your house?"

"If he slept with Liz, she might've let something slip about what the Macedonia Corp. wanted with the land outside of town."

Vince shook his head. "I don't want to think he's guilty of something like murder. Petty crap—yeah. I can see him taking some wild potshots at me. But murder and torture? Nah."

"I don't want to, either. But can we logically rule him out?"

"My brain may be going a little fuzzy, but ballistics rule him out. The hitman is on the hook for Liz and Barnes. My brother's not a hitman."

"Of course you're right." Still, she had to wonder if Chance had ordered the hit. She bit her bottom lip, rather than voice her thoughts. No point in troubling Vince with her speculations.

"You need to get some rest." He caressed her cheek. "I could use some too. My shoulder is asking nicely for another pain pill. I see a recliner in my near future."

"You should've stayed home today. The funeral was too much."

"No. *You* should've stayed home. But we *both* had our reasons for going, and they outweighed the woulda-shoulda-coulda."

"It means so much that you were with me. I'm not sure I could've made it through without you."

Vince shook his head. "You're tougher than you think. But I wasn't about to let you off this ranch without me."

"And I love you for it. You make me feel safe and protected like no one ever has."

"Don't reckon you ever needed to feel that way before now."

"And if you tell me we're going to get to the bottom of everything, I'll believe that too."

"We need to keep going through your father's papers. There may still be a clue we've overlooked." Now his cheeks were flushed where they'd been pale before.

"You mean *I* need to keep going through his papers, and *you* will take a pain pill and have a nap."

He gave her a sheepish grin. "Um, something like that."

She rose from the sofa, then leaned over to kiss his forehead, and was startled by how warm it was. "I'm going to get you some aspirin." She focused on the man in front of her. His eyes seemed dull, and that had developed in the last few minutes. Plus, he'd just pulled his shirt closed at the neck. He was shivering. "You're feverish."

"How can I be? I'm actually cold."

"That's because your temperature is going up." Where were the antibiotics the ER doc sent him home with? "Marti!" she called.

Marti poked her head into the office. "Yes?"

"I need a thermometer," she said quietly. "I'm pretty

sure Vince has a fever."

"Downstairs bathroom," Marti responded. "I'll get it and the *baby* aspirin."

"I'm not a baby." He folded his arms across his chest and jutted his chin.

"Then don't act like one. We'll take care of you." Abby nodded at Marti when she entered the room with the digital thermometer and aspirin.

"100.2 degrees," Abby said, after reading the thermometer. "Not alarmingly high but definitely elevated." She handed him two aspirin and his antibiotic. "You're going to bed."

Vince shook his head. "Recliner."

"All right. You need to drink plenty of fluids."

"A beer?" He grinned, somewhat bleary-eyed.

"No beer. Water and some juice."

"What if I'm hungry? I'll starve."

"Feed a cold. Starve a fever," Marti piped in.

"The important thing is to hydrate," Abby said with an emphatic nod. "But if you're hungry, you can eat. Proper nutrition is necessary for healing."

Before Abby could impart any additional wisdom, her cell phone chimed. "Drat." She straightened, pulled the phone from her pocket, and glanced at the screen. "I guess I need to take this. Rollo Moore. Wonder what he wants now?" She opened the door and walked outside onto the patio.

She punched the icon and answered, none too graciously. "What?"

"Abigail, my client was wondering if you'd rethought selling him your house. Since the fire and all."

"No means *no*, Rollo. Besides, the fire investigator hasn't released the house yet," she out-and-out lied. "I can't take care of repairs until he does, much less sell it.

Not that I will, anyway."

"His offer stands, even without repairs."

"Just who is this client? Maybe he's the one who set the fire, in the first place."

"Don't be silly." He gave a nervous bark of laughter. "I can't give you the name of my client. That wouldn't be ethical."

"Neither is setting a fire." She punched the disconnect icon. The real estate agent needed to get over it. Her house wasn't for sale. Not now. Not ever.

She slipped the phone back into her pocket then walked back inside the house.

Marti put a finger to her lips. "He's asleep in his man cave, but I'm a little worried."

"Sleep is what he needs. With the antibiotics, aspirin, and pain pills on board, he ought to have a nice nap. He'll be better when he wakes."

Marti's frown changed to a smile. "I hope so. He's my favorite of the boys. Don't tell him I said so."

"Mum's the word."

Chapter Sixteen

Only one more box to go through. Abby pulled the last of her father's boxes away from the corner, opened it, and sat on the floor cross-legged beside it. She checked the date on the top invoice slip. Maybe she should've gone through this box first. This invoice was dated just a week before her father had been killed. Probably nothing, but better leave no stone unturned.

More and more invoices. Beneath all the mundane papers, she found a locked file box. Feeling around the bottom of the box, she couldn't find a key. She stood and picked up the metal box. Marti might have something. She carried it into the kitchen where Marti was dredging chicken parts.

"Fried chicken?"

Marti beamed. "Not just any fried chicken. It's my special herbed fried chicken, but it's oven fried. Healthier that way."

"Sounds wonderful." Yes, Abby saw a membership at the local Weight Watchers in her near future. "Do you have anything that might open this file box? I can't find a key for it."

"No key, but I bet I have something that will do the trick." She opened a drawer and pulled out a small chisel.

"This ought to work."

Abby accepted the chisel. It seemed sturdy enough. "You keep a chisel in your knife drawer?"

Marti gave a quick nod. "Always prepared…for anything."

"Let's do it then." Abby tried forcing the chisel between the lid and the metal box. "Not having much luck."

"A little more elbow grease," Marti suggested.

"Right."

With more of Marti's "elbow grease," Abby managed to break the lock and open the file box. Inside, she found fifteen bundles of one hundred dollar bills, still bound with the local bank's currency straps. Each stack equaled ten thousand dollars, then multiplied by fifteen. Good grief—$150,000!

"Damn." Why did her father have 150-K in cash? Was this what the break-in and fires were about?

"Well…" Marti said, her expression as flabbergasted as Abby felt.

And was this the same cash that Vince's wife and the bank VP absconded with seven months ago? And other than the currency straps, was there any way to know if it was the same money? And why did her father have it? As for the answers, maybe she really didn't want to know. What had he gotten mixed up in?

Oh, Daddy. What a tangled mess.

Marti shook her head slowly. "I can't believe that money's been sitting here all this time, and we never knew. What're you going to do?"

"I don't have the least idea. I guess I'll wait until Vince wakes up. He'll know what I need to do next. I'll give Sam Dunaway a call too. He might know why Daddy had all this cash on hand."

The conversation with her father's attorney, didn't

reveal anything new. As for the cash, Sam told her the bank would likely have records of the serial numbers, especially money that had never gone into circulation. He suggested she notify the Texas Rangers who would determine the origin and whether or not it was counterfeit. More than likely, they would then notify the U.S. Secret Service.

What a can of worms she'd opened.

When she tiptoed into the man cave, Vince was still asleep. She lay the back of her hand on his forehead. Cooler, thank goodness. He'd kicked off the throw she'd covered him with when he was still shivering.

His eyes opened. He reached up and clasped her wrist. "Don't go."

"Feeling better?"

"You know it. With my own angel of mercy." His voice still had that pleasant drowsy quality.

"I'm no angel. You have to know that."

"Yeah, I know." He smiled up at her, a little bleary-eyed.

"I'm going to recheck your temp."

"If you must." He stifled a yawn. Should she tell him about the money right now or not?

Probably better now, even if he was half asleep. "I found something today in the last box."

"Mm, what?" He rubbed his nose and yawned again.

"One hundred and fifty thousand dollars. Cash. Still in the bank wrappers."

"Whoa!" He straightened. "Any chance? Are you thinking what I'm thinking?"

"Probably. The wrappers have the logo and the name of the Kenton Valley Bank and Trust."

He dug in his pocket for his phone. "I have to notify

Ben. The Secret Service will definitely need to be brought into the loop."

"If this is the missing cash from seven months ago, what was my father doing with it?"

"I hate to say this, Abby, but your dad must've been mixed up in something not quite on the up-and-up."

"I have the same feeling. And it's not a good feeling, at all."

She waited, anxious for him to make the call to Ben Rasmussen. Waited and paced. The only good thing about her father's being deceased was that he couldn't be arrested. His death, coming so soon after her mother's, had knocked her for a loop, but learning he was into something underhanded was even more of a blow. Whatever her loving, respectable father had been involved in, she wasn't sure she wanted to know.

And still, there was a hitman out there just waiting for the opportunity to complete his mission. But no matter who had hired him, someone else was still out there. While the ranch was a pleasant refuge from the hitman, having her movements restricted was the pits. Her business was suffering. Her family home was in dire need of refurbishing after the fire. Just so damn many things she needed to do.

Vince stood. Carefully. Damn.

His injured shoulder was a major handicap. He eased from the recliner to the French doors. He sniffed. "Is that Marti's herbed chicken I smell?"

"Yes, it is. I've been assured that it's oven-fried. I guess that means fewer calories," Abby said with a wiggle of her eyebrows.

He offered her a smile. Marti's cooking wasn't aimed at the weight conscious. "I'm going to record some of these serial numbers and then call Ben." He gingerly moved to the desk, then sat to record the numbers. As soon as the Rangers took the cash into custody, someone would have to record each and every single serial number. He didn't envy that person. He stood. "I'll be on the patio."

"Sure." Abby acknowledged with a nod.

Outside, he paced beside the pool, as he waited for Ben to answer.

"Rasmussen."

"Vince Tate here. We've come across a large sum of cash. Abby found it."

"How large?"

"150 large. Still in the currency straps from the bank."

"A hundred and fifty thousand dollars. Now, I have to say that's an interesting sum."

"Indeed it is."

"If you'll read off those serial numbers—just the first and last of each packet. I'll pull up the case and go over the serial numbers of the money that went missing when Barnes absconded."

Vince read off the numbers. "Now then, what about the money? I have a safe where I can secure it until you or the Feds pick it up."

"I'll get back to you as soon as I've checked the serial numbers. Tell me again where you found the money."

"Abby found it. We brought some boxes from her basement. Her father's things, mostly invoices and bank statements. It was in the last box she had to go through."

"The longer we work on this case, the more convoluted it becomes. Anyway, I'll get back to you as I'm through. Shouldn't take more than a few minutes. And by all means, secure it in your safe. I'll take custody of the funds tomorrow. "

"Ten-four." He terminated the call then walked back

inside the house. Abby stopped her pacing.

"Well?"

"We should hear something soon." He picked up the file box containing the money and carried it over to the wall safe. "All he has to do is pull up the case and check the numbers against the ones I just gave him." He opened the safe, concealed by the painting of a longhorn bull, and set the file box inside.

Abby's expression grew pensive. "And if there *is* a match, it means my dad was somehow involved in this mess." She shook her head. "I just don't understand."

She bit her bottom lip, making him wish he could kiss away her troubles. "But if there's a match, he must've had something to do with your wife's and Ed Barnes's murders." She sank onto the couch, burying her face in her hands.

He sat beside her on the couch, offering her a half of a hug with his good arm. Even half a hug was better than none when it came to holding Abby in his arms—correction—arm. "Not necessarily involved in their murders, but in something that got them all killed. It looks more and more like your father wasn't just killed by a druggie. It's more likely Tim Dill was another hired hand."

"But he never gave up who hired him? Who would wield that kind of power?"

"We need to have another run at Dill. After six months inside, he might be ready to give up his boss for better conditions."

Abby rested her head on his shoulder. The fresh citrus scent of her shampoo tickled his nose. "I'm having a difficult enough time believing my father was involved in illegal activities. I refuse to believe he had anything to do with any murders."

"Never easy finding out your father had feet of clay.

Somehow, he got in over his head. Did he ever gamble? Or have a problem with it?"

Her eyes widened. "My first inclination is to say no way. But honestly, I don't know. How sad is that. I don't think he did, but I wasn't around much for the last ten years or so. And what about that land? Could there be a connection to the money?"

"I've been hearing some chatter about the possibility of a new Indian casino opening. The Konawawak Tribe has two casinos in Oklahoma, but the tribe is originally from the Hill Country before they were forced out. They would have a good case to put forward."

"Is it possible the land was purchased in order to resell to the Konawawaks?"

"The Bureau of Indian Affairs would make the actual purchase and request the Department of the Interior to place the land in trust. And if that's the case, then someone is getting pretty antsy to get his hands on that deed. If your dad was the intermediary between the Macedonia Corporation and whomever he bought the land from, then whoever is left from the shell company is going to lose a ton of money, if he can't locate the deed of sale, the BIA will buy land from somewhere else and locate their casino there."

"This is beginning to make sense, if only a little."

"Whoever is driving this purchase is behind everything that's happened."

"And the resale of that land will make that person a fortune. I wonder what my father paid for it, whether or not he was a go-between. I haven't found a record of how much the land cost or how he paid for it."

"Could've been a strictly cash transaction. Someone trusted him enough to front the deal. We need to see *who* he brought the land from."

"Oh. I'd forgotten, but according to the county court clerk records, that 400 acres was just a part of the old Gardiner ranch. After Albert Gardiner died, his heirs sold everything. Land. Equipment. Right down to the stock."

"Then we need to see who else bought the rest of the ranch. They could want those 400 acres in addition to what they purchased."

"Trip to town?" Abby's eyes widened with interest.

"Not for you." No way would he allow her to leave the relative safety of the ranch.

"Oh please! I'm getting more than a little stir-crazy," she admitted. "And I need to have the house repairs seen to. I don't like the idea of it just sitting there."

"Normally, I'd agree and I'd go with you." He pointed at his injured shoulder. "I'm not one hundred percent physically if and when it comes to protecting your shapely butt. Can't risk it."

"Vince, please." She dragged out the please until it was two syllables. "This hitman has to know everyone is looking for him. If he has any brains, he's probably left the area, scuttling back to his hidey-hole, or wherever it is that hitmen hide."

"A hitman doesn't get all his payment until the job is done."

"Couldn't someone else go with me? What about one of your deputies? Don't you think Will would be happy to give me a hand at the courthouse and at the house?"

"I can delegate him to check the records at the circuit court clerk's office."

"But the house?"

"Telephone your insurance agent and your attorney. Delegate Sam to handle the contractors. That's the keyword: *delegate*."

"Look what happened when I delegated Darla to cover

for me at the drugstore. I don't want to place anyone else in jeopardy."

"No one could've predicted that." He stroked her cheek, wishing he could take away the hurt so visible in her every expression. "But now we know someone is after the two of us, it just makes sense that you sit tight for the time being."

"What about you? You're injured. *You* need to sit tight."

"Afraid I can't do that. I'm up for election in the fall, and I need to be seen doing my job, even with my arm in a sling."

"Surely you're not going back to work."

"First thing tomorrow. I have to turn over the money to Ben. It'll be off our hands then. Good riddance."

"Tomorrow? Why only this afternoon you were running a fever." Abby shook her head. "You are such a *man*!"

He let out a chuckle. "Hope so."

"Infuriating. Stubborn. Arrogant."

"I don't agree with those attributes."

"Blind, then. You lack self-knowledge."

"Keep on and you're going to hurt my feelings."

Her mouth formed a perfect kissable pout. "If you had any feelings, you'd see I need to take care of business in town."

"If you had any..." He let the words he wanted to say trail off, because they would only piss her off more than she already was.

"What? If I had any what?"

"Never you mind. I'll let your imagination fill in the blanks." He turned, more than ready to end the discussion. If anyone was infuriating and stubborn, it was the lady herself. Let her throw all the invectives she wanted. Still he couldn't help but admire her passion in more ways than one. Although he probably didn't have a chance in hell of experiencing a night of passion. Not after this disagreement.

Instead of risking another rebuff, he left her standing with her mouth open. That lovely mouth he could kiss for hours on end. He followed the aroma of herbed chicken and found Marti in her domain whipping up garlic-mashed potatoes.

His mouth watered and his stomach growled. "Dinner ready?"

The good woman looked at him askance. "You hungry for crow? 'Cause that's what you're gonna be eating if you plan on getting back in Abby's good graces."

So tiresome. Nothing was going as it should. He should have already sold the 400 acres to the BIA. They were making noises that while they preferred the Kenton Valley area, they could purchase another plot of land for the proposed gaming casino and reservation, returning the tribe to their place of origin. With that land placed into trust with the Department of the Interior, there would be no taxes paid on the income. Not federal, state, or local. But his bosses in Houston were even more insistent that the deal go through as planned. Apparently, they had even bigger fish to fry with the BIA.

In the beginning, it had been such a sweet and simple plan. Using Fields's misguided confidence about his gambling debt, he'd forced the pharmacist to act as a go-between and to buy the four hundred acres of land adjacent to the Gardiner land he'd purchased for his ranch. If he hadn't wanted to avert attention from his purchase, he would've bought all of it himself instead of using Fields and the Macedonia shell company.

But nothing was ever as simple as it seemed.

And now the hitman he'd hired was a loose cannon. Removing him from the equation wouldn't be easy.

Tom kicked back at the motel, watching porn on the TV. Not even good porn. Still it beat hanging out in the bushes across from the entrance to the sheriff's ranch. His burner phone rang. Had to be idiot who'd hired him.

He muted the porn movie, then answered, "Yeah?"

"Where the hell are you? And why aren't the sheriff and his bitch dead yet?"

"I'm on my break." Tom unmuted the porn.

"I'll break you!" He paused, then asked, "What the hell. Are you alone?"

"Told you I was on my break. And just so you know, I'd like to see you try breaking me. I really would. See here, I know what I'm doing. The sheriff and his bitch are holed up on his gated and guarded ranch. I can't do a damn thing during daylight hours. He's not leaving. And if she's smart, she won't either. Never fear. I have a plan."

"What are you going to do?"

"Under cover of darkness, I'll invade and you'll hear what happens. It won't be my usual method, but I'm tired of this crappy motel. Not nearly as tired as I am of talking to you." He terminated the call, then pulled out his prick.

Chapter Seventeen

Abby shot Vince a surreptitious glance over her plate of herbed chicken and garlic mashed potatoes. She'd already gained two pounds from eating Marti's delicious home style cooking. Comfort food was the right term all right. Every plateful was a very real symbol of the love and comfort Marti Mills brought to her cooking.

"More potatoes, Abby?" Marti asked, ready to pass the huge bowl.

"No thanks. Why don't you have another helping, Chase?"

"Me?" Vince's brother looked up from his plate. "Sure, the more the merrier."

"You can afford the calories. I can't," Abby said with a smile.

"Hmph." Vince speared his second piece of chicken from the platter, his expression priceless.

Being ignored served him right for being so pigheaded. "Protein. Good choice. You'll heal faster."

"Glad you approve." Was her ignoring him getting his goat a little? He'd been grumpy all through dinner. Speaking only to Marti and his brother, the one he *hadn't* kicked off the ranch.

"Where's Chance?" Chase asked. "I haven't seen him

since this afternoon."

"You won't be seeing him for a while either if I have any say about it. And I do."

"He's gone?" Chase's dark brows drew together, his forehead furrowed. "He never said anything."

"We had a disagreement. I'm buying him out."

Chase stood. "And if we have a disagreement, are you going to buy me out too? You want the entire ranch to yourself?"

"Hold on, cowboy. This was personal between Chance and me. He was the one who took those potshots at me. That and other things. It was time. *You're* my brother and a valuable part of this ranch."

"Same could be said of me, except about the potshots." Chase sat, his dark brows still furrowed.

"I'm not going into things any further."

"I thought something was up when he came down to the stable. Now I think about it, he seemed to be giving the place a once over. A final look." Chase snagged a piece of chicken. "But he didn't even say good-bye. I'm his twin. He should've said something."

Abby kept her gaze on to her plate. She'd caused enough trouble among the brothers. "Dinner is delicious, Marti. Thank you for another wonderful meal." She rose. "And no matter what you say, I'm loading the dishwasher tonight. If I'm going to live here, I'm going to help out."

"Many hands make for light work, hon. Thank you." Marti's expression was neutral, but her gaze flicked over to Vince who responded with a tiny nod.

If she couldn't work in the drugstore which would be closing permanently if they didn't find whoever was trying to kill them, she might as well brush up on her housework skills.

***

After unloading the dishwasher and putting away the dishes, Abby looked into the man cave. Vince and Chase were in the man cave engrossed in a Longhorns baseball game. She knocked on Marti's door. After hearing Marti's, "Come in," Abby opened the door and stuck her head in. "Dishes are done and put away. I'm going upstairs to read."

Marti shot her a smile and held up a mystery novel. "Good idea. I always keep a stash of murder mysteries and romance novels in the guest room, but if you don't see anything you like, then feel free to check out my private stash." She nodded toward a wide bookcase, each shelf packed double.

Abby smiled. "Good to know. It seems like I'm going to be under your feet for the near future."

"As much as I dote on those Tate boys, it's awful nice to have some female company."

"You're a treasure, Marti. It's no wonder they dote on you too. But you're right about having another woman around. I have girlfriends in town, and they're great, but I really, really miss my mom." She blinked away the sting of sudden tears.

Marti patted the loveseat beside her. "Anytime you need a hug, you just let me know. I have hugs to spare."

Abby sat beside her new friend. "I'll take one now, please." Marti's arms surrounded her, enveloping in a sense of comfort, home, and safety. Tears fell. But as they fell, Abby wiped them away. "You've been so sweet to me. I'll never forget your kindness."

"It's my pleasure and a joy to be kind to someone who deserves it as much as you. And, by the way, there's a man who needs your love far more than he knows."

"Oh, he's watching a ballgame. And even I know better

than interrupting during a game."

Marti nodded. "You'll make a lovely couple. Mark my words."

She sighed. "Maybe...if we survive long enough. We have quite a history. Lots of misunderstandings that we've recently settled."

Gray eyebrows rose. "I won't pry, but I'll just say *good for you.*"

Abby gave Marti another hug then got to her feet. She stopped at the door. "You're an amazing person as well as a wonderful cook. Tomorrow, I'm going to keep swimming laps just to keep the weight off."

Marti responded with a bark of laughter. "Remind me tomorrow morning, and I'll find you a swimsuit. I know there's bound to be something better than a pair of cutoffs."

"No need. I packed one after the fire. G'night." She shut the door behind her and headed upstairs. Having another woman around was exactly what she'd needed. Understanding and kind—that was Marti Mills personified.

During commercials and instant replays, Vince explained why he'd kicked Chance off the ranch.

"I had no idea," Chase said with a shake of his head. "I knew you and Abby fell out after you went off to A. & M. But I didn't know Chance had anything to do with it."

Vince considered his next question carefully. He didn't want to accuse his remaining brother, but he needed to know. "So you didn't have any idea why we broke up at the time?"

"No! I just figured it was one of those things that happens when one goes off to college. One thing I did know was he had a crush on Abby, but I never dreamed he'd gone to those lengths. Not that it did him any good."

"You sure about that? He said he slept with Abby after I left home. Did he?" Vince held his breath waiting for his brother's answer.

"No way."

Vince breathed a little easier, but he wasn't through asking questions. "He said he slept with Liz too." He waited for Chase's answer. While he and Liz hadn't gotten along for a couple of years before she ran off, he sure hoped she hadn't screwed around right under his nose. He'd never forgive his brother if he'd taken advantage of Liz.

Or had it been the other way around?

Chase hesitated. "I couldn't say for sure. She was flirty all right. And he's always liked to run his mouth. I never caught them at anything inappropriate." He shook his head. "Even Chase wouldn't go that far."

"No man likes to be made a fool of. Bad enough she ran off with Ed Barnes. I say *ran off*, because that's what I thought for months. But she was killed. Murdered. The same SOB who's trying to kill us now."

"Do the Rangers still think you had something to do with their deaths?"

"Nah. I passed the polygraph. Everything that's happened, including the break-in and fire at Abby's are all connected. It's a hell of a mess. I don't know if we'll ever get things untangled."

"You will—shit!" Chase almost bolted from his chair. "Did you see that triple play? Man-oh-man! That was something."

Vince chuckled. Chase was as avid as they came when it came to sports.

Before he could add to the conversation, the lights flickered and went out.

***

Abby froze. Darkness was absolute with a new moon that night. No sign of a storm, so this had to be a bad sign.

The hitman. He's here.

She sucked in a deep breath to steady herself, resisting the urge to rush downstairs to where Vince and his brother were. Where was the breaker box anyway?

No point in making it easy for the intruder. How had he gotten past the gate?

Think!

She ran to her door. Locked it. Okay. Now, in the dark, could she move the oak chest of drawers? Might as well try.

Loaded with linens and other clothing, the solid oak chest was heavy indeed. Still, using her body weight and her thighs, she managed to lift one side, then the other to walk it over to her bedroom door.

Leaning back, she huffed from the exertion. At least, that should slow him down some.

Below she could hear muffled shouts and grunts.

She felt around and found her phone on the bedside table. Dialing 911, she made her away across the room to the window. When the emergency service answered, she said, "Sheriff Tate's ranch. The lights have gone out, and I can hear sounds of a struggle. Send help, please." As soon as the EMS operator assured her someone was on the way, Abby was ready to disconnect the call, but the operator told her to find a safe place and stay on the line until help arrived.

Abby agreed, but set the phone aside to struggle with the window. With a heave she managed to raise it. Just as she'd thought, there was a section of the roof line she could get on and ease her way over to the jasmine-covered trellis. Once on the ground, she could—what, run away? Leave Marti and the rest to save her own hide? Besides the roof would be treacherous since it was metal. Cedar shakes would've provided some traction.

No such luck.

She wouldn't abandon her room for the roof unless she had to. With the window open, she could clearly hear the sounds of a major struggle.

Then the sound of gunfire. Oh, God. She closed her eyes and said a quick prayer for Vince or Chase—it had to be one of them. Maybe it was both.

Tom crouched behind a lounge chair in the breezeway where the fuse box was located. This would be the first place the sheriff or one of his brothers would come to check the power source.

He'd already taken care of the guard at the gate. One silenced shot to the base of the skull. He'd made his way up the long drive to the house. If the guard at the gate was all the sheriff had for security, this was going to be a piece of cake. No point in trying to blow the place up. He'd take them out, one by one.

Listening for sounds of someone coming, he leaned forward, his Glock ready.

"I'll check the breakers," Vince said, rising from the recliner. An uneasy sensation centered in his gut. He felt his way over to the book case, opened one of the doors, and found a Maglite. Switched it on, splaying the beam across the room. He opened another door and pulled out his service weapon. He checked the magazine, jammed it back into the grip, and pulled back on the slide. "Loaded for bear. Let's go."

"Wait. Let me get my sidearm," Chase said.

Handing the Maglite to Chase, Vince smiled. "You manage the flashlight. I'll manage the firearms."

"What about your shoulder?"

"Probably just a thrown breaker," he said, ignoring the agony in his shoulder every time he moved...and the uneasy feeling in his gut.

"The entire house?"

Vince pulled his cell phone from his belt and called the front gate. "Danny's not answering." The uneasy feeling in his gut maximized. "You check the perimeter of the house. I'll handle the breakers."

"But—"

"Go on. You heard me."

Chase shook his head. "Now *I'm* the gofer. Chance was right about one thing. *You're* the boss. Whatever." He exited the house through the French doors.

Vince fished a smaller Maglite from the cabinet. It would do for maneuvering inside the house. Taking care not to move his shoulder too much, he eased his arm from the encumbrance of the sling, looped it over his head, and tossed it aside. Now. He placed the lighter flashlight in his left hand. That might just work.

Okay, let's see what's going *on with the breakers.* He opened the door leading from the den to the breezeway. Somewhat shakily, he played the light around the breezeway. The door to the breaker box was open.

Not good.

Senses on high alert, he retreated a step back inside the house. First, a rustling, then an impression of movement. A dark figure sprang from behind a lounge chair, knocking Vince to the floor. Trying to cushion his shoulder from the fall, he lost hold of his weapon. It hit the floor with a *thunk* and slid out of reach.

Pain blossomed and took his breath away. Pain or not,

he had to reach his weapon before... He half-crawled, half-scrambled, pulling his body across the floor with his good arm and kicking at the intruder with his feet.

The intruder let out a bark of laughter. "Missed you once, you son of a bitch. I won't miss this time."

Instinctively, Vince cringed but kept moving away. Away. He had to get away. The tips of his fingers touched the cool metal of the grip. He grasped the butt, twisted his body, and fired once at the shadowy figure as a shot spit by him so close he felt the heat of the round as it missed his ear.

Vince fired three more times in rapid succession.

The intruder dropped, his body falling across Vince's feet and legs. Scooting from under the body, he called to his brother. "Get the lights!"

The lights came on, blindingly bright after the utter darkness. Chase stumbled breathlessly into the man cave. "Are you hit?"

He shook his head. "No. Close thing, though."

Chase knelt beside the intruder's body and felt for a pulse. "He's dead. You got 'im good."

The sound of sirens filled the night.

Vince cocked his head. "Did you call 'em?"

Chase shook his head. "Not me. Marti or Abby must've."

"Guess we'd better check on the women folk." Vince got to his feet, groaning with the pain in his shoulder.

"Yeah. Reckon we should. I'll check on Marti. I suspect she'll meet me at the door with that shotgun of hers."

"Right." Vince retrieved the sling he'd discarded earlier. "I'll take Abby. At least, she won't be armed."

He ran up the stairs and tried to open Abby's bedroom door. "Abby! Are you all right?"

Chapter Eighteen

The sound of Vince's voice, alive and well, filled her with gratitude. Now if she could just get the door open. "The chest of drawers is in the way," Abby said, gasping as she tried to move the stubborn piece of furniture. Certainly was a lot heavier than before.

"How the heck—"

"Must've been the adrenaline. Not so much circulating now." Finally, she was able to open the door a crack and see Vince's handsome face. "Are you all right? And Chase?"

"We're fine."

"I heard shots. Too many to count."

"He missed. I didn't. He's dead, Abby."

Dead. The hitman was dead. Relief shot through her, but before she could ask for more details, she heard a banging on the front door. "That must be the backup I called for. I was so scared you'd be killed."

"I'd better go open the door before they break it down."

"Go. I'll keep working on moving this chest."

She heard the reassuring thump of his footsteps as we went downstairs. Gathering her strength, she was ready to put her back into the task again when Marti tapped on the door. “Here, use these.”

“Furniture sliders. Thank you! I can just about manage these,” she said, “as long as I do one foot at a time.” She bent over, and using all her strength, lifted the bracket foot a half inch and slipped the first slider under it. Now just repeat three times, and she’d be home free.

Sure enough, once the sliders were in place, the large piece of furniture slid easily across the pine floor back to its former position.

Marti opened the door and entered the guest room. “Are you all right? I can’t imagine how you moved that chest of drawers without sliders.”

“Like I told Vince—adrenaline.”

“Whooee!” Marti slapped her knee. “Never seen so much excitement. You really lighten up the place.”

“More like I’m a curse, don’t you mean?” A curse on everyone who came into contact with her. Even with the hitman’s death, Abby wasn’t sure she’d ever get over feeling responsible for Darla’s murder.

Vince walked with Will out to the front gate. With the red lights flashing and its siren blaring, the ambulance was just pulling away with Danny Keene. “How is he?”

Will removed his cowboy hat, wiped his brow with the back of his hand, then replaced the hat. “He has a bullet in his skull. I don’t know how, but he’s still alive...barely.”

Not many survived a wound like that, much less recovered, Vince mused. “Too soon to know if he’ll even make it to the hospital. “We need to notify his mother.” Danny was twenty-two and one of the two guards supposed to be on the gate that evening. “Any sign of Raul Perez?” Raul was the other.

“Nope.”

Raul was the ranch foreman and one of the ranch's most dependable employees. Raul had a wife and family who lived in one of the smaller houses on the ranch. His absence was a major concern.

"We've got to find him and determine what kept him away from his duties tonight. I'll send Chase to Raul's place for a start. You go on to the hospital, check on Danny. I'll swing by his mother's place in town and bring her to the hospital. Let me know if there's any change in his condition."

Will nodded. "Will do."

"But first I need to update Abby." He could just imagine how news of another near death would affect her. She'd blame herself. Needlessly. But she would.

"She should be relieved it's over."

Vince shook his head. "I'm not sure it is." There was still the matter of who hired the hitman in the first place. While he might not be as deadly, he was ruthless and determined. Hiring a hitman proved that.

When he re-entered the house, he found Abby, along with Marti, in the kitchen. Abby had a cup of coffee sitting in front of her while Marti was slicing a ham to make sandwiches for his deputies.

He met Abby's questioning gaze and sucked in a breath. "He shot Danny Keene in the head. They've taken him to the hospital."

"He's alive?"

"For now. The coroner's on the way to take away the hitman's body. Will called the Ben so the Rangers will be here soon, doing the forensics. Don't touch anything in the den."

"As if..." Marti muttered, still slicing the ham with a

vengeance.

"What can I do?" Abby pleaded. "Please I have to do something."

"Nothing," Vince said. "For now, I'm going to pick up Danny's mother and take her to the hospital. Raul's missing. Chase is going over to see if his wife has any idea why he wasn't on the gate tonight. That's all I know right now."

"Do you think it's over?"

"No. But it is for tonight." He let out a heavy sigh. "Sorry. Gotta go." He beat a hasty retreat. Dealing with Danny's mother was next on his agenda. Dreaded it like the plague would be an understatement. Given the gravity of the injury involved, chances of his recovery were slim to none.

Abby watched Vince leave, feeling the tears come to her eyes. "Another life cut short."

"You don't know that." Marti set the butcher knife on the counter then walked to Abby's side. She placed a comforting hand on her shoulder. "You heard what Vince said. He's hanging on. That's gotta be something."

She gazed up at Marti through a sheen of tears. "I told you I was a curse. A bullet in his skull. He's not going to survive that. If he does, he'll require long term care. He'll have no quality of life."

"Darlin', you didn't pull that trigger. You've made choice to protect yourself. The killer—rot his soul—made a choice to shoot that boy, just like he made a choice to kill poor Darla Murray."

Frustrated, Abby clenched her fists. "I still don't know how all this comes together, Marti. But it's too much for mere coincidence." It had all started with two bodies and a break-in, and now was one tremendous mess.

"True enough." Marti resumed slicing thick slabs of ham, then turned to Abby, brandishing the butcher knife. "You know I'd like to use this on whoever set this in motion. I really would."

"I'd help you. I would." For all the good it would do. No punishment would ever bring back the lives lost. Or free her from the guilt that threatened to overwhelm her every time she thought about it.

Vince drove the SUV into the Los Marcos County General Hospital E.D. lot, then parked. He opened the door for Barb Keene, who remarkably hadn't fallen apart, but from her tight facial expression to her clenched fists, appeared to be about a hair's breadth from doing so. On receiving the news her son had been gravely shot, all she'd said was, "Why was Danny on guard alone? What good do you think one guard can do?"

"There were supposed to be two guards on the gate. Raul is missing. I don't know what happened to him...yet."

His phone dinged with a text from Chase:

Raul not home.

Wife says left to go on guard duty at regular time.

Crap.

He exited the SUV and opened the door for Barb. "Raul has a lot to answer for," she said, giving him a no-bullshit glare.

He sure as hell did. Better keep his thoughts to himself. It would only take a nudge to send Barb over the edge.

Before they could enter the E.D., the man himself, Raul Perez, emerged, appearing confused, glancing from Vince to Barb and back again.

"Where the hell have you been?" Vince stopped short, planting his feet apart. "How did you hear about Danny?"

"I don't know anything about Danny. I got a call from Chance saying my son was admitted with appendicitis and to get to the hospital fast. I rushed over. He isn't here. I just hung up with my wife. She says Joey's fine, but something went down at the ranch. What's going on, Boss?"

A call from Chance? How was his brother mixed up in this? "Got no time for explanations right now. Park your ass in in my vehicle."

"Sure thing, Boss." Raul nodded, then headed for the SUV.

Vince and Barb Keene entered the E.D. where the clerk directed them to the trauma one. The door was closed and the curtains pulled. Impossible to see anything.

"I need to see my son." Barb's tone was determined.

"Let me check. We don't want to get in their way while they working on him." He eased the door open and peeked inside. He could see three intravenous drips running as well as blood. He could hear the wheezing ebb and flow of a respirator, so Danny had been intubated. All it proved was the young man was still alive.

One of the nurses looked up, caught his gaze, and shook her head.

He shut his eyes for a moment, took a deep breath, let it out, then closed the door. "They're still working on him. He's on a ventilator. He's still alive, but I'll tell you it doesn't look good, Barb."

First her chin started trembling, then her entire body. Her face paled. Vince wrapped an arm around her waist to keep her from falling, then guided her to the nearest chair. She started inhaling and exhaling rapidly.

"Paper bag, please," he called out. "She's hyperventilating."

A nurse ran over with a paper bag, instructing Danny's mother to breathe in and out with the bag over her mouth and nose.

While Barb used the paper bag to normalize her breathing, he had more time to consider Raul's remark about the phone call from Chance, the call that pulled Raul away from guard duty. Was his brother be mixed up in everything that was going on? But how involved was he? Anger aside, how could he risk the lives of everyone on the ranch, his two brothers included?

"I think I'm all right now." Barb neatly folded the bag and slipped it into her purse.

"You sure?"

She nodded. "This is a mother's greatest fear, you know? I nearly went nuts when he started driving. But I never worried much about him working on your ranch. He loved it so. The horses. The livestock. Being outdoors. He never wanted to be anything but a cowboy. I never considered– I mean, I thought ranch work was safe. His being a guard never entered my mind."

Vince swallowed hard. "It was a new situation. The hands all took turns. Danny wasn't singled out."

"No, but Raul left him alone." Barb's fists clenched in her lap. "Raul said Chance called him away for an emergency. Why would your brother do something like that?"

Vince shook his head. "Don't know. Been asking myself the same thing."

"I-I'd like to call my preacher." Her chin trembled, but otherwise, she maintained her composure.

"Of course. Just tell me who."

"Brother Darwin at the Methodist Church. See if he'll come."

Vince walked over to the nurses' station. "I need a

phone number for Reverend Darwin at the Methodist church. Mrs. Keene would like to have him here."

A little ginger-haired nurse nodded. "I'll be happy to make that call for you, Sheriff."

He thanked her and returned to Barb's side. "The nurse is calling him now."

"Thank you, Sheriff." She sniffed and dabbed her eyes with a tissue. "I don't know what I'll do without Danny. He's my only child. His father ran off about ten years ago. Just the time when a boy needs his dad most."

"Yes, ma'am. I know that had to be rough." Dammit! Chance had a lot to answer for. "I need to make a call of my own. Will you be all right if I step outside for a minute?"

Barb nodded. "You go ahead. I'm all right, for the time being anyway."

Vince stepped outside and called Chance. He waited while the phone rang. And rang. The call rolled to voice mail.

After a rather rude answer message, Vince left one of his own. "I need to see you now. Specifically, why on earth did you pull Raul away from guard duty with a bogus call about his son? Danny Keene is near death, and it's looking like your fault. I'm officially telling you to haul your ass in for questioning. Or I'll do it for you." He disconnected the call.

That ought to do it.

Abby wrapped up the remains of the ham and set it in the fridge. "Why don't you go on to bed, Marti? I'll finish cleaning up the kitchen." Easy to see that Marti-the-Super-Bunny of housekeepers was wearing down. Her eyelids were drooping at half-mast. And each step the woman took was slower than the one before.

"You need your rest too."

"Maybe but I won't sleep a wink tonight. Not until Vince calls with an update."

"If I turn in, you have to promise to wake me if the news is bad."

"I will if that's what you want."

"*And* you have to promise me you won't sit out here and blame yourself for what's happened. None of this is your fault."

"That might be a little more difficult."

"Try." Marti patted Abby's shoulder.

"I'll try." Abby enveloped Marti in a hug. "Now, off to bed."

"I'm going."

Abby let out a sigh of relief when she heard the door to Marti's quarters close. She quickly wiped off the counters and table top. She made a fresh pot of coffee, then poured it into a thermos. That deed accomplished, she prepared the coffeemaker for the morning, programming it to come on at six. Now. She dried her hands on her jeans.

Vince had said it was at least over for tonight. That meant she was free to leave the ranch and check in at the hospital. Having one of his employees so badly injured had to be stressful. He needed her support...and some decent coffee.

And he was going to have it.

No news was good news...usually. But somehow Vince figured the doctors and nurses were too busy trying to save Danny's life to come out and give any kind of an update. Barb sat quietly in a far corner of the waiting room, an unopened bottle of water in her lap. He'd offered her coffee, but she asked for a bottled water instead.

Twenty minutes after being called, the Reverend Mr. Darwin came sweeping into the E.D. lobby, seemingly as grand as if he were the Pope. Perfectly cut hair. A suit that must've cost the church coffers more than a pretty penny. Snakeskin boots.

"Mrs. Keene? Where is she? I've been called." His voice boomed, as if preaching to an entire congregation instead of the much smaller E.D. waiting room.

The minister glanced around the lobby, overlooking Barb. Didn't he recognize one of his flock? Vince shook his head.

"Here, Brother Darwin." Barb waved to get his attention. "Over here."

"Ah, yes, my child. What can I do for you?"

"It's my son, Danny. He's been shot. It's very bad they tell me."

"How did this happen?" The preacher seemed to cut his gaze toward Vince.

Now what was that about?

Barb spoke low, but the minister was well into his performance. "We must pray for his soul."

Vince shuddered as the preacher prayed way too loud and way too long. Yes, Danny needed the support from all the prayers he could get, but Darwin's sincerity had all the hallmarks of a Shakespearean actor playing to the back of the hall.

Enough already.

He heard the *whoosh* of the E.D. doors opening. He turned.

Crap. What was Abby doing here?

Chapter Nineteen

Carrying a thermos of fresh coffee and a thick sweater—hospitals were always cold—Abby blinked at the bright lights of the Emergency Room. Now where—

Good grief! Brother Darwin was over in the corner of the waiting room, having what amounted to a revival meeting. That poor woman, the focus of the preacher's attentions, had to be Danny's mother. Her arms were bare, and she was shivering. Maybe from shock or from the AC. A sweater was just what she needed—maybe even more than the good reverend's highfaluting prayers.

Stepping carefully, so as not to disturb the gathering, she made her way to Mrs. Keene's side and slipped the sweater around her shoulders. The woman glanced up and mouthed, "Thank you."

Abby nodded and eased away from the group to find Vince.

His expression when she found him wasn't exactly one that said he was glad to see her. She pasted on her best smile. "Coffee. I bring fresh coffee."

"So I see." Setting his hands on his hips, he leveled his cool blue gaze on her. "Let me get this straight. You left the ranch, risked getting shot like Danny, just to bring me some fresh coffee."

"Most of all, emotional support. I have loads of that too. Besides, you said it—whatever it is—was over for the night at least. How's Danny?"

Vince's gaze darted toward the room where she assumed Danny was being treated. "Judging from the expression the nurse gave me, he's not doing too well."

"Let's go into the vending area. I see a table and some chairs. I'll pour you a cup of this coffee."

He frowned. "I need..."

"You'll be able to see the doctor from there when he comes out. Come on. You've had a long night." She took his elbow and guided him to the small round table and pulled out a chair. "Sit."

"I never noticed how bossy you are." He sat, not giving much argument and betraying how weary he must be.

"That's because you're too busy being bossy yourself." She removed the top from the thermos and poured a cup of the aromatic brew. She slid the cup toward him. "Drink."

"There you go again." He picked up the cup. Sucking in a breath, he inhaled the rich aroma.

"Better get used to it." She smiled. There were a lot of things about Vince she could get used to.

He took a sip. "I *could* get used to it all right." Smiling, his eyes crinkled at the corners. "Thanks." Shaking his head, he said, "You're reckless. Guess that's not going to change."

"Probably not." He looked so tired, but he'd never admit it. More than anything, she wanted to put her arms around him and tell him everything would be okay. Not appropriate, given he was on duty. "I was wondering, since the hitman is out of the picture, if I could re-open the drugstore. Before you say, 'No,' I just thought maybe—"

"Out of the question!" He slammed the cup on the table, splashing coffee. "Damn! Now I made a mess."

Abby jumped up and grabbed a napkin from the dispenser. "No problem. I don't mind cleaning up after you. I could get used to that too." *OMG! Careful. That was more than a little Stepford wife-ish, wasn't it?*

"I might hold you to it."

The door to where Danny was being treated opened. A doctor in dark blue scrubs emerged. Vince rose and strode over to meet him. Abby followed closely behind.

"How's he doing?"

Instead of answering Vince's question, the doctor asked, "Does Mr. Keene have family here?"

Vince nodded. "His mother is over there with her minister. Danny works on my ranch."

His mother came rushing over with the preacher close on her heels. "How's my son?"

"There's a quiet room. Let's go there." The doctor led the way to a room that wasn't a chapel, but was close to it. Carpet and soft furnishings in muted greens and grays. "Your son has suffered a traumatic brain injury. We are taking him to surgery to remove the bullet, but there is a great deal of swelling. The swelling is being treated with steroids, and part of his skull will need to be removed—just like they do with brain injuries from IEDs. You understand? To decrease the pressure and damage to the brain."

Mrs. Keene nodded, grasping the cross on the chain she wore around her neck. "What are his chances?"

"They're not good, but the fact that he's still alive gives room for some hope. If he survives the surgery, then he will need long term acute care and then therapy when appropriate."

Sinking onto a leather sofa, Mrs. Keene dissolved into tears.

"Let us pray," intoned Brother Darwin.

Abby eased from the room, unable to take anymore. A young man had come to work healthy with his entire life in front of him was now possibly—make that most likely—damaged beyond the power of modern medicine to repair. She'd help pay for his care. Yes, she would. Even if she had to sell her family home, she'd assume responsibility for whatever it was she'd set in motion.

After assuring Barb that Danny's care would be paid for by the liability and medical insurance Vince carried on all his employees, he left the quiet room. At least he hoped it would. Since Danny was a crime victim, insurance companies could get tricky when it came to payment. Whatever, he would personally see that Danny received the care he needed.

Ranger Ben Rasmussen strode down the hall toward Vince. "How's he doing?"

"Still alive. The E.D. doc is talking to Barb. Danny's headed for surgery as soon as papers are signed." Vince nodded toward an empty cubicle where they could talk in relative privacy. "Anything on our shooter?"

Ben nodded. "Ballistics on the round taken from the wall in your den show he was our hitman for sure. His prints were a hit in AFIS. His real name is Arthur Bradley aka Artie Brass aka Tom Dooley, and about ten more aliases if you're counting. He's a Gulf War vet with a bad conduct discharge in 2005. Known to work out of the Houston mob."

"But something tells me it's not over." Vince shook his head. "Someone hired him to kill Liz and Ed Barnes. They were up to their necks in something."

"Agreed. We need to find out if anyone here has a connection to the Houston organization. I'll get in touch with the organized crime unit in Houston."

Vince nodded, agreeing that would be the next feasible step. "I'm headed downtown to the office. I need to take a couple of statements. Arrest one of my brothers. Lots to do."

Ben shot him a skeptical look. "Uh, yeah. Sounds like it."

Arrest his brother. Like when had he ever considered that would be necessary?

While the lawmen shared information, Abby waited in the lobby to see if Vince was coming back to the ranch. Now that she was here, it was plain to see he was busy and not in any real need of emotional support. He was definitely in his lawman mode.

He emerged from the cubicle, making a beeline to her. "You need a ride home?"

"Home?"

"To the ranch."

She shook her head. "Uh, no. I drove myself here. I figured it'd be okay since our hitman was on his way to the morgue."

"You took a chance. I appreciate your coming, but..." Vince frowned. "I probably won't be home until sometime tomorrow. There's paperwork. And I need to have an in-depth conversation with Chance."

"Chance? I thought you'd already had a conversation with him."

"This is something else. Related to the investigation."

She ran her hand back through her hair. "Then I guess I'd better scoot along. At least one of us will get some sleep tonight." Although she doubted she'd sleep at all after all the excitement. And questions. She had a ton of those.

"That'd be good." His manner was distracted. Not meeting her gaze.

Now what was he being so mysterious about? How was Chance related to Danny's shooting—she assumed that was the investigation he meant at all?" Maybe she should give Chance a call. But remembering his attitude the last time they'd had any interaction, maybe not such a hot idea after all.

The ER doors whooshed open, and Chance strode in with a face like a thundercloud.

Now this would definitely be a good time to duck out and drive home. Getting between the two brothers was bound to be one of those no-win situations.

At least his brother had taken him seriously and not gone on the run. "Robert Chance Tate, you're under arrest for conspiracy in an attempted murder. You have the right..." He heard gasps from several in the waiting area, but refrained from acknowledging them. "...to an attorney." He finished reading his brother his rights.

"The hell you say." Chance's face paled. He backed up. Will Rasmussen stepped behind Chance and cuffed him.

"Take him downtown and book him." Shaking his head in disbelief, Vince turned away. Never in his wildest imagination had he ever considered he'd be forced to arrest one of his brothers.

"Vince!" He struggled against being manhandled. "You're nuts if you think you're going to treat me this way. What have I done? Is this about Abby?"

"Shut your mouth!" Leaning in, Vince got in his brother's face. "I'll talk to you at the Sheriff's office. For now, Will, get him out of here."

***

After Will left with Chance in custody, Vince headed outside to his SUV where Raul was still cooling his heels, a cell phone in his hands. “Still here, Boss. Wife’s called me a dozen times, but I still don’t know what’s going on.”

“Danny Keene was shot tonight.”

“Danny? No, man, no.” The disbelief in his voice sounded genuine. He held his hands up to his head, shaking back and forth. “No. No.”

“You say my brother Chance called you?”

“Yeah. He said my Joey was sick and at the hospital, so I left Danny in charge. I know I should’ve arranged for someone to take my place, but I was so worried about my boy.”

“And you’re sure it was Chance who called you?”

“Yeah. Well, y’know, it’s hard to tell the twins apart over the phone, but he identified himself. He did. Boss, you gotta believe me.”

Raul’s response had the ring of truth. “You need to come to the station and make a formal statement. Chance is under arrest for conspiracy to commit murder.”

Raul’s jaw dropped. “No, Boss. He wouldn’t do something like that. Not Chance. Had to be some kinda joke.”

“Danny Keene’s not laughing.”

Back in the Sheriff’s Department, Will Rasmussen handed over Raul’s signed statement. Vince read through it. Pretty much in line with what he’d said in the hospital parking lot. He nodded at Will. “Raul’s free to go. Take my brother to the interview room. You interview him. I’ll observe. I imagine the Rangers will re-interview him at some point, but I'd like to get a handle on how he's involved in what happened tonight."

"You sure about that?" Will's reluctance was evident from his defeated posture. "Doesn't seem right. I've known him all my life."

"That's why the Rangers will take the lead on this. We're too close. Hell, he's *my* brother." Honestly, he felt like kicking his brother's ornery ass, but he settled for kicking the waste basket instead. He waited until Will knocked on his door, signaling Chance was in the interview room. Vince rose, strode to the observation room next door and waited to hear why his brother had set Danny Keene up to be killed.

Still weirded out by the night's events, Abby kept a watchful eye on her review mirror for any sign someone was following her. Thankfully, she made it home without incident. Driving through the gate, she heaved a sigh of relief. Two guards.

She let out another sigh as soon as she made it safely inside. The house was dark, except for one light over the kitchen stove and another in the hallway by the stairs. She stopped to tap lightly on Marti's door. No point in waking her if she was asleep.

"Abby? I'm awake."

Abby opened the door and found the housekeeper curled up on a dark green leather sofa, a knitted afghan across her knees, and a paperback mystery on her lap. "How's Danny?"

"On his way to surgery the last I heard. But it doesn't look good."

"His poor mother." Marti shook her head.

"The preacher was with her."

"Which one?"

"Darwin."

"Hmph. Him. I got no use for that one. Don't know why. Just never liked him. Don't know why they hired him in the first place." She rolled her eyes. "That's not true. I was on the selection committee. His credentials were excellent. He even had a family connection to the Valley, but somehow..." Her words trailed off. "I guess it's neither here nor there—what I think. If he's some comfort to her during this ordeal, then I guess I should hold my tongue and my judgement."

Abby smiled to herself. Marti was nothing if not fair. "You can't please everyone. I thought he was over the top at Darla's funeral. Kind of old school...if you know what I mean."

"I do." Marti swept the afghan off her knees and laid her book aside. "Now that you're home safe and sound. I'm going to bed. Do I need to lock the front door?"

"No. I did. And thank you for lending me a key." She smiled, setting the key on the side table. "I'm off to bed too."

Marti nodded. "Breakfast comes early on a ranch."

"Vince said he wouldn't be back tonight." She paused, wondering if she should bring up the subject of Chance. Might as well. "He's awfully upset with Chance over something. I don't know what."

"No telling with that one." Marti shrugged.

"I feel like I've caused trouble between them. I hate that."

"My guess it would be the other way around. He's troubled. Different from his brothers. Never been able to figure out why. But he is." She made shooing motions. "You go on. Get some sleep if you can."

"I'll try." She shut the door and headed upstairs. After entering her bedroom, she locked the door behind her. Just in case.

Vince watched through the two-way mirror. Chance's entire aspect was belligerent. His jaw set. His fists clenched in front of him, where one of his wrists was cuffed to the table.

"Will you just tell me why my brother arrested me? I know he's pissed off, but that was a personal matter. I don't appreciate being arrested, even as a joke. Who the hell did I conspire to murder anyway?"

"No joke," Will said. "Danny Keene was shot tonight. He's in surgery. Right now, at the very least, you're an accessory to attempted murder, but if he doesn't make it, the charge ups to accessory to murder."

"Danny was shot?" Chance bolted upright. "What makes you think I had anything to do with him getting shot?"

"We have witness testimony that you called one of the guards and told him his son was in the hospital, leaving Danny alone."

"Raul—that shit." Chance leaned back, folding his arms across his chest. "Lawyer."

"You want a lawyer? That's fine, but it's to your advantage to talk to us. Explain yourself. If you know any mitigating circumstances..."

"Lawyer. Call Sam Dunaway."

On his side of the mirror, Vince gave a huff of disgust. Sam Dunaway was the attorney for the ranch. Representing Chance for a crime against a ranch employee was a non-starter. Conflict of interest.

Will rose, closing the file in front of him. What else

could he do? Once Chance requested a lawyer, the interview had to stop. Vince had hoped he'd have a better idea of how Chancc was involved before he lawyered up. But no such luck. Still something in his response nagged Vince. Was Raul more involved than he'd indicated?

Time for another conversation with his foreman.

Thirty minutes later, Vince observed Raul in the interview room. His foreman was looking mighty nervous. He twitched, glanced around nervously, and chewed his bottom lip.

Time to get some answers. Vince opened the door to the interview room. Raul started like he'd been shot. "What's the deal, Boss? I was almost home when I got the deputy's call to come back in for *more questions*? My wife's getting antsy. She's got questions too."

"First of all, I'd like you to know this interview is being recorded." He nodded at the camera in the corner with a blinking red light.

Shifting in his seat, Raul cut his gaze toward the camera, then gave a nod.

"Second, I'd appreciate it if, this time, you'd tell me the truth. Chance sold you out." Okay, that was a bluff, but a legal one frequently used by law enforcement. "But tell me your version, again, why you left Danny Keene alone in the guard house."

Raul's cheeks darkened. "Your brother's a real prick. I never thought he'd narc on me. There's this *chica*, waitress at the Los Marcos Cantina. She's hot for me, y'know? What's a man to do? So, Chance and I fixed it so he would call me with an emergency, and I'd duck out for a couple hours or so."

"How did you end up at the hospital? That's what sold

me on your first version."

"My wife. She texted. Said Chase was there and where the hell was I if I wasn't at work. Said something happened. Was I at the hospital? So I says, 'Yes, that's where I am.' So I gets dressed and heads to the hospital to see what's going on. Only the gal at the desk wouldn't tell me nothin'. So I'm ready to go back to work when I met you in the parking lot."

"So that's all this was. You two conspired to get you some time off so you could make some time with what's her name?"

"Yeah, that's it. That's the whole truth. Nothin' but the truth." Raul rose as if to make tracks.

"No, I mean *what's her name*? Have a seat. I need to check your alibi."

"Bettina Roja— Say, you're not going to tell my wife what I was up to, are you?"

"Not if I don't have to. Can't make any promises, though."

Raul glanced at the door, his expression hopeful.

"Like I said, you're not going anywhere until I check your alibi. What time did Chance call you?"

"Around seven, maybe five-ten minutes after."

"What time did you see Bettina Roja?"

"Twenty after seven."

"She must live close by. Her address? And what time did your wife call you at her place?"

Raul gave the address, a motel that catered to by-the-week trade located on the edge of town, then added, "Sonia called about quarter to nine. I got to the hospital about five to nine."

"I need to see your phone if you'll hand it over voluntarily. It'll help confirm part of your time line."

Raul frowned, then pulled it from his hip pocket and

shoved it across the table. “Sure.”

Vince opened the phone. “Password?”

Raul shrugged. “I don’t use one.”

Scrolling through the directory of recent calls, Vince noted his brother’s cell phone number at 7:05, then a call at 8:44 a text which he assumed was from Raul’s wife. He’d have to check that out. He called the number the text came from and waited.

Raul’s wife answered, “Where are you, Raul? I’m getting worried.”

“This is Sheriff Tate, Mrs. Perez. Raul is helping me with an inquiry. He’s all right, and he should be home in another hour or so. He’ll explain everything. Yes, he will.” Vince terminated the call, smiling at his foreman, who’d started to sweat.

“What am I going to tell her?” Raul wiped the beads of sweat from his brow.

“Tell whatever you’re comfortable telling her. The truth now, instead of maybe later?”

“Tell her the truth? Then you’ll have *her* in here on a murder charge.”

“You need to stay until your statement is ready for your signature, then you’re free to go.”

“Yes, Boss.”

“On that note, if you want to keep your job, I suggest you restrict your screwing around to your free time and not when you’re supposed to be working.”

“Yes, Boss.”

“If this comes to trial, you may have to testify. It’ll all come out then.”

“Might as well find me an undertaker and pay for my funeral.” He buried his head in his hands.

Vince shrugged. He didn’t feel sorry for his foreman, not in the least. If you play, you have to pay...sometime.

Tough lesson. Some men never learned. He'd never cheated on Liz, in spite of his suspicions that she'd been unfaithful. He couldn't ever imagine that he would ever cheat on any woman he loved. Certainly not Abby.

Chapter Twenty

Abby woke to the sound of her smart phone trilling. She gazed blearily at the screen. It was seven-thirty...already! She'd slept like the proverbial log. In fact, it seemed as if she'd fallen asleep the minute her head hit the pillow.

The phone trilled again.

This time she answered. "Hello. It's too damn early to be calling, whoever-the-hell-you-are."

"Rollo Moore, Abigail." He gave a light chuckle. "Charming as ever."

"You are really the last person in this crazy world I expected to call. What do you want? Spit it out so I can go back to sleep." Actually, now that she was awake, she was raring to go. But he didn't need to know that.

"It's about your house. I see that some repairs have started, and I wondered if I could show it to my client. He's *very* anxious."

"Hell no! I told you it's not for sale." Was the real estate agent behind all the dirty dealings and murder attempts? What lengths would he go to in order to sell her house? And why did he or his client want it so badly? Did he even have a client?

"Surely you don't want to stay there after the fire, or

after you marry the sheriff. Aren't you living with him now?"

"I don't know how my living arrangements concern you. That house has been in my family for over a hundred years. And I have no intention whatsoever of selling it. I've already told you that. So show your client some other houses. *Comprende?*"

"But he only wants to see *your* house. Couldn't I just show it to him, even though I'll make it clear it's not for sale? Maybe he won't even want it after he sees it. And I'll be out of your hair."

"Oh, for Christ's sake, show him the damn house! But I have to be there when it's shown." No way did she trust Rollo Moore and his strange client, who only wanted to *see* her house, to wander around at will.

"Now, Abby, he prefers to remain anonymous. That's how these things are done."

"I don't care. That's my one condition. If he wants to *see* the house, I have to be there. Just let me know when." She terminated the call.

Time for a shower and then breakfast. So hungry she could feel her backbone when she pressed on her stomach.

Well, almost.

By eight o'clock in the morning, Vince had verified all points in Raul's story. And Chance's. There was no point in keeping him in jail any longer. True, there were some grounds for filing obstruction charges, but there wasn't much point since his evasions had nothing to do with the actual attempted murder of Danny Keene.

Vince watched his brother saunter into his office and flop down into a chair, a smirk on his face. "So what're you going to do now, big brother? Have me shot at dawn?"

"Sit your ass down and shut the fuck up. You wouldn't have had to spend the night in a cell if you'd told me the truth about you and Raul's little arrangement."

Chance straightened. "He narced on me! I figured as much."

"Actually, I told Raul you narced on him first. After that, his main concern was whether or not his wife found out what he was up to while Danny Keene was being shot."

"I was just doing my friend a favor." Chance gave an eye roll. "We didn't know someone was going to try and kill Danny. Or maybe you're just mad because he didn't try to kill me too."

Vince slammed his fist on the desk. "Don't be ridiculous! Danny's fighting for his life. No matter how much you piss me off, I don't want anything bad to happen to you."

"He's still alive, then?"

"Yeah. For now."

Chance let out a sigh. "So I can go?" He stood, ready to head out the door.

"As far as I'm concerned you can. The Rangers might have more questions. "Where're you staying?"

"I rented a condo over on South Meadowlark."

"Leave your address with the duty sergeant...just in case we need to talk to you again."

"You're a real piece of work. My *own* brother arrested me. Man, that sucks." Shaking his head, Chance stormed from Vince's office.

Why was his younger brother so ornery? If Chance wasn't careful, sooner or later, someone would take real offense at his crappy attitude. It wouldn't be pretty. And he'd learn what real trouble was.

A few minutes later, Ranger Ben Rasmussen stuck his head in Vince's door. Vince waved him inside. "That money is still in my safe. After what happened last night, it was better to leave it there."

Ben nodded. "I can pick it up, if you'll let your housekeeper know I'm coming. Not to change the subject but I see you let your brother off the hook."

Vince gestured for the Ranger to have a seat. "It's true Chance diverted Raul from his duties, but the only conspiracy was so Raul could get his ashes hauled. Seems a senorita who works at the Los Marcos Cantina can alibi him." He shoved the file over to Ben's side of the desk. "I've verified everything."

Ben read through the statements with a shake of his head. "He's kind of a lowdown dog, your foreman."

Vince's brother, too, but that was entirely another issue. "Yeah, but if Raul cleans up his act, he's too good at his job to get rid of."

His forefinger tapping on his knee, Ben smiled. "I have some news for you."

"I'm listening." Vince rubbed his eyes and yawned. "Sorry."

"How long since you had any sleep?"

"Night before last. No matter. What do you have?"

"I had one of my rookie Rangers doing some in-depth research on new arrivals to town over the last year, concentrating on the time before your wife and Barnes disappeared."

"Thinking a newcomer initiated these business dealings?"

"Correct." Ben nodded. "Someone struck me as odd, or I should say, struck my rookie as odd, to give him credit."

Vince shrugged. "Our population is pretty stable. Who'd he come up with?"

"Only one person of any prominence in the community moved into the Valley in the last year."

"Okay, I'll bite. Who?"

"The Reverend Mr. Jamison Darwin. According to his C.V., he graduated from the Saint Paul School of Theology, Overland Park, Kansas, in 2002. But here's the kicker. Photo in the yearbook looks nothing like the man we know as Reverend Darwin."

"You don't say. So who is he?

"Seems to be a matter of a stolen identify. However, we've been unable to trace the real Reverend Darwin, so I'm certain foul play's involved. Now that we know the real Jamison Darwin is missing, we can obtain DNA from his family. Maybe he's an unclaimed John Doe in one of the surrounding states. Next, I would love to get some fingerprints and DNA on our imposter."

"If we bring him in and ask for prints and DNA..." Vince paused, rubbing his chin. "He's bound to get a mite suspicious."

"True. And we don't want to tip him off."

"I know of a way to get his prints and DNA. Abby would help I'm sure. He'd be more inclined to leave his prints and DNA in a social situation."

"If he's as dangerous as we suspect, I'm hesitant to use a civilian."

Vince leaned forward. "We'll have someone in place in case he gets suspicious. Here's my idea."

Abby was in the office going through the last box of her father's papers. After finding the box of money, she hadn't given the other papers a thorough going-over. Hearing what sounded like a vehicle, she stood and walked to the door. "Marti, is that Vince?"

"Yes, but it's weird. He just drove around the house and parked behind it."

"That *is* weird. Wonder what he's up to?"

She didn't have long to consider. Vince opened the door from the breezeway. He entered, followed by Will Rasmussen who was carrying what looked like some kind of audio equipment. Vince smiled, his sky blue eyes shining with excitement. "I have a mission, should you choose to accept it."

"Not impossible is it?" she asked with a smile. In spite of his shining eyes, he looked way beyond tired. He certainly hadn't had any sleep.

"No, but it may be tricky."

"Sounds like fun." She hugged him from his right side, not wanting to bump into his injured shoulder. "Then after the mission, will you get some rest? You look like you're ready to collapse.

He brushed off her concerns. "I'm fine."

After giving Abby the details of the mission, Vince asked, "Are you sure you can handle it?"

"Of course." After all he'd done for her, she couldn't fail him now. Besides, it might be fun to put one over the smarmy rev.

"Tell me again what you're going to do."

"I'm to call the good rev and tell him I'd like to set something up for Danny Keene's medical bills and ask him to help me. I'll invite him to the ranch for coffee or tea and Marti will serve those orange Danish rolls of hers."

"And?"

"After he leaves, I'll collect his coffee cup for his prints and DNA and place it in an evidence bag."

"And if he gets suspicious, or you feel you're in any danger whatsoever, you use the words 'fresh fruit,' and I'll be right there."

"You don't really suspect the preacher of being behind all these dirty dealings? Really?"

"Don't jump to conclusions. I just want to know if he's who he says he is."

"Why would you think he's not the preacher? He preached a heck of a sermon at Darla's funeral." Okay, so Darwin was one of those over-the-top evangelists. That wasn't any reason to suspect him of being a criminal.

Vince's expression was noncommittal. "I can't go into my reasons."

"Whatever... Yes, I know what to do."

"Good. I'm going to place a couple of microphones, here in the kitchen, and one in the living room, just in case you decide to serve coffee in there."

Her enthusiasm for the operation grew. "Will I have to wear a wire?"

"No. Will and I will just be in the office down the hall. The bugs Will placed in the dining room will be sufficient."

"Call him now?" Excitement and adrenaline coursed through her body, picking up her heart rate.

"No time like the present."

Abby picked up her cell phone and looked up the number for the church. The church secretary, Carrie Underhill answered on the second ring.

"Hey, there, Carrie. This is Abby Fields. May I please speak to Brother Darwin?"

Fine time for her mouth to go dry. She licked her lips while she waited for him to come to the phone. "Reverend Darwin, this is Abigail Fields. I have a proposition that might interest you."

He gave a little chuckle. "I find that rather surprising."

"Double entendre not intended," Abby said with a small chuckle. "This is about assisting the Keene family. He's one of the employees here on the ranch, and I'd like to set up a fund to help with his medical expenses. I thought you'd be the perfect person to chair the fundraising efforts."

"That's very commendable, Abigail. When would you like to get started?"

"As soon as possible." She glanced at Vince, who nodded his approval. "Could you drive out to the ranch this afternoon? For reasons I'd rather not go into, it's difficult for me to leave."

"What about four?"

"Perfect. We'll have tea or coffee which do you prefer?"

"Coffee would be fine."

"Wonderful. I'm sure I can convince Ms. Mills to serve some of her wonderful Danish rolls."

"See you at four, Abigail. I'm really looking forward to working with you."

"As am I, Brother Darwin." She terminated the call and turned to Vince. "How'd I do?"

"Great. Did he sound suspicious?"

"Not at all. In fact, he sounded as if he were practically salivating. Smarmy git. I wish you'd tell me why I'm doing this."

"If it works out, I'll tell you."

"Then Marti and I better get busy with those rolls." She glanced at the clock. "It's two now. Can Will set everything up? You need to take a nap. I'll wake you as soon as the preacher man hits the front gate."

Will nodded. "Amen to that. I'm good with the equipment. You get some rest."

"I'll nap on the couch in the office, otherwise I might not wake up when it's show time."

Abby surveyed the table set with a pink chintz-patterned china. The tablecloth was white with Battenberg lace trim. Fresh cuttings from the fragrant lavender-blossomed butterfly bush, arranged by Marti in an antique hobnail milk glass vase, had been set in the center of the table. She could tell from the spicy sweet aroma that Marti's orange cinnamon rolls were about ready to pull from the oven.

"Abby?"

She looked up. "Yes?"

Potholder in hand, Marti said, "The guard at the front gate called. Preacher Darwin is here. Is everything ready?"

"Yeah." Abby flashed a smile. "Time to wake Vince." She ran to the office. Even though she hated to wake him from such a sound sleep, she tugged gently on his good arm. "He's here."

Vince groaned, then sat up, settled his feet on the floor. "I'm not sure two hours was enough." He glanced around. "Where's Will?"

"Everything's in place. Will's on the patio. He didn't want to disturb your nap." She tapped on the French door, then opened it. "He's here."

Will jumped up from the lounge chair with a wide grin. "Show time."

Once inside the office, Will handed Vince a set of earphones and settled another set on his head. "We're ready."

Smiling, and feeling a buzz of excitement, she shut the door to the office.

Show time, indeed.

Back in the kitchen, Abby surveyed the table again. "Coffee. Danish. Silverware. Battenberg lace napkins. Evidence bags in the drawer." She smiled. "Looks like we're good to go."

"These are ready to come out." Marti bent over to pull

the hot rolls from the oven. "Just in time to ice them. They'll be runny though."

Remembering their gooey goodness, Abby licked her lips. "That's how I like them."

Marti set the hot pan on a cooling rack, then cut a sharp glance at Abby. "Do we want to know why we're doing this?"

"Apparently, it's need-to-know, and we don't."

"Oh, all right. I never liked him much anyway. Seems like they're all cut from the same cloth, spouting the same platitudes. At my age I'm fed up with same old, same old."

Abby patted her friend's shoulder. "It'll be all right. He won't be staying long."

Marti nodded, chuckling as she left the room.

As soon as the preacher's knock sounded, Abby ran to the front door. She opened it, offering him a wide smile that in her mind was patently false. "Welcome, Brother Darwin. Please come in."

"Thank you Abigail. This is a good thing you're doing. I know Mrs. Keene will be very thankful. He removed his Stetson.

Wow. In Texas, even preachers wear Stetsons.

"Something smells awfully good."

"That would be Ms. Mills's Danish rolls. Come this way." She led him into the dining room just off the large ranch kitchen.

"My-oh-my, this *is* a lovely dining room you have here. He pulled out a chair and sat.

Abby poured two cups of coffee. Gazing at him over the rim of her cup, she tried not to hold her breath—or choke—while he took a sip from his. *Yay, DNA.*

"Wonderful cup of coffee," he said.

Marti slipped into the kitchen and placed the plate of rolls on the table.

Abby looked up at Marti. “Please join us. You’ve worked so hard getting this ready.” She poured a third cup of coffee. “By the way, I’d like Mrs. Mills to have a role on the board of this foundation, as well.”

“Of course.” He touched the napkin to his lips. “I’m sure she’ll be a valuable asset.”

Yay, more DNA.

“Just how much were you thinking of investing in this foundation, Abigail?”

Guess the time for small talk was over. Abby smiled widely. “It seems I’ve come across some *extra* funds, so I’d like to donate all $150,000 to kick the fund off.”

He blinked. “A hundred and fifty thousand, you say?”

“Yes, and I’m sure Sheriff Tate would consider a similar sum. Just to get the ball rolling. Then we can raise more funds and invest those. I’m sure Danny’s expenses will be a great deal more than that especially if he requires long-term care which they seem to think he will. And then there’s the possibility of the additional rehab expenses if he progresses.”

He cleared his throat. “That certainly sounds feasible. I would be more than happy to work on this project with you.”

“Excellent. I’ll contact our lawyer and get him started on whatever paperwork it takes to accomplish something like this.”

He took another sip from his coffee, then cut into a roll with his fork every so precisely, when she was certain what he wanted to do was cram the entire roll in his mouth.

He wiped a bead of icing from his lip with his napkin.

Yay! Even more DNA. Go for it, Rev.

Finally, after more banal pleasantries, it was past time for him to go, in her book anyway.

He picked up the cup, turned it around in his hand, a

smile tweaking his lips. "This is such a lovely old-fashioned pattern. What's it called?"

Fingerprints. Nice.

Marti smiled. "It's some type of chintz pattern. Very popular once upon a time. I've been told they first belonged to the Tates' great-great grandmother, I believe."

He set the cup down on the saucer. "It's always nice to hang on to these precious objects from the past."

"Yes, indeed," Abby said. "In fact, someone has been bugging me to sell my house. It's been in my family for over a hundred years. I just wish he'd go away."

"Well, it's certainly a lovely home. I don't blame you for wanting to keep it, but it's rather large for a single person."

She arched a brow. "Maybe I won't always be single."

He gave her a smarmy smile. "Don't give up. There's always room for hope."

Enough of this conversation. Time for the bum's rush.

She rose from her chair. "I know you're a busy man, so we won't keep you any longer. As soon as I have paperwork from the attorney, I'll give you a call."

"I look forward to serving with you and Mrs. Mills." Darwin nodded and replaced his Stetson.

As soon as the front door closed and he was in his vehicle, Abby rushed back to the kitchen to find Marti waving the evidence bags. "Lots of lovely fingerprints and DNA. I just know it."

"I think you must be right, Marti."

Vince emerged from the office. "Good job, ladies. Did you notice any change when you—very slyly I must add—mentioned the money you'd found?"

"He blinked, but that was it."

"A blink is as good as a wink," Will said. "Or is that a nod's as good as a wink?"

"The latter is correct," Abby said.

Vince rubbed his hands together. "All right, let's get this stuff bagged and tagged."

Marti wagged her finger. "Mind you take special care with that cup, Vince. I just imagine Starlight Tyler Tate would haunt your hide if you or one of your cohorts break it." She gave a brisk nod for emphasis.

Vince flashed a grin. "I'll be careful. No need to threaten my hide with great-great Granny's ghost."

Pulling a pair of Latex gloves from his pocket, he carefully lifted the rev's cup and placed it into the first bag. He then repeated the procedure, to place Darwin's fork into a second bag. Darwin's napkin went into a third bag. "These should tell us who Darwin is."

"And what if he's who he says he is?" Abby wrinkled her nose. "Just playing the devil's advocate here."

"Won't be an issue." He sat at the table to label, seal and sign the evidence bags.

Well, that said a lot. Abby glared at Vince. "You already *know* he's not the real Brother Darwin."

His cagey expression told her she was right. So who was he really?

Vince stood. "Bagged. Tagged. Ready for the Rangers."

"You need to go to bed."

"Not going to happen until I hand this evidence over to Ben."

"Why can't Will do that. You need to get some rest. You're dead on your feet. Or a very good imitation of it."

"Simple matter of chain of custody," he said, brushing aside her concerns. "The fewer links, the better."

"You are so freaking stubborn!" Grabbing a Danish, Abby flounced from the kitchen. Honestly, the man could out-stubborn a billy goat. She walked out onto the patio, ready to collapse into one of the chairs beside the pool.

How was it that she had been in the water only once? It was so cool and inviting, that much she knew from experience. She slipped off her sandals and walked over to the side of the pool and sat. Dipping her feet into the water, she sighed. The day was hot and steamy, perfect for a swim. She hopped up and ran back inside the house.

Ten minutes later, she'd changed into her swimsuit. She dove into the water, slicing through the cool depths. When she came up for air, Vince was standing, hands on hips, watching her.

So what. She gave a kick and started swimming laps. The pool wasn't Olympic sized, but it was long enough to get in some decent laps.

As she neared the opposite end, she heard him. "Go ahead. It's all right. Ignore me. Procedure is procedure, doll. I'll be back in a couple of hours."

She flipped and turned, heading back to his end of the pool. Never, ever was there a more stubborn man who seemed determined to ruin his health. His shoulder was nowhere near fifty percent, much less one hundred. He had no business being on duty. He simply wasn't fit. What if something happened?

Vince shook his head. Abby was pretty PO'd, but she'd get over it. Once he returned and got a good night's sleep, she'd stop worrying. Things would get back to normal between them. Whatever normal was.

Time to get the samples to the headquarters of Company F in Waco. The sooner he turned the samples over, the better. Too many things could happen. He carried the samples back in side, setting them on the kitchen table where his deputy was stuffing a Danish in his mouth. He nodded at Will, then pulled his phone from his pocket to call Ben.

"I have fingerprint and DNA samples of our imposter. I'd like to get them into your hands ASAP. Are you back in Waco?"

"You're in luck." Ben chuckled. "I'm over at my mom and dad's place."

"Will and I will see you soon, then." He terminated the call. "Let's get these over to your brother. There've been too many incidents and accidents lately. I'll rest easier once they're in Ranger hands."

He walked back into the office and gazed out the French doors for a final glimpse of the woman he loved. The same one who drove him crazy most of the time. She was still swimming laps. Reckon she'd quit when she got tired.

Abby's phone rang as she was changing from the wet bikini. Glancing at the Caller ID, she noted it was Rollo *again*.

"Yeah?" she answered, none too graciously.

"My client has agreed to your condition. He wants to see the house at seven. "

"In the morning. That's awfully early."

"No tonight, Abby."

"I have to work something out. I can't get there by seven. How about seven-thirty?"

"He says that's fine, but no later."

Rollo's client was damned demanding when *she* was the one doing the favor. "It's my house. If he wants to see it, he can jolly well do it when it suits me. I'll be there..." She glanced at her watch. "...at eight." She ended the call.

Eight o'clock should give Vince time to get back home and go to bed. Then she'd sneak out without his knowing wiser.

A curl of unease spiraled in her stomach. Maybe sneaky wasn't the way to go, after all.

Vince shifted in his chair. His shoulder ached like an SOB. He hadn't brought any pain pills with him. A couple of ibuprofen would have to do. Grimacing, he glanced at his watch. Nearly seven thirty. He'd left his deputy and the samples with Ben at the Rasmussens. The handover had gone smoothly. Ben had left immediately to transport them to F Company HQ in Waco. It wouldn't be long before there was at least a hit on one of the data bases.

His private phone rang. He winced when he saw it was Abby. He answered, "I know I said I wouldn't be long, But I'm waiting on some results."

"No matter. I'm coming into town to meet that pesky real estate agent at my house. Long story. I'm not going to bore you with the details. But now that I've made this appointment, I'm feeling a little leery about going there. I just wondered if you'd meet me at my house at eight. I'll tell you more when I see you."

"I don't think you should—"

"Bye!"

Damn! He hit the return call button, but she didn't answer. He opened the ibuprofen bottle and dry swallowed a couple, grabbed his Stetson, and was ready to head out when his office phone rang. He grabbed the phone, more from habit than any desire to know who called. "Sheriff Tate."

"Vince, we've a hit in AFIS."

Chapter Twenty-one

Abby pulled up to her house and parked. No signs of the workmen. Not so odd since they seldom worked after three-thirty. Still she'd expected to see more evidence that they had been working. Sometimes, a contractor might pull a crew off to work on another job that was more pressing, even more likely in her case since she'd said she was in no real hurry to move home.

Rollo's BMW was parked on the street in front of the house, so he must already be inside with the client. For once and all, she was going to make sure he and his contrary client understood her house wasn't for sale at any price.

Wondering if she should wait for Vince, she sat in the car to give him a few minutes. It wasn't quite eight yet. No. She might as well go on inside. Vince was only a few blocks away. How long could it take him?

She tested the door knob. New door. Still needed varnish. And not locked. Whoa! How had Rollo and his client gained access without a key? She'd not given him one. Perhaps, the workmen has left it unlocked. She'd have to speak to the contractor about securing her property.

More and more, Rollo was fast becoming too much

trouble to fool with. She opened the front door and stepped inside. "Rollo," she called out. "I'm here. Where're you?"

She eyed the living room and the foyer where the major fire damage was. The living room walls had been primed, the woodwork around the windows stripped, and the window glass replaced. Good. At least some of the work had taken place. She walked through the living room into the kitchen.

At the far end of the kitchen island, she saw the soles of two shoes sticking out. She sniffed the metallic odor of blood.

Whoa!

She took a step back and bumped into someone's chest. Gasping, she whirled around to face... "Brother Darwin. Are *you* the client? What's happened to Rollo?"

He smiled that sanctimonious smile of his. "I'm afraid my realtor is lying down on the job."

His attempt at humor notwithstanding, she panicked. Her mouth dried. Tried to swallow. Her pulse pounded in her ears. She raised her fists to protect herself.

Darwin grabbed both wrists in one large hand. "You didn't think your little tea party fooled me. No. No. Much too obvious. I suppose by now your sheriff boyfriend thinks or perhaps even *knows* I'm not a preacher man." His eyes were a flat, dead brown. Why hadn't she noticed that before?

Afraid of the answer, she asked, "What *are* you?"

"I'm a business man. And I'm running out of time. Where's the deed? And where's my *money*?" He shook her hard to jar her teeth.

"I don't know what you're talking about!" She struggled, trying to free her wrists, but for a *preacher man*, his grip was incredibly strong.

***

"Repeat that please." Vince listened, although his gut was screaming for him to slam down the phone and rush over to Abby's.

"Edward Barrow aka Eddie the chameleon. Member of the Houston mob. That's how he knew your hitman."

"And that's probably who Abby's meeting at her house right now. Gotta go." He slammed down the phone and ran from his office. "Dorothy, I need a BOLO on Rev. Darwin."

The dispatcher gaze up at him with a dumbfounded expression. "You need a BOLO on *who*?"

"You heard me. Dawwin's an imposter. Consider him armed and dangerous."

The door opened. Will strode toward Vince.

Thank God. "Will! You're with me. Dot, call for back up. Abby Fields' address."

"Here in town or out at the ranch?" she asked.

"Town, of course." He ran for the door with Will on his six.

Think. Focus. Keep him talking.

Except terror had dried her mouth to sand, and her bones were about to liquefy. "You don't really think I came here without telling someone who I was meeting, do you?"

"So?" He shrugged. "You were coming to meet our hapless friend Rollo. The sheriff will think he killed you and then offed himself. Otherwise, I'll have to take my chances." He dragged her across the kitchen, forcing her down onto a chair. He zip-tied her hands behind her and her ankles to the chair legs. "Now, tell me about the deed and that extra hundred and fifty thousand dollars it seems you've come across. Or were you baiting me?" He shook his head. "No. You're not that smart." He reached into his jacket and pulled out a semi-automatic weapon.

A gun. She *hated* guns. Funny how she'd made that decision so quickly. "Think again." She glared up at him, her heart pounding. "You're right. By now, your fingerprints and DNA are at the Texas Rangers headquarters in Waco. Everyone will know who you really are and what you've done. I just wish I knew *why*."

"Don't think I don't know you're stalling for time. You think your boyfriend is going to rescue you. He isn't."

"Yes, he will. He'll be here before you can get the hell out of Dodge. And then, you're headed straight for death row. You know we execute convicted murderers in Texas, or hadn't you heard?"

"They'll have to catch me first. Now *where's* that damned deed?"

She let out a theatrical sigh. "I never found the actual deed. Just a record at the courthouse where my father recorded it. According to my lawyer, as things stand, *I* own the land, and I'll be selling it to whichever tribe wants to build a gaming casino on it. I expect to make a lot of money on that deal once *I* find the deed."

"And the cash?"

"Safety deposit box in a bank in Austin. Nice to have a little nest egg." A propensity for telling big whoppers had always gotten her in trouble as a child, but given her current situation, the talent came in handy.

"I will tear this house apart. Heaven knows I've tried a couple of times."

"And you made a pathetic job of it. Very slapdash, if you ask me."

"*You*!" He accented the word by slapping her across the face. Her head snapped. Her eyes watered and stung. "Are an absolute a waste of time and space. I should've choked the life out of your the first time I had hold of you."

"So that was you, *Brother* Darwin." She reined in her rage. Fat lot of good it would do her now. "I was always tempted to tell you how horrible your sermons were. They were the real reason I stayed away from Sunday services." She cringed waiting for another blow.

He laughed. No. He roared.

"Like I cared what you or anyone in that wretched group of congregants thought. They all had their secrets. Even the holiest of them. Even your *father*. Man oh man, did he ever make a mistake by confiding in me. Oh, he had a gambling problem. Didn't you know?" He got down in her face, his fetid breath turned her stomach.

"My father had a gambling problem?" Finally, it was coming together.

"How do you think he paid for that fancy renovation your mother wanted? His first trip to the Kickapoo Lucky Eagle Casino, he won big. Really big. Beginners luck. It didn't last." He chuckled. "He made it so easy for me to use him as a go-between to buy that plot of land outside of town."

"I don't believe a single word you say." She had to keep him talking long enough for Vince to arrive. And what was taking him so long, anyway?

"Too bad his conscience got the better of him. Too bad for him. But he was stubborn. Too stubborn. Said his conscience started bothering him. So, he refused to hand over the title. Refused to give me back the money he had left over from the land purchase. Even after my friend from Houston tortured him, he wouldn't reveal where he'd hidden it."

"What about the man who's sitting in jail awaiting trial for my father's murder?"

"If you must know, I made him an offer he couldn't refuse. I planted evidence. His part of the deal was he didn't have to confess, just not fight too hard. His common law wife helped frame him. That's another story and *you're* running out of time."

"Then tell me, at least, what the sheriff's wife and the banker had to do with everything?"

"More confessions. They were having an affair and he was embezzling from the bank. Together they had already formed a series of shell companies to launder money he'd embezzled. I blackmailed them, too. They tried to back out and run away. My pal Tom caught up with them. Had some fun with them, then I kept them on ice until I buried them on the sheriff's land.

"But you had the hitman kill Darla Murray. She didn't have anything to do with any of this."

"I had nothing to do with her. Tom did that one on his own. If you'd stayed where you belonged, he wouldn't have bothered with her. Her death's on you."

Tears sprang to her eyes. Abby's shook her head. No. Not her fault. "He didn't just kill her. He *tortured* her!"

He shrugged, brushing off Abby's horror like a worrisome gnat. "As I said, that was his deal entirely. Not mine. Although I have to say I'm sorely tempted to see if a cigarette burn here and there would change your story or improve your appearance." He ran his hand over her cheek and then down her forearm as if looking for a good place to start.

She cringed at the thought of being tortured. Not particularly brave. Oh yes, she had a smart mouth, but physical torture? A whole other deal entirely.

"What good will it do you if I had the deed to give you? No matter what you do to me, you're finished in the Valley the second those fingerprint and DNA results come back."

With a growl, he pressed the gun barrel under her chin, forcing her head back against the chair splat. "What *good* will it do me? I'll tell you. I'll hand it over to my boss. He'll do whatever the hell he wants with it. Job well done. And I get to live a little longer. And then, I get to disappear."

"Now..." He pressed the gun harder. "...if you want to see another sunrise in this desolate pit of humanity you so lovingly refer to as *the Valley*, you'll tell me where that deed is and *where the hell my money is*!"

While Vince sped along the quiet streets of the Valley, Will called for local SWAT backup.

"She should've waited for me." Vince swore when he saw her empty vehicle parked in the drive. "We have to assume either the real estate man or his client is behind everything that has been going on locally. Obviously the Houston mob is in this up to their necks. Why would organized crime seek out this sleepy little Texas town unless it involved gambling or drugs? He'd seen no evidence of an increase of drug trafficking. Nothing above the usual levels of weed and meth busts.

He'd never liked Rollo Moore. The man was entirely too slick and well-oiled. But being involved with the preacher might be a sign of his utter gullibility. But then, Darwin had fooled an entire congregation of folks.

He braked to an abrupt stop in front of Abby's house. The two storied house would be a wonderful home in which to rear a houseful of kids, as would the Tate ranch.

But only if Darwin didn't act true to form and kill Abby. *Not going there. No way.*

"I'm calling Abby's cell phone," he told Will. "See if I can determine what's going on inside the house."

He hit the speed dial for her cell number. It rang once. Twice. A third time. "Hello, Sheriff Tate."

Not Abby. Definitely Darwin's unctuous tones or Eddie, whoever the hell he was.

"Darwin, I want to speak to Abby."

"I'm afraid she's all tied up."

"If you've hurt her..."

"Not much...yet. I am considering it, though."

"What do you want, Darwin. You're surrounded. The Texas Rangers are on the way. Give me your terms now before this gets complicated with SWAT snipers and the Rangers."

"Don't want much. Deed to a certain plot of land, and I want the cash."

"We haven't found the deed. If it's anywhere, it's still in the house. The money I can have that here in—"

"Ten minutes or she dies."

From the corner of his eye, he saw his deputies clearing the nearby residences. Another deputy was in the process of setting up a perimeter. The Los Marcos County SWAT van was pulling up inside the perimeter. Will signaled that two snipers were getting into place. "Ten minutes isn't enough time. The money's in my safe. It'll take at least ten minutes just to get back to the ranch."

"Nine minutes."

"Let me speak to Abby. You know how this works. I need proof she's still alive, otherwise we'll blow that damn house up with you in it."

"Eight minutes."

Through the phone, he heard some rustling. "Vince? I'm okay. But Rollo's dead."

At that bit of news, Vince's gut twisted. He'd failed to keep Abby safe. And now, she was in the hands of a mad man.

More rustling, then Darwin's voice. "Time's a-wasting, son. Changed my mind. I want ten million and a helicopter."

"You might as well shoot her now. The nearest helicopter is in Waco. That'd be easy enough, but no one in this county, much less this town, has money like that." Had he just suggested to a known killer that he go ahead and shoot Abby? Darwin only had leverage as long as Abby was alive. He wouldn't shoot her until he thought he had a surefire exit strategy.

Or had Vince miscalculated? With no way out, would Darwin shoot her and turn the gun on himself?

Darwin guffawed, the sound of it so evil, it unsettled Abby's already dicey nerves. "I'm glad you find something about this situation amusing."

"Your sheriff said I should go ahead and shoot you. Now that's what I call true love."

What was Vince thinking? *Go ahead and shoot me*? She squared her shoulders and wrestled with her wrist restraints. *Now think.* She was all the leverage Darwin had. Vince had to be counting on that fact. "He's probably right. No one around here has that kind of cash. I doubt even the bank has that much in the vault." So much for the final nail in her coffin.

Pacing the kitchen and muttering to himself, Darwin seemed to be on the verge of losing it. Not good. If he did, likely he'd kill her first. That sobering thought sent a wave of nausea roiling through her body. Facing death, certain or uncertain, hadn't been on her agenda today. If she'd thought about her death at all, it was somewhere in the distant future. Even with recent threats looming over her, she'd never, ever, thought them real.

Until now.

***

Vince climbed into the SWAT van. “Can the snipers get a bead on him? Where are they?” he asked the Tom Miller, the SWAT commander and negotiator, a no-nonsense man in his forties.

“In the back of the house.”

“That’s the kitchen. Can they see Abby?”

“Negative. Subject is pacing. We need him to stand still to get a clear shot.”

“I’ll call him again,” Vince suggested. “Maybe that’ll slow him down.” In the meantime, he could see the SWAT team moving around, covering the front, side, and the rear means of exit.

Miller nodded. “Go ahead.”

This time he called Abby’s land line. If he remembered correctly, the kitchen extension was wall-mounted next to a window.

Darwin answered on the third ring. “Got that helicopter already? And the ten mil? Man, you’re quick.”

“Chopper’s on the way, but there’s not enough room for it to land in this neighborhood with all the trees. We’ll need to transport you to the ball field a couple of blocks from here. How would you like us to do that? You’re in charge. We don’t want anything to happen to you or to Ms. Fields.” Fifty percent of that was true.

He glanced at Miller. “Anything?” he mouthed.

Miller spoke calmly into his headset, “Do you have a clear shot?” He shook his head. “Take it as soon as you’re clear.”

“Ball field?” Darwin yelled. “Are you freaking serious? I might as well shoot her right now.”

“You don’t have to do that. There’s still time to work this out,” Vince pleaded.

Miller murmured, “Take it.”

Trying to talk to Darwin and listen to the Swat Commander at the same time, Vince jumped at the sound of a shot. But in the confusion, he couldn't tell whether it came from a sniper's rifle or from inside the house.

The remaining members of the SWAT team breached the door. Yes, she'd need another new door. He found himself running up the sidewalk to the house, his heart in his throat. What would he find? Was his future waiting for him alive and well?

Chapter Twenty-two

The shot came so quickly and out of nowhere that, for a second or two, Abby's heart felt like it stopped. With the sound, blood spatter simultaneously hit her face. She blinked. Darwin dropped like a stone.

Her breath came in ragged gasps.

She heard the front door smashed. Men in black—SWAT—rushed into the kitchen.

The men and the kitchen seemed to swirl around her. Realizing she was on the verge of fainting, she bent forward to get her head lower than her heart.

"Abby!" Vince groaned, calling her name and falling to his knees in front of her. "He's killed her."

Her head clearing, she straightened to meet his gaze. "I'm all right. I just got woozy for a second."

"There's blood."

"His."

"And Rollo?" he asked. "I—I thought you were dead. I wanted to die too."

"He wasn't involved. He was just trying to sell my house." At that moment, her hands were freed by one of the SWAT team. She cradled Vince's face in her hands. "*I'm* all right. Truly."

He stood, pulling her to her feet. She could've gotten

lost in cool blue depths of his gaze. "I'll never let you come to harm. You know that." He lowered his mouth to hers for a hot and hard kiss. Her knees nearly buckled, but he held on tight.

Then she pushed him away. "As soon as I catch my breath, I have a bone to pick with you. You told him to go ahead and *shoot me*!" She gazed up at him with a smile. "I mean really..."

"I was pretty sure he wouldn't."

"But not a hundred percent?"

"Let's say ninety-nine percent."

She balled her fist and popped him a good one on the chest. "Yeah!"

He gathered her small fist lovingly in his larger hand while he glanced over at Darwin's body. "If I could, I'd kill him again."

"Thankfully, you won't have to."

He swept her from the kitchen, through the living room, still full of various members of SWAT, and through her splintered front door. "Here, let's get you checked out. Are you sure you're not hurt.

"Just my wrists where I was trying to get loose. You know those zip-ties are hard on a gal's delicate skin."

"And you have *very* delicate skin," he murmured softly into her ear, then nipped the lobe.

More than aware of two staring EMTs, Abby said, "Enough. You're going to embarrass yourself if you're not careful." She extricated herself from Vince's arms and offered her injured wrists to Suzanne, the female EMT, who was trying not to laugh.

"Why should I be embarrassed? This woman is totally hot. Who wouldn't take advantage?" He glanced from one EMT to the other. "Right."

"Right," they agreed simultaneously.

Abby smiled while Suzanne cleaned and bandaged her wrists. Vince could always make her smile, even at a time like this.

After Suzanne released Abby, Vince gathered her up. "I'm taking you home. You can make your official statement tomorrow."

She glanced over her shoulder at the Fields' family home. The one place she'd always thought of *home*. Now and always, it would be tainted by the knowledge of the events that had occurred there, as well as the reasons. "I'm going to sell it. My house, that is."

"You won't need it." Vince pulled her tighter into his arms.

"I won't," she agreed, ignoring for the moment what his statement implied. "I think I'll buy something a little more manageable."

"There's no rush."

"No. there isn't. Take me home."

"I am."

Home. Truly in her mind, home *was* with Vince. But he might have other ideas.

On the drive to the ranch, Vince listened while Abby told him what she'd managed to get out of Darwin. The sun shone, glinting off the hood of the SUV. It was a perfect summer day. Puffy clouds drifted across the horizon like cotton bolls.

"What will happen to Tim Dill now that the rev confessed? I mean he confessed to me, not to anyone in law enforcement."

"We'll have to talk to the DA, but based on your testimony, after all it was your father he was supposed to have killed, he'll probably be released before too long."

How could he have gotten everything so wrong? A rush to judgement—just what the rev ordered.

"Do you think it's finally over? Will they just send someone else to threaten and kill us?"

"I don't think the Houston mob is going to send anyone else. There's been too much trouble for no result. The Rangers will definitely be looking into Darwin's contacts and associates in Houston."

"I doubt I'll ever find the title, but if I do, I think I'll donate the land to a charity. Some kind of good needs to come out of all this."

"He must've hidden it damned well or destroyed it." Before he could expound any further, his phone rang. His mood plummeted as he listened. "Thanks for letting me know." He let out a sigh.

"What is it?"

"Danny Keene died a few minutes ago."

"Oh, no. Do you need to notify his mother?"

"No. She was at the hospital."

"I'm so sorry."

Sorry didn't come close to how he felt. He should've dug deeper into the first murder, Abby's father. Instead, he'd rushed to judgement, taken the easy road. In spite of the evidence, planted by Darwin. Now he knew. The rest of the murders wouldn't have taken place. "Danny was a fine young man. Showed a lot of promise for ranching. I'll see his mother is taken care of."

"*You're* a fine man, Vincent Tate."

"No. I'm responsible for the rest of those who lost their lives. I didn't do a proper investigation into your father's murder. Not like I should have. I should've..." He couldn't bring himself to say more. Anymore and she would blame him for the death of the other pharmacist, her friend.

He turned into the ranch and drove up to the house. It

was the same summer day. Same brilliant blue sky. Same white clouds. But internally, a storm was brewing.

Vince had descended into some sort of existential fog. His gaze was inward as he exited the SUV, and he seemed to have forgotten she was with him. She didn't blame him for Darla's death, no more than she blamed herself. Well, maybe she still blamed herself a little. No. The preacher and the hitman were responsible for the deaths that had ensued after her father's murder.

"Vince," she called after him. "None of what's happened this week is your fault." She caught up with him on the porch then grabbed his wrist. "Sit." She motioned him to one of the porch rocking chairs. Taking the one next to his, she took his strong work-hardened hands in hers. "You followed the evidence when you arrested Tim Dill. You had no way of knowing the evidence was planted to frame him. He was an addict. The perfect patsy. I believed he did it. Hell, everyone in town agreed."

Vince shook his head slowly. "That's just it. I'm the sheriff. I'm supposed to get it right."

Hoping to soothe his frayed soul, she stroked the back of his tanned hands. "You're human. You're not perfect. No one is."

He squared his shoulders, and started to rise. "But—"

She shook her head. "Stay with me. If you want to assign blame, what about my father? There's plenty of blame to go around if that's what you're of a mind to do. I loved my father with all my heart, but because of his actions, he has his share of responsibility. His weakness set some of these events into motion."

"Hold on now. In the end, your dad tried to make it right. That's what got him killed."

"There's no way to change the events of the past. What counts now is how things have turned out. We have what you LEO types call a 'positive result.' What matters now is what happens in the future. No one else is going to be murdered. Tim Dill will be released. Although I think that so-called wife of his should be charged with something since she helped the rev frame him."

"Speaking of what happens from here on out?" Vince smiled, a somewhat mischievous smile at that.

Finally, a smile from the man.

"What do *you* want to happen? Do you still intend to sell your family's home and buy a smaller place?"

"Yes, that's exactly what I want to do." Liar. Liar. Could she really have what she wanted? A home. This man to love her forever.

This *man* who was *kneeling* before her. Like right *now*.

"Since we're talking about the future, I can't imagine mine without you. And being as I *am* down on my knees, will you marry me?"

"By all means, save time, so you don't have to get down there twice." She laughed, a laugh tinged by a tiny dose of hysteria. How she loved this man. His shining eyes. His engaging smile. His heart so full of love.

All for her.

"That's not an answer."

His sky blue eyes danced with excitement. Her heart pounded as if it might burst from her chest. Blinking back tears of joy, she swept her arms around his neck, and knelt before him, face-to-face. "This is my answer: Yes, I'll marry you, Sheriff Vincent Tate. I'll marry you with all my heart."

He slanted his mouth across hers. She threaded her fingers though his hair. Dissolving under the assault of his lips, she moaned with desire.

Finally, she and Vince would have a life together. The life they were supposed to have started and shared over ten years ago. So what if their happy ending was a little delayed. And now, so much the sweeter for it.

Chapter Twenty-three

A week later

Abby moved the ladder closer to the high shelf where her father's collection of antique apothecary jars were displayed. "That should do it," she said to no one in particular. Her cashier Ellen was at the front of the store. Business had picked up a bit since she'd been able to re-open the store. They would still have reduced pharmacy hours since she was the only pharmacist. She wasn't quite ready to hire another. She imagined the interviewee's question, "Why did you last pharmacist leave?" and her answer, "She was murdered" wouldn't go over all that well.

No. Not the way to hire a new pharmacist.

She climbed up the ladder. Time to give Dad's collection a good dusting. Swiffer handy, she sneezed at the first round of dusting. Ah, heck, some of the jars were simply too delicate to just dust willy-nilly. In fact, she might as well give them a good handwashing. But the thought of climbing up and down the ladder innumerable times, one jar at a time, didn't exactly appeal.

"I could help you with that."

Startled, Abby jumped and almost fell off the ladder. "Chance. I didn't know you were in the store, much less behind me." Vince still hadn't forgiven his brother for his dirty tricks and lies. And the small matter of Chance's taking those potshots at him.

"Careful. I didn't mean to startle you."

"I just didn't expect you." An understatement if there ever was one.

"I meant what I said about giving you a hand." He reached out. "Hand 'em to me, and I'll set 'em wherever you want."

"The breakroom will be fine." Why was he really here? What was he up to now?

Mumbling a bit, he said, "I also wanted to apologize for being a jerk."

"And for lying about your brother after he went off to college. That too?"

He hung his head, gazing at her with puppy dog eyes. "Yeah, that too."

As big a pain as Chance had been, maybe he'd learned his lesson. Coming between the two brothers had never been on her agenda. "I'm willing to overlook it and move forward, as long as you mend your ways. Think you can do that?"

"I'll try."

"Your brother, though, he's another matter. You'll have to work on him yourself."

Chance shook his head. "I don't know. Vince isn't the forgiving kind."

She smiled. "Then I recommend a big slice of humble pie. Marti probably has a recipe for it." Abby chuckled. "Sorry. I know it's not funny, but if anyone has that recipe, she does."

"Yeah, I miss her cooking too."

"Well then, that settles it. Make nice with your brother and stop being such an ass."

"Yes, ma'am."

They worked quietly for a few minutes. "This one has something in it." Chance held up a tall milk-glass apothecary jar. Sure enough, something rattled when he shook the jar.

Abby climbed down. "Let me see." She removed the stopper, pulled out a rolled up piece of paper, and unrolled it.

After all this time, the title to the land. Time for a mental happy dance.

You sure picked a good hiding place, Daddy. I never would've found it if I hadn't decided to do a little cleaning.

"I can stick around and help you put them back up," Chance offered.

"Don't you have something you need to be doing?"

"Nah. Vince bought me out of the ranch, so I'm kind of at loose ends. I put a down payment on that condo at the end of Meadowlark. It's nice, but it's not home yet."

"Then do some good with your funds. Don't blow it all. Get your head out of your ass and make a plan. Invest it."

"Like it when you talk tough, Abby." Chance chuckled. "You don't mince words. So now that you've found the deed, what are *you* going to do with the land?"

"I'm certainly not going to turn it over to the Houston mob. I have the land, but I don't have the money to develop it. I'm not exactly anxious to see a gambling casino on the outskirts of town, so maybe I'll just hang onto it until I think of something. Something worthy."

Chance let out a low chuckle. "If I'm not careful, you're going to be a good influence on me."

"So take my advice and start with your brother then." Abby locked the title away in the office safe.

After helping her wash the jars and replace the collection on the shelf, Abby thanked him. "You're going to talk to your brother, sooner rather than later—right?"

"I guess so."

"No. You have to promise."

"All right. For Pete's sake, I'll talk to him."

"Soon."

"Yeah. Soon." Shaking his head, he turned and left the store. "Crazy woman," he muttered.

"I heard that." There was hope for the bad-boy twin, after all. Now if Vince would only relent and forgive his brother, she would have accomplished something positive for the time being, anyway.

Back at the ranch, Abby dived into the pool. She'd have to make a daily habit of swimming laps if she was to keep ahead of Marti's calorie-laden meals. She sliced through the water, each stroke smooth and powerful.

Now that she closed the pharmacy section of the store at six, she could enjoy the benefits of a regular schedule. In other words, she could have a life.

She swam until the cares of the day and the last couple of weeks were drained from her entire body. She pulled up at the end of the pool to see two cowboy-booted feet.

"Doll, I'm home."

She hoisted her body from the pool and got to her feet. "Mm." She gave a little purr. "So I see." She shook the excess water from her hair.

Vince hopped back a couple of steps. "Watch it. You're wet."

She let out a laugh and sat on one of the lounge chairs. "I always heard lawmen were observant." She wrapped a towel around her head, soaking up the excess water. "It just feels so good not to have a cloud hanging over my head—no, our heads," she added.

He crouched down beside her. "Does feel pretty good. How about we set a wedding date. I'm thinking September. That give you enough time?"

"Hm." She cocked her head to one side. "What do you say, we discuss plans after dinner? Marti's about to ring the dinner bell, and I need to shower and change." Giving him a quick wink, she eluded his lunging grasp.

After another of one of Marti's sumptuous dinners, Vince poured a glass of white zinfandel for Abby and snagged a beer from the fridge for himself. "Outside woman. We have wedding plans to discuss. C'mon."

He led the way to the shaded area by the pool where a redwood pergola stretched overhead. He sat on the settee and patted the cushion beside him. She sat, pulled her feet up under her, and snuggled in his arms.

She let out a sigh. "This is a perfect time and place to discuss our wedding plans. But September? That will mean I have to hire another pharmacist right away, if we're going to have any kind of honeymoon."

He nudged her chin upward with a touch of his forefinger. Her gaze widened, her jade green eyes darkened with emotion. "Hold on now. Are you going to be one of those crazy brides?"

"Not at all. We can keep the arrangements simple, but it'll still take time to find a place to get married. The church is out—uh, no minister."

Recalling that he and Liz had eloped, wedding planning wasn't exactly his favorite sport. "What about here on the ranch?"

"You know," she said with the sweet smile he loved so much, "I don't really care where or when as long as, at the end of the day, I'm married to you."

His heart swelled as she uttered those words. "I could ask Judge Sewell if he would perform the ceremony. We could hold it in Central Park and decorate the gazebo. Then the whole town could come or not, then back to the here to the ranch for a big Texas barbecue."

"Sounds perfect." She lay her head on his chest, nestled in the crook of his shoulder.

"You know, doll, any day that ends with you in my arms is perfect."

"You really are a mushy guy, aren't you?"

"Nah. Just know who makes me happy."

She straightened. "Maybe I shouldn't bring this up right now and spoil the mood, but Chance came by the drugstore today."

Vince couldn't help it. He bristled. "What the hell did he want?"

"All he wants is to make amends."

She ran her fingers along his thigh. Dang. Didn't she know how her slightest touch affected him? His jeans grew snug in the crotch. He stirred to allow more room. "So there's a twelve-step program for jackasses?"

"Jackass or not, he's your brother. I believe he's really sorry. He even gave me a hand at the drugstore today. Oh, and we found the title to the land."

"Talk about burying your lead. You're just now telling me?"

She smiled up at him so sweetly. "Your presence is very distracting. I forgot. Anyway, I decided to give daddy's jar collection a good dusting, and then I decided to wash the ones that didn't have those little paper labels. Chance helped me with the washing and everything."

"You're kidding." Talk about a soft touch—Abby personified. "I don't trust him. He's bound to be up to something."

"Of course, he was feeling me out. He's going to try and make things right with you soon. He promised." She curled back into his arms again.

"Yeah? He sent me a text this afternoon. Didn't say much. Reckon I'll have to listen to what he has to say." Talking wouldn't be enough. He'd have to prove himself.

"You know you don't want to stay at odds with your brother. Not forever. "

"So you're the peacemaker now?"

Abby nodded. "If you like."

"Like? Doll, love is what it is." He leaned back, pulling her over him. He could drown in the sweetness of her lips.

She pulled away and stood, but then she pulled him to his feet. "We need to take this upstairs, Sheriff. Don't you think?"

"If justice is to be served, I'd say so."

"Then by all means, let justice be served."

Epilogue

Six weeks later from the Kenton Valley Gazette.

Fields - Tate

Abigail Fields and Vincent Tate were married September 17, 2016 in Kenton Valley Central Park, his honor Judge Chatham Sewel officiated. The bride is the daughter of the late Mr. and Mrs. Robert Tate. The groom is the son of Nathan Tate of Galveston, TX, and Helen Tate Williams of Tulsa, OK.

The bride wore an ivory dupioni silk gown trimmed with lace and wore her great-grandmother's pearl necklace. As befitted a Texas bride, she carried a bouquet of yellow roses.

Following a reception at the Tate ranch, they left for Hawaii. After their honeymoon, the couple will reside at the Tate ranch outside Kenton Valley.

The bride graduated from the University of Georgia in Athens. She is employed as a pharmacist and owns Fields Drugstore in Kenton Valley, TX. The groom graduated from Texas A&M. He has served as the Los Marcos County Sheriff since his election in 2014.

As soon as the Sunday paper was delivered, Abby snatched it and ran inside. She tossed aside the rest of the *Gazette*, keeping only the Features section. “Look, Vince. Here’s our wedding announcement. Front page, above the fold.”

Vince took a sip of coffee, then smiled. “Big news. Not everyday the local pharmacist marries the most eligible man in town.”

“Oh, so you’re the most eligible man in town, are you? On the other hand, you could say the sheriff snagged himself a successful business woman.” She swept her arms around his neck, hugging him from behind. “Gosh I love you.”

“Back at ya, doll!” He rolled up the Sports section and swatted her behind. “You’re late!”

“Uh-uh. The drugstore doesn’t open until one on Sundays now.”

“So what on earth will we do with an entire morning to ourselves?”

“Got an idea.” He rose from his chair. “Last one to bed has to give a full-body massage.”

Abby gave a squeal and darted for the stairs. “I’ll win that race.”

“That’s what you think.” He raced after her, caught her in his arms. “I’ll be the real winner.”

Her heart full of love, she smiled. “I think it’ll be a tie.”

The End

About the Author

Marie-Nicole Ryan was born in a small western Kentucky town, but after college and marriage, she said "Good bye" to small town life. After spending three years as an army wife, she landed in Nashville, TN, where she spent several decades working as an R.N. and case manager. Finally in 2002, she achieved her lifelong dream of becoming a published author.

She loves all lawmen and detectives and writes erotic historical western romance and contemporary romantic suspense. TOO GOOD TO BE TRUE, won a 2008 EPPIE for erotic romantic suspense. In addition, her mystery/suspense novel, ONE TOO MANY, was a 2009 EPPIE Finalist.

She returned to her old hometown in western Kentucky in 2010. When she's not slaving away at her current work in progress, you might find her walking her dog Kelsea, a Sheltie rescue, or at the Y. But you won't ever find her in an airplane. No, not ever.

She's a former member of Romance Writers of America® To learn more about Marie-Nicole Ryan, please visit her web site at marienicoleryan.com. To keep up with her latest releases, new, and contests, send an email to Marie-NicoleRyanNews-subscribe@yahoo.com Or you may follow her on:
Facebook: https://facebook.com/marienicoleryan.author
Twitter: @MarieNicoleRyan

www.ingramcontent.com/pod-product-compliance
Lightning Source LLC
Chambersburg PA
CBHW020235260626
47156CB00002B/683

* 9 7 8 1 3 9 3 0 9 9 2 1 5 *